W9-ATF-011

From the best-selling book *Tell Me the Secrets* written by Max Lucado, created by Ron DiCianni

The Song of the King

Max Lucado

Illustrated by Toni Goffe

CROSSWAY BOOKS • WHEATON, ILLINOIS
A DIVISION OF GOOD NEWS PUBLISHERS

PUBLISHER'S ACKNOWLEDGMENT

The publisher wishes to acknowledge that the text for *The Song of the King* appeared originally in *Tell Me the Secrets*, written by Max Lucado and illustrated by Ron DiCianni. Special thanks to Ron DiCianni for the idea and vision behind the creation of the series. For more stories in the "Tell Me" series, *Tell Me the Story* and *Tell Me the Secrets*, both published by Crossway Books, are available at your local bookstore.

The Song of the King

Copyright © 1995 by Max Lucado

Published by Crossway Books
              a division of Good News Publishers
              1300 Crescent Street
              Wheaton, Illinois 60187

Cover illustration: Toni Goffe

Creative Direction: Brian Ondracek

Art Direction/Design: Mark Schramm

First printing 1995

Printed in Mexico

Library of Congress Cataloging-in-Publication Data
Lucado, Max.
    The song of the king / Max Lucado : illustrated by Toni Goffe.
        p.   cm.
    Text appeared originally in Tell me the secrets.
    Summary: Three knights set out on a perilous journey to reach the king's castle, but the only one to reach his goal is the one who was wise enough to listen to the song of the king.
    [1. Kings, queens, rulers, etc.—Fiction. 2. Parables.] I. Goffe, Toni, ill. II. Title.
PZ7.L9684So 1995   [Fic]—dc20   95-12970
ISBN 0-89107-827-4

03	02	01	00	99	98	97						
15	14	13	12	11	10	9	8	7	6	5	4	3

Dedicated
with love to
J. T. and Carra.

May you hear the
song of the King.

$\mathcal{T}$he three knights sat at the table and listened as the prince spoke.

"My father, the king, will give the hand of my sister to the first of you who can prove himself worthy."

The prince paused to let the men take in the news. He looked at their faces—each weathered from miles and scarred from battles. The three had much in common. They were the strongest warriors in the kingdom, and they each wanted to marry the daughter of the king. The king had promised each a chance—a test to see which was worthy of his daughter. And now the time for the test had arrived.

"The test is a journey," the prince explained, "a journey to the king's castle by way of Hemlock."

"The forest?" one knight quickly inquired.

"The forest," answered the prince.

There was silence as the knights thought about the words. Each felt a stab of fear.

They knew the danger of Hemlock, a dark and deadly place.
Parts of it were so thick with trees that the sunlight never found
the floor.

It was the home of the Hopenots—small, sly creatures with
yellow eyes. Hopenots were not strong, but they were clever,
and they were many. Some people believed the Hopenots were
lost travelers changed by the darkness. But no one really knew
for sure.

"Will we travel alone?" Carlisle spoke—
a strange question to come from the
strongest of the three knights. His fierce
sword was known throughout the
kingdom.

But even this steely soldier knew better
than to travel Hemlock alone.

"You may each choose one person
to travel with you."

"But the forest is dark. The trees make the sky black. How will we find the castle?" This time it was Alon who spoke. He was not as strong as Carlisle but much quicker.

He was famous for his speed.
Alon left trails of confused enemies.
He had escaped them by ducking
into trees or scampering over walls.
But quickness is worthless if you
have no direction.

So Alon asked, "How can we
find the way?"

The prince nodded, reached into his sack, and pulled out an ivory flute. "There are only two of these," he explained. "This one and another in the possession of the king."

He put the instrument to his lips and played a soft, sweet song. Never had the knights heard such soothing music.

"My father's flute plays the same song. His song will guide you to the castle."

"How is that?" Alon asked.

"Three times a day the king will play from the castle wall. Early in the morning, at noon, and again in the evening. Listen for him. Follow his song and you will find the castle."

"There is only one other flute like this one?"
"Only one."
"And you and your father play the same music?"
"Yes."
It was Cassidon who was asking. Cassidon was known for his
alertness. He saw what others missed. He knew the home of
a traveler by the dirt on his boot. He knew the
truth of a story by the eyes of the teller. He
could tell the size of a marching
army by the number of
scattered birds in flight.

Carlisle and Alon wondered why he asked about the flute. It wouldn't be very long before they found out. "Consider the danger and choose your companion carefully," the prince cautioned.

And so they did. The next morning
the three knights mounted their horses
and entered Hemlock. Beside each
rode the chosen companion.

For the people in the king's castle, the days of waiting passed slowly. All knew of the test. And all wondered which knight would win the princess. Three times a day the king sent his song soaring into the trees of Hemlock. And three times a day the people stopped their work to listen.

After many days and countless songs, a watchman spotted two figures stumbling out of the forest. No one could tell who they were. They were too far from the castle. The men had no horses, weapons, or armor.

"Hurry," the king commanded his guards, "bring them in. Give them medical treatment and food, but don't tell anyone who they are. Dress the knight as a prince, and we will see their faces tonight at the banquet."

He then dismissed the crowds and told them to prepare for the feast.

That evening a joyful spirit filled the banquet hall. At every table the people tried to guess which knight had survived Hemlock Forest.

Finally, the moment came to present the winner. At the king's signal the people became quiet, and he began to play the flute. Once again the ivory instrument sang. The people turned to see who would enter.

Many thought it would be Carlisle, the strongest. Others felt it would be Alon, the swiftest.

But it was neither. The knight who survived the journey was Cassidon, the wisest.

He strode quickly across the floor, following the sound of the flute one final time, and bowed before the king.

"Tell us of your journey," he was instructed.
The people leaned forward to listen.

"The Hopenots were crafty," Cassidon began.

"They attacked, but we fought back. They took our horses, but we continued."

"What nearly destroyed us, though, was something far worse."

"What was that?" asked the princess.

"They imitated."

"They imitated?" asked the king.

"Yes, my king. They imitated. Each time the song of your flute would enter the forest, a hundred flutes would begin to play. All around us we heard music—songs from every direction."

"I do not know what became of Carlisle and Alon," he continued, "but I know strength and speed will not help one hear the right flute."

The king asked the question that was on everyone's lips.
"Then how did you hear my song?"

"I chose the right companion," he answered as he motioned for his fellow traveler to enter. The people gasped.

It was the prince. In his hand he carried the flute.

"I knew there was only *one* who could play the song as you do," Cassidon explained. "So I asked him to travel with me. As we journeyed, he played. I learned your song so well that though a thousand false flutes tried to hide your music, I could still hear you. I knew your song and followed it."

ROGUE Angel

Alex Archer

PROVENANCE

A GOLD EAGLE BOOK FROM

W**O**RLDWIDE®

TORONTO • NEW YORK • LONDON
AMSTERDAM • PARIS • SYDNEY • HAMBURG
STOCKHOLM • ATHENS • TOKYO • MILAN
MADRID • WARSAW • BUDAPEST • AUCKLAND

First edition March 2008

ISBN-13: 978-0-373-62129-3
ISBN-10:   0-373-62129-9

PROVENANCE

Special thanks and acknowledgment to
Victor Milán for his contribution to this work.

Printed in U.S.A.

THE
LEGEND

...THE ENGLISH COMMANDER TOOK
JOAN'S SWORD AND RAISED IT HIGH.
The broadsword, plain and unadorned,
gleamed in the firelight. He put the tip against
the ground and his foot at the center of the blade.
The broadsword shattered, fragments falling
into the mud. The crowd surged forward,
peasant and soldier, and snatched the shards
from the trampled mud. The commander tossed
the hilt deep into the crowd.
Smoke almost obscured Joan, but she continued
praying till the end, until finally the flames climbed
her body and she sagged against the restraints.

Joan of Arc died that fateful day in France,
but her legend and sword are reborn....

1

A burst of automatic rifle fire in the grand ballroom shattered the band's bright dance music like a crowbar smashing glass figurines from a shelf.

People screamed. Men in tails and white ties and women in elegant evening gowns threw themselves to the floor or clung to each other and trembled. Heads turned to stare at the half-dozen black-hooded men in loose green-and-black camouflage-pattern clothing who had burst in like wolves among pheasants.

And here I am practically naked in this ridiculous dress, Annja Creed thought, arched over backward with her hair almost brushing the elegant blue-and-gold carpet and only Garin Braden's strong right arm keeping her from falling.

SHE HAD THOUGHT the evening had started inauspiciously.

"How good of you to join me," Garin murmured when she presented herself at his table. Actually, she was presented by a bowing and scraping steward who acted as if he were giving a supermodel as a gift to a maharajah. Except a maharajah would probably not have received quite such deferential treatment.

Annja felt eyes sticking to her like clammy clumps of seaweed. She felt exposed in the clinging sheath of flame-colored silk he had picked out for her. Her long chestnut hair had been swirled atop her head by the cruise ship's expert staff of hairdressers. She suspected it made her look as if she had a soft-swirl ice-cream cone for a head. Around her slender neck she wore a delicate gold chain with an emerald pendant that Garin assured her would bring out the green highlights in her amber-green eyes. She knew it was exquisitely tasteful, just too small to be gaudy. But she could practically feel the weight of the money it had cost. It felt like an anchor.

"As if I had a choice," she said snidely as she allowed herself to be seated.

Garin laughed a rich baritone laugh. He was a charismatic devil, she had to give him that. And devilishly handsome. The catch was the consistent way *devil* kept creeping into her thoughts about him.

"There's always a choice, my dear," he said. "That is one thing life has taught me in no uncertain terms."

As always Annja felt conflicted about Garin, as she smiled and accepted the menu from the head-waiter. In his immaculate tuxedo with the star-sapphire stickpin, h_s black hair and goatee and dancing black-diamond eyes, Garin was admired by every woman in the room. He was charming, breathtakingly well-read and witty. He was vigorous, and as CEO and majority shareholder of the monster oil company EuroPetro he was, officially, richer than God. He was what most women in her position would consider one hell of a catch.

But *hell* was the operative word. That was the catch.

First of all, Annja had sworn off having affairs with men significantly older than she was. Not that he *looked* over the limit. Annja was in her mid-twenties. Garin appeared to be in his early thirties. But his real age belied that appearance—by centuries.

And then, of course, there was the fact that, while he sometimes helped her—indeed, she was paying off one of those debts at that moment—he also had the unfortunate habit of trying, at entirely unpredictable intervals, to kill her.

Around them people chatted and drank wine from immaculate crystal and ate five-star food. The cruise ship *Ocean Venture* was the most modern and luxurious ocean liner yet built.

"I can't believe I let you blackmail me to serve as arm candy for some business negotiation," she said.

"*Blackmail* is an ugly word," Garin murmured

over the top of his menu. "Besides, I believe *extortion* is more correct under the circumstances."

She glared at him through slitted eyes.

"You really must try the Pinot Noir. A splendid vintage. In any event, if you wish to keep your scruples inviolate, you can always choose to believe that you are here of your own free will. It's true, of course."

He held the crystal goblet up, where the light from the chandelier struck bloody highlights through the wine. "See? As I've told you, my dear. There's always a choice."

She winced.

He ordered for them. She didn't mind. It was the role he was playing. She was secure enough in her own independence not to feel threatened—least of all by him.

She did have something he wanted. And she did keep it coyly and carefully hidden from public view. But it wasn't what most people would think.

It was a complicated dance they danced.

The food was excellent but Annja ate mechanically. Distracted by circumstances, she scarcely noticed what she consumed. Growing up in an orphanage in New Orleans' French Quarter, she had learned not to be picky about what she ate. As she spent more time on the Crescent City streets she had learned to appreciate good food. Subsequently, as a graduate student and then archaeologist on innumerable digs, and in the last few years trotting the globe as staff talking head and resident voice of reason on *Chasing History's Monsters,* she had learned to be quite adventurous about what she ate.

She was preoccupied, on the evening of the first full day at sea in the Caribbean.

"So why *do* you have me here?" she asked.

Garin smiled. "Reasons of my own."

The reason she was there was that he had called in a favor. A big one. A save-your-life favor—not to mention the life of an innocent girl who'd depended on her.

Of course in the process of doing her that favor he had increased his wealth and influence almost exponentially. To his mind that failed to diminish the moral obligation one iota. What was worse was, he knew full well it didn't in her mind, either.

At some point in the future, when she wasn't still miffed about having her arm twisted, she would have to admit to herself there were worse fates than getting a free ocean cruise with a movie-star-handsome man who happened to be one of the world's richest. If she was a captive bird her cage was very well gilded by any standards. And her captivity, to call it that, would last no more than the four days of the cruise. But her fiercely independent nature bridled at it anyway.

"Come on," she said, spearing a piece of asparagus. "You owe me a better explanation than that."

He shrugged a broad, tuxedoed shoulder. "Perhaps you're right, Annja dear. I have no wish to torment you, after all. I am not a cruel man, you know—I worked that out of my system long ago."

She tried not to shudder, and tried harder not to envision just what he meant.

"Although I'm maintaining a low profile on this voyage," he said, "and the world at large still does not know my face—an expensive status to maintain, but well worth the investment—I have a certain image to project to those with whom I'm carrying out a certain, most delicate negotiation."

His accent was vaguely and indeterminately European. She suspected it was an affectation. He no doubt could speak English better than she could. He'd had long enough to practice.

Nonetheless it did contribute to making him devastatingly sexy. Curse him anyway, she thought. This could turn out to be a *very* long voyage.

"Aren't you concerned about doing that under the noses of the Venezuelans?" she asked. The *Ocean Venture* had just steamed past Aruba in the Netherlands Antilles, and was scheduled to make landfall at Willemstad on the island of Curaçao the next morning to allow sightseeing and, of course, a spree of shopping. Venezuela's north coast lay less than a hundred miles to the south.

"How do you know those aren't the ones I'm negotiating with? Their oil holdings might prove of interest to EuroPetro. They certainly do to the Chinese."

She looked at him hard. "Am I just arm candy?" she asked. She shook her head in almost reflex negation. "You could have your pick of supermodels or Hollywood stars. If you crooked one finger,

Nicole Kidman would kick Keith Urban back into rehab and fly at you like somebody's wristwatch to the inside of an MRI machine."

He laughed with a gusto that made heads turn. He paid no mind. He did few things by halves. "You've a gift for unexpected expression," he said. "Indeed, you've a positive gift for the unexpected. Is it not enough to know that I savor that? Because I do. Not to mention your beauty, which to my sorrow you constantly denigrate, and which possesses, to these jaded old eyes, a freshness few celebrities—especially the flavors of the week—can match."

Annja snorted in a most unladylike way. "Flattery," she sputtered.

He scowled and she recoiled slightly. She feared a lot of things and a lot of people—she had seen and experienced far too much not to—but she was intimidated by no one. He came close, though.

"Please, my dear," he said, softening a degree or so, "never say such a thing again. I never flatter." Then that grin, youthful and ageless, returned. "It implies I need to."

"Point taken." Finding her plate empty, she set down her fork, propped her elbows to either side, laced her fingers in their flame-colored long gloves and rested her chin on them. "Now, give. Why is it so important to have me along?"

"Perhaps I feel the need of additional security," he said, with a roguish twinkle in his eye. Well, even more than usual. "You make a most exemplary bodyguard, as well as a—shall we say—*disarmingly* lovely one?"

She snorted again. "I don't want to set off that touchy Renaissance pride again," she said—she was something of an authority on the Renaissance, it being her period of professional specialization as an archaeologist and historian. "But that seems rather hard to believe. You can afford to travel with a phalanx of top security men. And you do—I've spotted a few of them on the boat. Immaculately dressed bald guys with wires in their ears."

"Ship," Garin corrected automatically. "Without meaning to denigrate your own falcon keenness of perception, don't you think potential evil-wishers can do at least as well spotting such men? Whereas you are an extraordinarily gifted amateur, some of them are lifelong professionals at the craft."

"Hel-*lo*," she said quietly, "you're immortal."

He chuckled. "Being immortal doesn't necessarily mean I can't die," he said. "It just means I haven't."

He made an easy gesture with one hand. "I am extraordinarily tough to kill, I grant. But there are certain fates that might make me wish I could die. What if I was trapped at the bottom of the sea? So that I was perpetually drowning, but couldn't quite die? That would be like hell, would it not? So you see, I've plenty to fear. And of course, there is always my concern, now that you've claimed the sword, that my gift—the one that old rake Roux perversely prefers to consider a *curse*—of immortality might evaporate."

Annja's blood ran cold. She could never forget that Garin would—if he could—wrest the mystic sword of Joan of Arc away from her and break it to pieces again, as had the English soldiers who had captured St. Joan so many centuries before.

"Fear not, fair lady," Garin said, eyes dancing as he finished his wine. "So long as I continue to wake up each morning feeling hale and whole—you can continue to wake up in the mornings. Shall we dance?"

"You're a bastard," she told him as he held her chair and helped her to her feet.

"Born that way," he acknowledged, "although I like to think I've earned the title on my own merits, over the years."

When the band, perched on its podium to one side of the great ballroom, struck up a tango, Annja thought for sure the evening couldn't possibly get any worse.

"I don't know how to tango," she snarled in Garin's ear.

"You'll be fine," he said. "You're a natural athlete. And a trained martial artist. Remember your *taijiquan* balance training."

"I don't do *taijiquan* in heels," she said. She knew now why they called them *stilettos*—they were like daggers stabbing her feet at every step. As much experience as she had wearing heels—very little—she walked in them with all the grace of a drunken baby duck. Whereas she danced in the high spike heels, she thought, like a water buffalo on skates. But a *tango*— "I'll break an ankle!"

He laughed softly. "Follow my lead," he said. "It's worked splendidly for you so far."

She struggled to keep her irritation from showing on her face. Her gown was backless, and its bodice consisted of what she tried not to think of as bunny ears from just south of her navel upward, diminishing to bitty strings tied behind her neck. It was held in place either by some kind of surface tension, like a bubble, or through magic. And she didn't believe in magic.

She'd seen the tango sequences in *True Lies*. She secretly identified with Jamie Lee Curtis, a sort of standard-bearer for gawky women who could still be darned sexy. But once Garin started flinging her around she feared it would be mere seconds before her boobs came flying out of the dress like startled pigeons.

"*Trust* me," Garin said with a wicked grin.

"Yeah," she whispered furiously. "It's not like you've tried to kill me."

"Not recently," he said. "And most assuredly not here."

The preliminary violin strains died away. She felt his hand burning at the small of her bare back as if heated in a forge.

The tango began in earnest. He leaned forward. In response she leaned back, bent over his strong grasp. She felt her breasts ride up her rib cage and thought, *This is not good.*

That was when the terrorists barged in and fired a burst into the ceiling.

2

"Nobody move!" a black-hooded man shouted in Spanish-accented English. "We have commandeered this vessel in the name of the People's Revolution!"

"How tedious," Garin murmured, his face inches from hers. "It seems we're being hijacked."

"I'm almost relieved," Annja murmured. Her heartbeat, already accelerated, spiked. But she wasn't in any danger of losing her presence of mind over a little full-auto gunfire, even though it hurt her ears in these close confines.

At least it wasn't aimed at her.

With deliberation Garin straightened his back. He brought Annja upright as if she weighed nothing.

"You think they're trying to kidnap you?" she asked softly.

He frowned slightly. "I think not. Trust me, I'd sense their intention."

"How?"

He smiled. "Long experience. This is something else."

He let go of her hand. The other stayed at the small of her back. She found it strangely reassuring. "Now let's play along like good little lambs," he said.

She knew how he thought. "Until…?"

His smile widened. It made her think of a lean black wolf contemplating a staked lamb. "Until it's time not to, of course."

More armed men crowded into the room. They carried what Annja recognized as Kalashnikov AKMs, some with folding stocks, some with fixed wooden stocks. She had learned they were generic weapons for terrorists—or people who wanted to pose as terrorists. Something about the men struck her false. Maybe they're just pirates, she thought.

She looked to Garin. He was looking elsewhere. She saw him give his head a barely visible shake and realized he was telling one of his security men to stand down. For the moment.

At least a score of men in black ski masks had bustled in tothe ballroom. They broke up in to several groups. One rousted the musicians off the platform. In different circumstances it might have been funny to see the men and women in their penguin suits scurry off clutching their instruments to their breasts. As the gunmen on the platform covered the crowd, other knots of two, three and four began to move among the dancers, cutting them into groups of a dozen or so like cattle-herding dogs.

One of the men on the dais grabbed a microphone from its stand. "You are now the People's prisoners of war," he declared. "If you follow instructions you will be treated properly. Do not try to be heroes. If you resist you will be considered an unlawful combatant, and will be killed."

Garin's expression hardened. "Another unfortunate legal precedent we have to thank your government for," he murmured.

"Why are they separating us?" Annja asked under her breath. "Wouldn't it be easier for them to keep control if they kept us together?"

"Dividing the hostages into groups and dispersing them throughout the ship makes it harder for counterterror teams to effect a rescue," he said.

"Oh." Annja glanced down at her feet. She really wanted to ditch the heels. She always hated it in the movies when a heroine tried to run—or do anything more demanding than a runway turn—in heels. She'd hate trying to do anything herself if the crunch came down, encumbered with what she thought of as torture devices.

But the lightweight gold pumps had straps that crisscrossed past her slim ankles halfway to her knees. She knew they looked sexy. But they also meant she had no chance of kicking off the shoes quickly. She would have to bend over—which might cause misunderstanding among their captors. And

Annja made it a principle never to court misunderstanding with people toting automatic weapons.

Two men thrust themselves between Annja and Garin, jabbing at them as if their heavy Russian-made assault rifles were pitchforks. They might as well have been, for the alacrity they elicited from people shying away from their menacing black muzzles.

Annja found herself amongst a dozen—ten passengers and two stewards, the latter a man and a woman, both with painfully young faces sheened with nervous sweat. Of the group, six were elderly and four Annja's age or a little older, which seemed a representative sampling of the passengers.

The captives were being split up without regard to who was with whom. One thirtyish man with a blond crewcut tried to stay with a female partner who was being prodded from his side. A terrorist clipped him in the face with the butt of his rifle.

Annja winced. She knew the AKM was nearly nine pounds of hardwood and stamped steel, with a steel plate capping the butt. The man went down as if shot, although a moment later he was being helped to his feet by a fellow passenger and a steward whose crisp white jacket was never going to be the same with all the blood pouring on it from the man's smashed nose.

A pair of terrorists herded Annja's group to the galleys. One guard preceded them, kicking open the double doors. She caught a glimpse of Garin in a different group going out a side entrance. Then she was in the humid gangway, all white and stainless steel, redolent of cooking food and dishwashing steam. Stewards and chefs in their puffy white hats emerged from side doors, to vanish like rabbits down holes when the terrorists barked at them and pointed their rifles.

As their captors, shouting, herded them down the gangway, figures from the cruise line's brochures played through Annja's mind as she tried to encompass the tactical situation. Ocean liners always reminded Annja of skyscrapers toppled onto their sides into the ocean. The *Ocean Venture*'s vital statistics did little to belie that image. Over one thousand feet long and one hundred feet wide, more than two hundred feet from keel to funnel, grossing over 125,000 tons. With fifteen decks she accommodated two thousand passengers and over one thousand crew. She contained gyms, two swimming pools and even a water park.

It really was a horizontal, ocean-going skyscraper, plain and simple.

How many men do they have? Annja wondered. It would take a huge force of highly trained special-warfare operators to really secure something this huge with so many people aboard. She was no professional herself but she was still sure it would tax the resources of a full U.S. Navy SEAL team to do so.

No way did the terrorists—or pirates—have that many men aboard. No way did they have that kind of training and discipline. That was just practical reality, she knew.

So they would try to secure important locations, such as the bridge and engine rooms—and they would grab some hostages. They probably preferred the richest of the passengers—who happened to be attending the fancy-dress ball. She presumed they'd ordered everybody else to go to their rooms and stay there. They'd enforce the order by sending random patrols of men with guns to threaten anybody who poked their heads out.

As Annja's group proceeded, the doors that weren't opened by curious staff were yanked or kicked open by the terrorist in the lead. He seemed to be looking for something. Suddenly he dived into a room. A pair of white-clad staff erupted out like flushed pigeons and raced away down the hall. Apparently the men had all the hostages they felt they needed.

The lead terrorist emerged again. He had long kinky black hair flowing out the bottom of his ski mask. His eyes, visible through the holes, were dark. They showed a lot of white, like a frightened horse's. Annja didn't think that was a hopeful sign. A hyper-adrenalized state, a finger in the trigger guard, an automatic weapon with the safety off and crowded quarters was a potentially explosive combo.

"In here!" he shouted, gesturing with his rifle into what Annja could see was a storeroom lined with shelves of fat, institutional-sized cans.

Annja strode forward, wobbling only slightly.

Sharp pains shot up her calves. She held her head high and her face impassive.

From somewhere distant came the thud of a single gunshot.

GARIN BRADEN smiled and nodded encouragingly to the dowager with the blue-white hair and the gaudy string of pearls. His group had three gunmen herding nine prisoners, including a little girl of perhaps nine. From their stature and quick motions Garin surmised, not surprisingly, all three were young. Two carried AKMs. The third, who seemed to be a sort of officer, carried a handgun, a Beretta or the nearly identical Brazilian Taurus. They were highly excited. Perhaps more than even the circumstances called for. That concerned him.

Something about these self-proclaimed terrorists— or People's Revolutionaries—struck him as phony.

He took no more interest in the conflicts of human ideologies for their own sake than a normal adult in the battles between the red ants and the black. As with cruelty, it had taken him what he now frankly regarded as an unseemly amount of time to outgrow an adolescent interest in that sort of thing. But outgrow it he had, now centuries past.

He took the same sort of interest in politics and its attendant shooting conflicts that a canny sailor or pilot took in the weather—with a wary regard for potentially lethal storms. Unlike airmen or seamen, though, he also sometimes kept a weather eye peeled for potential profits from those situations.

He was particularly suspicious about Spanish-accented revolutionaries cropping up right off the coast of loudly socialistic Venezuela. Indeed, for self-proclaimed revolutionaries to pull so drastic a stunt within air-strike range of Venezuela smacked of an attempt to discredit or embarrass the government—or even a false-flag attempt to justify violent U.S. retaliation.

While Garin knew of the existence of various parties who might have the means and inclination to do such a thing, he doubted that was the case, either. His gut response told him this was really about ransom. Or *extortion* might be a better term, as he was amused to recall having told Annja in what now seemed a hopelessly trivial context, not an hour previously. The hijackers would systematically rummage the ship for valuables—the obvious, such as cash, jewels and credit cards, and the far less obvious, such as high resale-value prescription drugs both from ship's stores and private staterooms. Then they would negotiate a stiff cash settlement from the cruise line to get their ship back, as well as their passengers.

Part of the settlement would entail an agreement by the shipping line not to pursue the matter through the courts, nor to cooperate in any ensuing investigation. It was not legally enforceable, nor would it ever be admitted—but it would be most scrupulously kept.

It would be neither the first such deal struck nor the last. Garin knew the cruise lines were obsessed with keeping a positive public image above almost all else.

As far as he was concerned that was fine. The cruise company's craven but entirely understandable capitulation would make it difficult if not impossible to recover the cost of his own valuables through insurance. On the other hand the sum of it, including the little bauble with which he had chosen to grace Annja's charming swanlike neck, amounted to scarcely more than pocket change.

Should the terrorists actually annoy him, they'd find out that as a true son of the Renaissance, Garin had forgotten more about exacting vengeance than these modern upstarts would ever know. His reach, should he really wish to extend it, was as long as his memory.

And the fact he had forsworn cruelty for its own sake hundreds of years ago by no means implied he was averse to making examples of those who crossed him.

"Move it! Move it!" the leader of the gunmen screamed as they pushed the group of captives out the doors of the grand ballroom and into the corridor. Spittle flew out the mouth hole of his mask.

He struck at one older man with his pistol. Garin grimaced. It's not a club, you half-wit, he thought. He hated to see anything done badly, and anyway, his action was inviting accidental discharge. The man was barely in control of himself, and that was the worst thing.

The little girl, wearing a prim but visibly expensive blue silk dress, her blond hair pulled into painfully tight pigtails, suddenly broke away between the other two masked gunmen and raced back toward the doors of the grand salon screaming, "Mommy, Mommy!"

The leader of the gunman shrieked at her to stop. When she didn't he raised the handgun.

Garin frowned. "Wait," he said, and stepped in front of the masked man, holding up his hands.

The man shot him in the chest.

3

The men deep in the immense ship's brightly lit cargo hold paused in their work as gunfire clattered through the ship. It had a faraway sound, like hail on a neighbor's roof.

"Idiots," remarked one. Like the self-proclaimed revolutionaries above, his head was encased in a ski mask.

The resemblance ended there. The dozen men working in the hold wore casual street clothes appropriate to the Tropics. All of them were much calmer than the raging, rampaging, camouflage-clad hijackers—even the several who stood guard holding MP-5 submachine guns with their barrels thickened by built-in sound suppressers.

Their leader was a short man with a powder-blue shirt open to reveal a thick thatch of dark chest hair, silver-dusted and growing down toward a hard, aggressive paunch. He took a lit cigar from the mouth of his own ski mask.

"Hey," he said in a New Jersey accent. "Give 'em some credit. It's supposed to be a diversion. What's more diverting than a damn firefight?"

"Or a massacre," a third man said from behind the controls of the front-end loader. The others laughed.

The first man, who had fair skin, seemed sour. The ponytail sticking from the mask down the back of his neck was dark blond. "It's all good fun until the chopper-loads of SEALs start falling on the boat from the sky."

"Ship," one of the guards corrected.

"Shut up," the guy with the chest hair on display said. It came out emphatically but without heat. "That's just all the more reason to hurry up and get that bad boy loaded on the forklift." He waved the cigar at a large yellow-pine crate lashed to hold-downs.

"Boss," the driver said, leaning out of the little roll cage, "it's a front-end loader."

"Who asked you?" the leader said. "What is this, remedial English? Now move it, you assholes. We got us a boat to catch. Boat, not ship, Mr. Teach and Learn Network. And watch your fingers—that crate weighs a ton."

THE PISTOL SHOT echoed in the gangway. As Garin fell passengers screamed in horror.

Slowly, Garin picked himself up off the carpeted deck. He reached to the ruffled white front of his tuxedo shirt to the protective shield over his heart. His fingertips came away bloody. He scowled thunderously.

"You stupid bastard," he said to the gunman. "You've got no idea how badly that stings."

The hijacker's eyes almost bugged right out through the holes of his balaclava-style mask.

Garin moved. He had no extraordinary physical abilities other than his longevity. What he had was *practice.*

The gunman simply stood stunned, as if he'd taken a bat to the side of the head. He had no chance. Garin skipped forward. He batted the handgun offline with a quick swipe of his right hand. Then, closing fast, he clenched the hand to deliver a back-fist to the side of the mask-covered head with a snap of his hips and all the power of his big, well-muscled body.

The gunman's head whipped around from the blow. A string of saliva trailed from his bearded lips. A pair of his neck vertebrae snipped one of the arteries threaded through them like scissors.

With an arterial break that close to the brain, incapacitation was instantaneous, death almost so. The man simply fell straight down as if the tendons holding his joints together had dissolved.

Garin's left hand had grabbed the wrist of the man's gun hand. He caught the pistol as it slipped from lifeless fingers. Then he twisted counterclockwise and snapped his arm straight out.

The other two hijackers were still staring in slack-jawed amazement.

Garin shot one between the eyes. His head whipped back. His eyes rolled up. He sank to the deck. Though his finger was still on the trigger of his big Kalashnikov, he didn't fire. A hit in what counterterrorists call the "ninja mask" region of the head had punched through his *medulla oblongata* and instantly switched off his nervous system.

His partner was a little quicker on the uptake. He grabbed an elderly lady around the waist and tried to shove the muzzle brake of his AKM under her ear. It was a stretch, but he was well-motivated.

"Drop the gun," he screamed, "or I'll blow this old bat's head off."

From somewhere off through the bulkheads Garin heard a rattle of automatic fire. That will be dear Annja swinging into action, he thought. *I hope.*

Garin swung his arm around until the terrorist's staring right eye, visible inside a curl of his hostage's white hair, was perched like a plum atop his foresight post. He squeezed the trigger.

The eye vanished in a red splash. The terrorist dropped out of sight behind the woman.

She turned and looked down at her captor. Then she looked back at Garin. She seemed more startled than afraid.

"That was a remarkable shot, young man," she said shakily.

"I learned from the best," Garin said. I wonder

what she'd say if I told her that meant Wild Bill Hickok? he thought, amused.

Then he winced. It felt as if he'd been kicked by a mule. His body armor, worn from habit because his business dealings had a tendency to turn nasty, couldn't prevent bruising from the impact of such a close shot.

"You folks should find someplace to hide," he said. He quickly subvocalized commands to his security force, whom he had earlier ordered to stand easy and await events, via a high-tech and very well-concealed phone. Events having begun, he ordered them to move quickly to neutralize the other hijackers. He had faith they would do so with discretion and brutal effectiveness. He knew how to hire skill.

ANNJA'S HEART JUMPED into her throat. Garin! she thought. The guard with the long kinky hair was starting to bring up his rifle. His body language suggested he was about to start shooting.

Who are these people? she wondered. Terrorists were vicious by definition and usually crazy, but most of them knew not to massacre their hostages except as a final dying gesture. It not only burned all their bargaining chips, it ensured the authorities, when they inevitably landed on them, would be in a vengeful frame of mind. They'd shoot first—and probably not ask any questions. Ever.

Annja was already moving. Her total lack of coordination on those ridiculous spiked heels acted to her advantage. She tottered a couple of quick steps toward the gunman, then stumbled against him.

He caught her reflexively with his left arm. It left him still clutching the Kalashnikov's pistol grip with his right hand, and his finger still on the trigger. But in grabbing her he automatically dropped the weapon offline. It no longer threatened the innocent hostages.

His eyes went wide and his pupils dilated inside his mask as his left hand closed around Annja's right butt-cheek. "Ah!" he exclaimed. "It'd be a waste to shoot a hot *chica* like you."

"I think so, too," she said.

Annja snapped a right backhand into the hijacker's Adam's apple.

He fell back against the bulkhead, clutching his throat and emitting a rattling gasp. If she'd succeeded in collapsing his windpipe, he'd be dead in minutes unless he got an emergency tracheotomy—unlikely under the circumstances, however the events of the next few seconds played out. If not, he was still going to be way too preoccupied with a trivial little matter like trying to breathe to shoot anybody.

As Annja turned away from him she formed her right hand in a fist and exerted her will. Obedient to it, the hilt of her sword filled her hand, summoned from the otherwhere where it rode, invisible but always available.

The other gunman had turned to gape back down the gangway at the sound of the far-off gunshot.

Turning back, he goggled at Annja, struggling to swing his heavy rifle up to shoot her.

Somehow Annja managed to execute a flawless high-line lunge in her heels. She drove the sword through the man's sternum to the hilt.

He bent over as he took the blade. Or it took him. His eyes stood out of his head. He was literally dead on his feet, his heart virtually cut in two.

Annja let go of the sword. It vanished back to its private dimension. She grabbed the Kalashnikov as it fell.

Letting the man slump, she spun. Blessing the universal thug propensity to carry a weapon with the safety off at all times, she snapped the rifle up.

Still clutching his ruined throat with his left hand, the young man Annja had stunned was raising his own assault rifle to shoot her. She fired a burst from the hip. He fell backward as three metal-jacketed 7.62 mm slugs lanced through his chest and belly.

Glancing around the shocked faces of her fellow hostages, she quickly settled on the young steward with the prominent forehead as the calmest-looking of the lot. "You," she said in a voice that acknowledged no conceivable possibility that he'd do anything but what she told him. "Take the gun. Get the people in the storeroom and guard them."

He nodded and quickly knelt to recover the second Kalashnikov. Its owner was clearly dead, huddled against the base of the bulkhead. Annja wasted no pity on him—he was a victimizer of the innocent. He had gotten what he deserved.

"And watch where you're pointing that!" Annja snapped at the steward.

"Oh! Right. Sorry." Hastily he lifted the muzzle away from Annja's navel, where he was pointing the weapon because he happened to be looking at her. She smiled to take the sting from the tone she'd used.

"No problem. You might want to shake him down for more weapons and extra magazines."

"Sure." He seemed excited, eyes wide and bright, and dark cheeks flushed, as anybody would be. He seemed in no danger of losing it.

"What about you, young lady?" asked an older man with a salt-and-pepper beard and a substantial belly pushing out his white vest beneath his tailcoat.

She thought like mad as she finished searching the man she had run through for other weapons, finding none, and spare magazines, coming up with two.

"You never saw me," she said. Then she frowned. Where am I going to carry the magazines? she wondered.

"But that sword you used," said a blond woman about her own age in a floor-length blue gown. "Where'd that come from?"

Annja looked at her and forced a conspiratorial grin. "What sword?" she asked, and winked broadly.

She settled on unfastening the dead man's web belt. It was bloody. She grimaced but pulled it out from under him. She'd learned not to be squeamish since the sword had entered her life. Darn, she thought. And I became an archaeologist so I wouldn't have to deal with bodies that were still juicy.

She stood up. Everyone was staring at her with a combination of fear and awe. She felt hurried relief that, in apparent violation of the laws of motion, her breasts had not escaped custody in all the commotion.

"Listen, people," she said, "this is secret stuff, okay?"

Everybody nodded.

"I know," the young steward said. "You're some kind of special operator."

She gave him a smile. "I was never here," she said. "Okay?"

"Anything you say, ma'am," he breathed. He seemed to be working on not hyperventilating. She reckoned she had probably tripped the switches for all his adolescent male fantasies at once.

She turned to look at the others again. They seemed mostly to have huge saucer eyes, like alley cats who have been awakened to find themselves nose-to-nose with a grizzly bear.

"What you saw," she said, "is a big bald guy in a tux take these two down." That was a fair description of pretty much any random member of Garin's squad of bodyguards. "You didn't see any details because you were busy ducking like the smart people you are. You really don't remember it clearly anyway—you're so traumatized and all. Do you understand? This is extremely important."

They stared.

"Nod," she said.

They nodded.

"Breathe," she said.

They breathed.

"Great. Now—you, what's your name?" She turned to the steward.

"Tommy."

"Great," she said. "You nice folks all go in here and do what Tommy tells you. And Tommy will keep watch, and take care of you, and remember his responsibility is to stay with you and not, under any circumstances, to play hero. Right, Tommy?"

"Yes, ma'am!"

"And you." She turned to the female staffer. "What's your name?"

"Tina, ma'am," she replied confidently.

"You help Tommy take care of these people and keep them calm and safe. Are we good?"

"Oh, yes, ma'am," she said, eyes shining. "Very good."

Annja nodded decisively. "Okay. I'm going to go deal with some more of these bad guys. And once more, you never saw me, because I was never here!"

"Oh, yes," they chorused. "Didn't see a thing."

It'd be nicer, she thought as she buckled the gory web belt around her narrow waist, if this getup didn't make me look like a direct-to-video prom queen from hell. But we do what we have to do.

4

Steam wisped from Annja's mug of hot chocolate as she emerged from the small but well-organized kitchen of her Brooklyn loft. She wore a dark purple sports bra and white terry shorts. Despite the air-conditioning holding the flat summer day's heat at bay, her skin was sheened with sweat from her morning workout.

Finding a spot at one end of her sofa that was clear of books and manuscripts, she plopped down. She picked up the remote from the coffee table, its glass top also loaded down with artifacts, magazines and stacks of printouts. She clicked on the television.

One of the cable news channels came up. There weren't many kinds of daytime television she could bear to watch. Actually, most of her viewing consisted of watching DVDs, either of movies or occasionally whole seasons of TV series. She hated only being able to watch part of a story, and she hated commercial interruptions, although she did find some ads entertaining.

Not like I have much time to watch, she thought.

The modest wide-screen set showed a long, gleaming white ship shot from above. Helicopters swarmed around it, including the shark shapes of gunships. Boats of various sizes surrounded the huge luxury vessel.

Annja grimaced. She didn't have to read the white letters at the bottom of the screen. It was the *Ocean Venture,* where criminal investigators and counterterrorism experts from the Netherlands, the U.K. and the U.S. were still trying to sort out what had happened.

She muted the sound. It wasn't as if they were going to tell her anything she didn't already know. She just felt sorry for the passengers and crew, still stuck on board while authorities grilled them.

"WE'RE CLEAR TO GO," Garin had said, when he walked into her stateroom without knocking.

"What?" she replied, shocked.

He smiled that devil's smile of his. "I pulled some strings," he said. "Amazing what's available to be pulled when one is CEO of one of the world's largest oil companies. I could get used to it."

She narrowed her eyes. "You talked our way out of interrogation? What, did you bribe the SEALs? The Royal Navy? All of the Netherlands?"

"None of the above," he said. "It's always easier and cheaper to bribe the media. Listen and learn, young Annja."

The terrorists had never known what hit them. By the time the first SEALs swarmed over the stern from their fast STAB craft in the wee hours of the morning—they'd beat the Royal Dutch commandos by half an hour—the hijackers were all being guarded by Garin's highly professional security team in the cruise liner's ballroom. Garin had communicated with the rescuers in advance, using the ship's radiotelephone. Captain Nygard, who had started the rescue rolling by surreptitiously pressing a concealed panic-transmission button when the masked men burst onto the bridge, was very cooperative. One of Garin's bodyguards, himself a former Royal Marine commando, had dropped the hijacker aiming at the captain's austere silver-haired head with a head shot of his own. Garin's call had prevented any unpleasant incidents. Under normal conditions a counterterror team hitting a hostage situation would automatically kill anyone they saw holding a weapon.

Annja had captured several hijackers. She hadn't had to kill any more. Having a beautiful woman wearing a bloody and not very substantial evening gown burst in and aim an assault rifle at them got their attention. Especially since the rattle of gunfire hinted how very far wrong things had gone for them.

The presence of almost a score of far more

professional armed thugs in the midst of their intended victims had taken the hijackers utterly by surprise. They'd obviously expected the cruise liner to be a soft, undefended target. Civilian vessels usually were.

The total butcher's bill had been nine hijackers killed, three wounded. Almost twenty more had been taken prisoner. One of Garin's men had been wounded slightly when a mettlesome but over-wrought female passenger, believing him to be a hijacker despite his evening dress and lack of a ski mask, nailed him above the right eye with the spike heel of her shoe. I knew those things were danger-ous, Annja thought when she heard that.

Once the ship was secured, and the antiterror units converging on the liner had been alerted to the fact, Annja and Garin had returned to their cabins to change out of their incriminatingly bloody clothes. En route Annja wiped down her AKM and magazines for fingerprints and hid them in a broom closet. She showered and then had a fit of the shakes.

A pair of SEALs paid a visit to her cabin half an hour before Garin showed up. She was sitting in a chair wearing jeans and a short-sleeved blouse and the most innocent expression she could muster. They had been briskly professional as they searched her cabin for lurking terrorists, told her to stay put and await further instructions, and left.

She fully expected to spend hours being grilled by spooks and operators from half the nations of the earth. When they had rendezvoused briefly after the ship's recapture, Garin explained that the Americans were coming because they had the closest operational team available. The Dutch were sending men because the ship was in their territorial waters and the UK was getting an oar in because a lot of its nationals were on board the *Ocean Venture,* and anyway it still liked to imagine the Caribbean belonged to the Royal Navy.

And then Garin came waltzing in to tell her they were free to go. A EuroPetro helicopter was descending toward the afterdeck helipad to lift them off.

SITTING SAFE AT HOME in the air-conditioning of her loft, Annja blew at the hot cocoa, as if that would actually do any good, then tentatively sipped. As always it was hotter than she suspected and scorched her lips and tongue.

She winced and set the cup down. It was all part of the ritual.

She still remembered the surreal feeling as the blue-and-white Dauphine leapt gracefully off the *Ocean Venture*'s deck while Dutch commandos on guard stood by as unresponsive as statues, as if their camouflage battle dress wasn't being whipped and their very eyeballs blasted by helicopter rotor-wash.

"Why are they letting us go?" she asked Garin.

He smiled. "I told them something far more compelling to their minds than mere truth," he had told her. "I told them what they wanted to hear."

The media, courtesy of Garin's bribes or not—
Annja took what he told her with a grain of salt,
although experience had shown her that the more out-
rageous what he said sounded, the more likely it was
to be gospel truth—were asserting that the would-be
hijackers had fallen for a multinational sting operation
designed to trap modern-day pirates of the Caribbean.
It wasn't as far-fetched as it sounded—on the flight
to Curaçao Garin explained what a huge and growing
problem piracy was worldwide, although largely un-
reported even by the sensation-hungry news media.

She could also see how the nations of the multinational antipiracy task force would be more than
happy to take credit for what they believed had been
accomplished purely by Garin's security team. They
couldn't be happier than Annja. She'd spent way too
many uncomfortable hours answering pointed questions from sweaty men in uniforms.

For their part, the "People's Revolutionary" terrorists had reportedly confessed to being pure pirates,
interested only in looting the wealthy passengers and
gouging a vast hush-payment out of the cruise lines
to get their ship back. She knew not to take anything
in the news at face value—she'd seen what *really*
happened far too often. But she suspected that much
was straight. She hadn't bought the "revolutionary"
line from the outset, and gathered Garin hadn't, either.

Garin. At least he seemed to be done with her semi-
coerced services as escort. That was a relief, too. She
hadn't really been able to enjoy the cruise anyway….

To what extent Garin would consider she had returned his favor was an open question. But then, so was Garin. He had off-handedly explained that he had felt compelled to act when a little girl broke away to try to rejoin her mother, from whom she'd been separated. "Don't think it was a good deed on my part," he'd assured her. "I was simply worried that, once the hijackers started shooting, they wouldn't stop."

It was entirely plausible but she didn't believe it for a minute. Sitting in her own living room she still wasn't sure what to believe. Sometimes Garin seemed an embodiment of evil. Sometimes he seemed merely to be totally selfish—and she had seen enough authentic evil not to buy into the currently dominant wisdom that the two were one and the same. Many of the worst monsters she'd met believed what they thought was right so selflessly that they didn't care how many people they had to kill for their own good.

Sometimes Garin seemed almost chivalrous. She suspected that was illusion, too.

But she didn't *know*. I don't know anything where Garin's concerned, she thought. Except that our destinies are entwined, and going to stay that way so long as I carry the sword.

The TV switched to show a man with one of those boyish-gone-middle-aged hardcase faces under a crewcut the color of a steam iron. The screen identified him as spokesman for the Cruise Line International Association. She guessed he was about to very earnestly, and with great sincerity, lie across his bow tie about how the cruise lines would never, ever pay hush-money to terrorists.

She'd had enough. She turned off the television and picked up a recent copy of *The Journal of Forbidden Archaeology.* Thumbing to an article on crystal skulls, she began to read.

MEETINGS WITH the *Chasing History's Monsters* staff ate up Annja's afternoon. Her producer, Doug Morrell, had been in fine form, flitting around the meeting room like a butterfly.

"I don't really think," Annja found herself saying at one point, "that we need to address the issue of whether the Loch Ness Monster is actually a shipwrecked alien from a water world." Although he gets credit for unusual imagination for that one, she thought.

"GIRLFRIEND," Clarice Hartung said, leaning forward over the table, "I don't see how you manage to eat that much and stay that slim."

Annja chewed the mouthful she had bitten out of the specialty of the house—a prime rib sandwich, blood-rare, on toasted sourdough, with just a touch of horseradish—and shrugged. "I mostly seem to have trouble keeping weight on," she said.

Clarice shook her head in mock despair. She was a production assistant on *Chasing History's Monsters.* She had milk-chocolate skin, a cloud of reddish-brown hair that was more curly than frizzy, big dark brown eyes and a wide smile. "I'd kill for a problem like that."

"You look great," Annja said, taking a bite of pickle.

"For a full-figured woman, you mean?" Clarice said.

"No. Seriously." To Annja's eyes her friend was no more than pleasingly padded. Certainly not fat. And even Kristie Chatham might envy the décolletage threatening Clarice's Caesar salad from her golden-tan blouse. Had Kristie ever deigned to notice lowly production assistants.

Annja thought of saying as much. It just wasn't her. She could *think* catty. But she seldom voiced it.

"It's the starch," Mindy Llewellyn said.

"Say what?" Clarice asked, in the middle of taking a bite from her roll.

"Your problem is the amount of starch you eat," Mindy said. She was a somewhat hyper young woman, with ash-blond hair hanging straight to frame a gamine face with big blue eyes. She did makeup for several shows, including *Chasing History's Monsters*.

The closest thing Annja had to real friends on the show, the pair had prevailed on her to accompany them to Corrigan's, an Irish pub near the studios and consequently favored by the crew—although not, for the most part, the on-air talent—for a bite to eat after the production meeting. "To decompress from Doug," as Clarice put it.

Annja found it a pleasant enough place, with its dark-stained wood paneling, muted Celtic music and the prints on the walls, most of which seemed to celebrate not just leprechauns but worldwide specimens of what alt.archaeo, Annja's favorite newsgroup, liked to call "the fairy faith."

"Girl, I don't even want to be as thin as you," Clarice said. Mindy was toothpick-thin. Annja worried a little about her health.

Mindy shrugged. "I never seem to have much appetite," she said. She had ordered a salad, too, and a mineral water. She picked at one and sipped at the other. "But if you're really concerned about your weight, you want to stop obsessing on fat and start looking at the amount of starch you eat. Take those fat-free yogurts you're always snacking on. Have you looked at their contents?"

"Hey, they're healthy," Clarice said.

"Are they? They have the same amount of calories as the normal, full-fat yogurt. What they replace the fat with is starch."

"But carbohydrates are brain food."

"If you sit on your brains. Some are okay, but starches go straight to your blood sugar. And your hips. Like that roll. And the croutons."

Clarice looked at the roll, frowned and replaced it on the bread plate. "Are you trying to rob me of my simple pleasures in life?"

"I'm just saying," Mindy said. She shifted restlessly on the booth seat where she sat next to Annja.

Clarice sighed. "Well, the truth is, I worry about our Annja spending too many nights alone on her couch with museum samples and moldy manuscripts," she said. "You're going to turn into a mummy, girl. And not the kind that goes with a daddy."

"Too bad the only bones you're handling are long dead," Mindy said. She snickered. "I can't believe I said that."

Annja favored them with an exasperated half scowl. "Thanks so much for your votes of confidence. You sure know how to give a woman confidence in her own sexuality."

"Oh, you've got loads of sexuality, Annja," Mindy said. "Men throw themselves at you like moths at a flame. And you swat them like moths."

"I think it's more like they smash their little antennaed moth heads in against the glass wall of her apparent indifference," Clarice said.

"I am not indifferent!"

Clarice smiled an extra wide "trapped ya" smile. "You're right," she said. "The word is *oblivious*."

Mindy's skinny butt bounced on the bench. "Good one!"

Annja sat back and crossed her arms. "I'm so glad we had this time together," she said.

"Oh, don't take it so hard, Annja," Mindy said. "We tease you because we love you."

"And we wish you'd give some nice man a chance to."

Annja sighed. She'd *given* some a chance. But they had a tendency to not stick around.

Or to die.

But she couldn't tell her friends that. Even though their well-intentioned teasing was like sticking a knife in an open wound.

"What you need," Mindy said, swirling a plastic sword with a piece of lime impaled on it in her tumbler of mineral water, "is a nice, rich oil sultan. But not one of the religious fanatic ones. Or a fat one with oily skin and too many rings. A handsome, dashing young sultan!"

"Right," Annja said. "And they exist where?"

Clarice cocked an eyebrow at Mindy. "You been playing Prince of Persia on your PlayStation Two again?"

"All right, how about just a billionaire? I mean, a nice *young* billionaire. I'm not talking Donald Trump orange comb-over here."

"If you just believed in yourself you could catch one," Clarice told Annja. "Get him to take you for a nice cruise— What?"

Annja shuddered.

"You look like you've seen a ghost," Clarice said.

"That's one way to look at it."

Clarice set her generous mouth. "All right. Be that way."

"She will," Mindy said, spearing a bit of lettuce. "She always is."

BACK IN HER LOFT Annja stood gazing at her couch by the light of a lamp with a black metal shade. She had changed to russet sweats, a green T-shirt and running shoes. "Do I really spend too much time here with my papers and artifacts?" she wondered aloud.

Of course not, she assured herself. She trotted the globe almost incessantly, both for *Chasing History's Monsters* and on adventures of her own that were far less publicized.

But the evenings she spent on her sofa reading papers and arcane journals—not to mention alt.archaeo and alt.archaeo.esoterica—struck her now as sadly symptomatic of a major hole in her life. She couldn't escape it even by racing around the world.

Get off this track in a hurry, she told herself sternly.

Her eyes strayed to the end of the couch. The emerald pendant Garin had lent to her that night on the *Ocean Venture* was strung over the heavy wood frame like a cheap Mardi Gras trinket from New Orleans. He had insisted she keep it. When she tried to demur, saying it made her feel uncomfortable, he only laughed.

"Our destinies are intertwined anyway," he told her. "A bauble more or less makes no difference either way, don't you see?"

He had a point, she had to admit. She had hung it there, in plain sight, almost defiantly. She figured in the event anyone burgled her loft they'd leave it alone, figuring it had to be paste and gold paint.

She sat down on the couch, clicked on the television. Tuning it to a station that was showing a documentary on sea turtles—innocuous enough—and turning the volume just low enough to provide a reassuring murmur of background noise, she opened her notebook computer and went to download her e-mail.

She had just gotten engrossed in the current flame war regarding the true origins and purpose of the famous giant stone Olmec heads when her skylight exploded in a tinkling cascade of gleaming glass shards, and men dressed all in black came sliding on ropes into her living room.

5

Annja pushed the computer off onto the couch and leapt to her feet. Her rational mind was grid-locked. This is totally impossible, this can't be happening, things like this don't happen, it doesn't make any sense—

Fortunately her body had long since learned how to react to immediate danger without relying on her brain. The sword appeared in her hand almost as if by its own accord.

The men descending from the shattered skylight in a downward roil of humid air were dressed in black, from boots to masks. Unlike the balaclavas worn by the *Ocean Venture* hijackers these lacked mouth holes. The intruders carried what looked like submachine guns of a design unfamiliar to Annja.

Two landed in the middle of her hardwood floor. They turned to her. With her left hand Annja scooped up a heavy fossil of a large chambered nautilus that a paleontologist friend had given her. She threw it at the one on her left. He raised a black-clad arm to protect his face.

The heavy stone crunched when it hit his arm. Whether it broke the bone or not he reeled back, off balance. His partner seemed nonplussed by the fury of her counterattack—and by the sight of her suddenly swinging a broadsword with a three-foot blade in her right hand.

Belatedly he started to lift his weapon. She slashed him diagonally across the neck. He fell back clutching at his blood-spurting throat.

Taking the sword's hilt in both hands Annja screamed her fury at the violation of her sanctum and swung with all her might at the man who had deflected the fossil with his arm. That arm dangled. He tried to aim at her one-handed. Her blade caught him at the juncture of neck and shoulder and bit deep into his torso. He dropped to his knees.

He was wearing body armor. It didn't surprise her. It also gave little protection against her sword, which struck at the edge of his shell and found flesh. Hard-shell armor would bind her blade worse. She put her hips into yanking the weapon free.

The man fell onto his masked face. His blood soaked into her throw rug.

It occurred to her that if this was some SWAT team she was in big trouble. In her anger she didn't care. She respected the police, but she also respected a document some people seemed to think irrelevant—the Bill of Rights. She couldn't square masked paramilitaries kicking down people's doors and invading their homes without presentation of warrant with the protections supposed to be guaranteed to Americans—which no act of Congress nor stroke of presidential pen was supposed to be able to contravene. No matter what kind of "official" sanction these men could have, to her mind their actions made them nothing but violent criminals.

And if she had to flee the country, live on the run—well, Garin and her mentor Roux had been living outside the law for centuries. She would learn from them, or learn on her own.

Two more men rushed at her. Beyond the light cast by her lamp she saw more figures descending from the skylight's jagged blackness. Her heart sank. How many of them are there? she wondered desperately.

She parried an overhand sword cut from the nearer man, on her left. The sound of steel on steel was ringing in her ears before the realization struck her—there was no SWAT team anywhere in the United States whose members carried short-swords slung in scabbards over their backs. Belatedly she realized she had seen the hilts protruding above the shoulders of the first two men she had cut down. Her mind had refused to assimilate them at first, so unexpected were they.

Reflexively she had thrown her right hand up any

which way in response to the stimulus of seeing the two-foot straight blade flashing toward her eyes, and stopped it with the flat of her own weapon. Shouting again in anger she spun right, dropping her weight as she did so. Her sword sang a rising, skirling song as it slid across the other's edge and whipped free. The second man, trying to close on her right, danced back to avoid its downward-slashing tip.

She went low, scything out with her right leg in a spinning sweep. The first attacker did not expect the move. It took him in the side of the right calf and knocked both legs right out from under him.

She completed her spin, driving with her left leg, coming up from the floor, slashing up and right with her sword. The second man hacked at her. Metal rang like a bell, a high pure note. Then the intruder was staring in stunned amazement at the stump of his sword blade, cut off clean from his cross hilt.

Another intruder vaulted over the man she'd swept. She spun back into him, slashing him across the torso. He uttered a hoarse shout, muffled by his mask, as his legs flew out from under him. He fell across his comrade on the floor even as that man tried to regain his feet.

At the same time Annja fired her right leg in a back kick into the man whose sword she had broken. He staggered back.

Swordsmen surged toward her. How many she couldn't even tell. Motion yanked her eye upward, above them. A man was sliding down a rope and aiming his machine pistol at her. She turned, darted a few steps and dove over the back of the sofa.

As she landed on her tucked-in shoulder and rolled over she heard a stuttering. It sounded more like an air gun than a suppressed firearm, even one firing subsonic rounds. It sounded almost like a paintball gun.

To her surprise no bullets punched through the sofa after her. The wooden backing was pretty solid, but she didn't think it would stop bullets.

Her assailants left her little time to puzzle over that. She sensed someone looming over the couch. She turned, drew her legs in and kicked the heavy sofa over, back to front. The top of it slammed into the man's thighs, knocked him down and pinned him.

Annja got her legs under her and launched herself in a mad sprint the several steps to her kitchen. Spice jars on a metal rack hung from the wall shattered as a burst barely missed her. At the kitchen's far end a window led out onto a fire escape. Expecting at any instant to feel bullet impacts hammering her back she yanked it open and swung herself legs-first onto the landing.

She went down the first few metal steps on all fours, like a monkey. She was scarcely aware of having released the sword back into the otherwhere. There were just too many intruders to fight. Her only hope lay in flight.

Though the rungs and rail were slick with an

ever-renewed coat of pigeon droppings she sped down them, released the last stage to drop with a clang. If anyone shot at her as she pounded down the last few steps and dropped the several feet to the alley they missed her.

She ran.

FOR A DAZED INTERVAL she wandered the fever-humid nighttime streets, ducking in and out of alleys and trying to avoid the lights and other pedestrians as much as possible. She did not want to be seen. She wasn't sure whether or not she was soaked with blood.

That it all belonged to her attackers was certainly a comfort. It wouldn't make it any easier to explain to the authorities, though.

Despite the mugginess she hugged herself as if she were cold. Her teeth actually chattered.

It took an unknown span of time before she began to wonder at the strength of her own reactions. Being attacked so suddenly and violently in her own home was an emotionally devastating experience. She felt at once violated and unmoored from reality.

Her part of Brooklyn was largely given to settled but run-down residences and businesses just scraping by, interspersed with pockets of gentrification and gaping wounds of derelict buildings. That was one of the reasons she was able to afford the space she had.

The streets were never truly deserted there, any more than anywhere else in the five boroughs. But most businesses closed at night, and concentrations of foot or vehicular traffic were relatively rare. It simplified her task of staying out from in front of anybody's eyeballs.

The few people she did encounter tended to take one look at her and walk quickly in another direction.

Eventually she found a recessed doorway in a dark alley and simply slumped in it. Should anyone see her, with any luck they would take her for another of the homeless who haunted Brooklyn. And if anyone took her for prey, for a mugging or worse—well, that would be the worst mistake of their life. Not to mention the last.

She started to cry. The intensity of the emotion pouring out of her amazed her and scared her all over again. But she knew better than to try to fight it. She just let it out in ragged sobs, trying no more than to keep herself from making too much noise and attracting attention.

At last she vented enough terror and anger and despair to get control of herself. She sucked in great breaths of garbage-flavored alley air. It contained just enough oxygen to begin to clear her head.

What happened? she asked herself. She shook her head as tears stung her eyes again. There simply weren't any answers. Not rational ones. Certainly not good ones.

Misdirected no-knock raids, based on lies from paid informants eager to pass information on to their handlers so they would get paid, or get their next fix, or on something as banal as a mistyped address, were becoming a disgraceful commonplace event across the country. A SWAT raid targeting Annja might not even be a mistake. She had skirted a hundred laws in a score of countries, had poked her nose into places and matters where it most definitely had no business, in official eyes. In her own exacting estimation she had done nothing *wrong*. But not everything she had done was strictly legal.

But this was no police raid. Not with swords. While the apparent fact her attackers weren't any kind of law enforcement officers was good news, from the standpoint of her not going away to jail, it made things much worse by way of explanation.

Who used those kinds of weapons? Along with her brushes with authority, in the course of her knocking around the world doing battle with those who would oppress the innocent, she had run afoul of any number of scary people. If they—or their survivors—had identified her and tracked her back to Brooklyn, an all-out attack on her residence would certainly not be beyond their moral scope. But in this day and age, who attacked like that?

She put her face in her hands for a moment. Then she smoothed her hair back and took another deep, malodorous breath.

It doesn't make any sense, she thought. If they wanted to kill me, why not just open fire through the skylight? Or shoot me as they rappelled down from the ceiling.

Whoever attacked her had wanted to capture her alive. The thought gave her a fresh set of the shivers. What were they going to do with me once they caught me?

She shook her head. "All right," she said out loud. "I have lots of questions I don't have any answers to right now. So the question I need to ask is, what do I do now?"

She stood and took quick stock of herself. She was bruised in various places, mostly, she guessed, from diving over the sofa. She couldn't find any punctures, though, and nothing seemed broken. She had blood spatters on her arms and suggestive sticky spots on her face. She wiped those away as best she could with her hands. Or at least smeared them enough so that they wouldn't be readily identifiable She hoped. As for the spots on her clothes she could do little except be glad she wore blue jeans. Her tan short-sleeve shirt was less fortunate.

She started walking again, with no particular destination in mind. She had no cell phone, no money, no credit cards—and no apartment keys. She could probably rouse Wally, the building superintendent, out of bed to let her in. He was a decent old guy.

Of course, he might have some uncomfortable questions if she turned up knocking on his door at weird o'clock in the morning looking as if she had just engaged in a swordfight with a bunch of guys dressed like ninjas. She knew she could be quite persuasive, but she had limits. And she did not want him becoming suspicious of her.

More by accident, or subconscious design, than intention, she found herself within a couple of blocks of a little neighborhood tavern she had been in a couple of times. She wasn't well-known there. That was a start.

The place was loudly crowded and had big motor-cycles parked outside. That was bonus. She tended to get along with all kinds of people, even fairly rough ones. She had learned that polite friendliness, offering neither submission nor challenge, went a long way. More to the point, the patrons would probably not be too nosy.

She was wrong about that. About the male ones, anyway; too many heads for comfort turned to track her as she squeezed through the laughing, shouting throng. And far too many women gave her the evil eye. She was surprised by that, as she usually was by male attention.

But it was blessedly dark inside the tavern, and the butt-to-belly crowding, if more intimate than she usually cared for, served her as well. The combination made it impossible for anyone to get a good look at her condition. And the fact that any blood left on her had long since dried, combined with her ministrations in the alley, meant she didn't leave blood trail on the people she brushed against.

The bathroom was lit by a single yellowish bulb. Apparently the owners were concerned about energy

consumption—it seemed to draw about five watts.
She caught another break in that no one was using
the sinks when she slipped in, although a pair of
women in the stalls were having a loud conversation
about how nobody worthwhile was hitting on them.

In the grimy mirror she smeared the blood spots
on her shirt beyond recognition as anything out of
the ordinary with the aid of water quickly dashed on
from a cupped hand. Suspicious matting in her hair
got more or less rinsed out. Most overtly alarming
was the condition of her face—her eyes were puffy
from her intense bout of crying. She looked as if
she'd gone five rounds in the ring. Some more water
thrown on her face and a brisk rub helped some.

She managed to escape before the loud women
emerged from the stalls.

OKAY, SHE SAID to herself, walking the lonely streets
again. *Now what?*

The responsible, conventional, good-citizen thing
to do would be to find a pay phone and call 911. And
say what? Hi, I'm out on the street without any
money or credit cards because my home was invaded
by ninjas. Yes, *you* know. Ninjas. Like those Japanese
assassin guys. Except I'm fairly sure they weren't
Japanese. No, this happened several hours ago....

And how am I going to explain all the dead bodies
and bloodstains in my apartment? she wondered.

The strong desire to return home came over her.
She doubted her attackers had hung around long

once she fled. Even in New York the sounds of pitched battle might be expected to draw attention. Although it occurred to her the whole affair had been pretty quiet, all things considered, and the soundproofing was actually quite good in her building, testament to its industrial-grade construction. But in any event her attackers would not want to risk getting caught.

She hiked back to her apartment. It wasn't that far. Her wanderings had been more winding than linear.

The fire escape still hung low, unsurprisingly. A faint light shone from her window. She jumped up, caught the bottom step, hauled herself up. Then she climbed the metal stairs, moving carefully to make no noise.

The window had been closed. She put her back to the wall and risked a three-second look inside. A lamp burned in the living room. She saw no sign of anyone.

She summoned the sword and tried the window. It was unlocked. She caught her breath when it creaked as she raised it. Then she bent over and stepped inside.

She straightened. Something was *wrong*. Alarms yammered in her skull. Yet she did not turn and bolt back out the window and down the fire escape.

Because she realized that what was wrong was that—nothing was wrong.

The kitchen was clean. Intact spice jars lined the racks. They looked vaguely out of order, and she thought there had been more. But the floor was not a crunchy carpet of broken glass and cinnamon and thyme.

Cautiously she moved to the living room entrance. She smelled the sharp tang of disinfectant.

There were no bodies, no bloodstains, no shattered glass on the floor. The couch sat upright. The skylight overhead was intact.

It was as if nothing had happened.

6

Morning sunlight streamed through the window, bringing its peculiar vivid-edged glow. The sky was clear except for a few white clouds. Down in the street the traffic rumbled and honked.

Annja sat on the window seat and tried to concentrate on notes she was trying to type up for the show. It was all so normal she wanted to scream.

Normal it may have been. But all was not as it had been before.

There were little things out of whack. The papers and periodicals were stacked on two-thirds of the couch as haphazardly as usual. But the cushions on the couch were new, the colors and patterns different from what they had been before. Similar—but distinctly not the same. Likewise the throw rug. The one that had been comprehensively bled upon was just an inexpensive throw she'd bought at Wal-Mart.

This one, again, resembled the old one. But it wasn't the same. Aside from lacking bloodstains.

The semblance of normalcy did nothing to diminish her creepy feelings of violation. They only added an edge of eeriness, as if the old *Twilight Zone* theme played constantly in the background.

Aside from the mind-fry elements, Annja had to admit a certain elegance to it all. It made reporting the incident to the police even more problematic. Hello? Remember me? Ninja girl? Well, it turns out the ninjas took all the dead bodies with them and cleaned up the bloodstains. They even replaced my throw rug and the contents of my spice rack!

Mentally replaying the hypothetical conversation for about the tenth time she shook her head. That conversation would not end well.

Why? she thought, for far more than the tenth time. *Who?* She sighed. She didn't even know where to start investigating.

She tapped at the keys a bit more.

Investigate recent reports from the Republic of the Congo of sightings of a large animal which allegedly resembles a dinosaur. If there's anything to it, it may be the model for the mysterious creature, the dragonlike *sirrush*, represented on Babylon's ancient Ishtar gate….

She stopped. "I can't concentrate," she said aloud. "I may just have to go out to get anything done."

She picked up the remote to click on the TV. It felt like an admission of defeat.

The 24/7 news channel had finally gotten over the abortive *Ocean Venture* hijacking. It was back to showing the usual processions of disaster and despair, interspersed with the standard assurances that all would be well, if only the viewers trusted the government. She sighed and turned it off.

Her phone rang and she answered it. "Hello."

"Hello." The man's voice had a mannered, almost English accent. "My name is Cedric Millstone. Am I speaking to Ms. Annja Creed?"

"Yes, you are, Mr. Millstone," she said, secretly glad of the interruption. "What can I do for you?"

"I'd very much like to meet you and talk to you, Ms. Creed."

Uh-oh, she thought. He sounded a little older than her usual obsessed fan. "I'm sorry, Mr. Millstone," she said. "I'm pretty tied up right now. I have a number of very pressing commitments."

It was true. Annja couldn't—honestly—claim she never lied. But she tried to tell the truth.

"I'm sorry," the mellifluous voice said. "I know how this must sound. I could tell you I am a man of some standing in the community, a man of considerable means, but I fear that might only tend to confirm your altogether natural suspicion that I harbor improper intentions. I can provide you references, but doubtless you are aware the voice that

answers at any number I give you might not be
whom he portrays himself to be."

"You're right, Mr. Millstone. I have to tell you,
that's almost exactly what I'm thinking," Annja said.

"Then let me tell you I wish to offer an apology,
and an explanation, for your recent inconvenience."

She drew in a sharp breath. She felt a complicated
mixture of fear and anger.

"Inconvenience," she said. It was almost a hiss.

"An inadequate word, I grant. As I say, I shall
endeavor to explain, and insofar as possible, make
amends. May I call upon you?"

Don't do it! the ever-cautious voice at the back
of her head cried. Nothing good can come of this.

She felt her mouth stretching in a tight-lipped expression that someone near-sighted might mistake
for a smile in bad light. I can rationalize about how
it's a matter of personal security to find out all I can
about whoever attacked me last night, she thought,
but the truth is I'll go crazy if I don't find out.

"We'll meet," she said.

ARJUNA'S COFFEE SHOP was a favored hangout of
Annja's, in easy walking distance of her loft and
convenient to the subway station where she caught
the train to Manhattan to work. It managed to be at
once spotless and cozy, not an effect all that easy
to achieve and not too common in this part of
Brooklyn. The owner, Mr. Brahmaputra, was a stout,
friendly, voluble man who always wore an apron

over his capacious belly, and had slightly protuber-
ant, heavy-lidded eyes behind thick round lenses.

Annja associated India with chai, not coffee. She'd
once asked Mr. Brahmaputra why he opened specifically a coffee shop, instead of a *chai* emporium.
"Because I like coffee better," he replied. Both the
coffee and chai he sold were excellent, as was everything else. That and the friendly ambience of the
place had helped him build a loyal clientele over the
years, enabling him to withstand repeated efforts of
a well-known chain to displace him.

Despite the café's name, Arjuna wasn't Mr.
Brahmaputra's first name. It referred to the Hindu
hero-god, whose charioteer in battle was no less
than the god Krishna, who was always lecturing
him about karma in *Bhagavad-Gita.* Reproductions
of some fairly alarming traditional portrayals of
Arjuna adorned the walls, many with Blue Boy
crouched at his side, nagging away.

"So, Mr. Millstone," Annja told her companion
through the steam rising from her freshly filled cup
in the artificially cooled air, "I believe you had in
mind to apologize and explain. Given the enormity
of what you have to apologize for and explain, I'd
say you have your work cut out for you."

Cedric Millstone, or at least a man who bore a
decent resemblance to the pictures she'd seen in a
quick Google search, nodded his head. He had a
large face, more sideways-oval than round, red as
a brick beneath a wavelike coiffure of hair as white

and perfect as a marble sculpture. His dark blue suit was expensive-looking, his nails recently manicured, his watch a Rolex. His cuff links resembled the exposed works of a small watch, gilded. Annja was disappointed the little gears didn't turn.

"There has been a terrible misunderstanding," he said. He had the kind of plummy voice that always suggested its owner was chronically constipated to Annja.

"I'll agree with the terrible part," she said.

He nodded as if accepting a passed sentence. "Truly, I know, there can be no restitution for what was done to you."

"You could make a start," she said, sipping her coffee and savoring its strong taste, "by cutting out the evasions and getting to the point."

He showed her a pained smile. "Quite. I'm sorry. This is rather difficult, you see—although not, of course, nearly as difficult as what you have been put through. I represent a certain private international society devoted to humanitarian works."

"Humanitarian? Is that what you call breaking through people's skylights in the middle of the night and trying to kill them?"

"Not kill, Ms. Creed. I assure you. The men who…attacked you…had been given strict instructions not to harm you."

"They shot at me." It was perhaps a testament to the sort of life she'd been living of late that it didn't take any particular effort to keep her voice down. If anything, she was way more upset about the violation of her personal space. People shot at her all the time. It no longer particularly bothered her. So long as they missed.

"Tranquilizer projectiles only," he said quickly. "A…proprietary design. Quite painless and free of distressing side effects."

"Aside from being captured like—what? A black bear who's wandered into the suburbs? And if all they wanted was to capture me, why did they come at me with swords?"

"I surmise, in an attempt to intimidate you into surrendering. Obviously, an ill-advised course of action. Terribly so, in light of what happened. Nor in honesty can I blame you for the actions you took. You defended yourself and your home against a violent invasion. You acted within your rights. Laudably, even," Millstone said.

"What did they intend to do with me, once they intimidated me, or knocked me out?"

"Question you concerning a certain artifact that vanished during a very recent attack on a luxury cruise liner off the Netherlands Antilles," he said. "Despite the play the incident received in the global media, certain details have been altogether glossed over. As you're no doubt well aware, Ms. Creed."

"Oh," she said, almost under her breath.

"I am, as I believe I have indicated, well-connected. My society possesses resources far in excess of my own. We were able to ascertain that you were aboard the vessel, despite the fact your name appeared nowhere on the passenger lists. Indeed, the cruise line had no record of you in their computers at all."

She had blessed Garin for his efforts in making them disappear from all the attention, both official and media, focused on the hijacked ship. Now the law of unintended consequences had apparently swung around to whack her in the back of the head.

"That disparity, combined with your mild international notoriety in connection with a rather sensationalist television series which concerns itself with arcane matters, led us to suspect you might be involved in the disappearance of our holy relic."

"I might be offended at that characterization of me," Annja said, "except nobody's ever referred to me as notorious before. I kind of like it but, did you say *holy* relic?"

He nodded. "What disappeared from the *Ocean Venture*—was stolen, to be quite candid—was an artifact of great antiquity. It has been in the possession of my society for centuries. It is a casket, containing the bones of a certain very holy man. Legend says they possess miraculous abilities."

He made a dismissive gesture with a well-scrubbed pink hand. "But that, of course, is legend. Whatever the case, it does hold a great religious significance. For us," he hastened to add.

Pieces fell into place in Annja's head so hard she could almost hear them click. "So the hijacking was just a cover all along," she said. "I thought there was something wrong with the whole setup. I mean, aside from the screamingly obvious."

"Indeed. As closely as we can piece the story together, the people who attacked the ship legitimately, if I might use the word in such a context, intended robbery and extortion. It appears unlikely they realized they were being employed as a noisy and, in the event, highly lethal diversion. The men who stole our relic appear to have been most helpful in alerting the would-be pirates to the prospect of hijacking the *Ocean Venture,* as well as in planning the operation."

He tipped his splendid head to one side. "They might have been wise to question their benefactors' motives a little more closely. Then again, pirates are not historically noted for their wisdom."

"So you thought I was one of these *benefactors,* who helped set up the raid—the real raid?"

"Not I, personally. Certain more volatile members of our confraternity, however, did jump to such an ill-advised conclusion."

She sighed. "And I thought getting flamed in the network chat rooms by Kristie Chatham fans was the biggest downside of my gig for *Chasing History's Monsters.* So I take it you've decided I wasn't involved?"

"Yes. I speak for all our brothers in this. Leaving aside certain persistent rumors flying among the passengers and crew—which I will say, I now find less incredible than I might, in light of your actions last night—no one with the ability or the connections to disappear off that vessel like a will-o'-the-wisp could possibly be involved in the attack or the theft. A party with access to such resources would have no need of employing such crude means to rob us, frankly. Or having chosen to set in motion such a scheme, taken the ridiculous risk of actually being on board when the operation occurred."

"That makes sense," Annja said. "In hopes of stemming speculation, I'll just say that I'm fortunate in my friends. And that's all I'll say."

She hoisted her cup to her lips with both hands, sipped, then frowned down at the dark liquid as if she saw tadpoles swimming in it. Unaccustomedly she was drinking it black today. It fit her mood.

She returned the cup to the tabletop with exaggerated care. "So what do you want of me now, Mr. Millstone?"

"First, to express how truly sorry I and all my brothers are that these things were done to you. That you were put in the horrible position in which you found yourself. We are willing to pay substantial sums by way of reparation."

She held up a hand. "I wouldn't feel right."

He nodded briskly. "I suspected as much. Very well. You are an archaeologist of some repute and achievement despite your tender years. You also have investigative talent, as manifest in your work for *Chasing History's Monsters*. And, clearly, you have certain highly advantageous connections. We should like to hire you to recover our stolen artifact, Annja Creed."

"No," she said without hesitation.

He smiled. The expression was almost bitter-sweet. He actually seemed like a nice man. She knew well just how little that could mean.

"If you would be so kind as to give the matter some thought—"

"My home was invaded, Mr. Millstone. Men *died*. All as a result of this little mix-up of yours. I killed them. I won't pretend or evade. Nor for that matter do I feel the trauma we're all assured will over-whelm our lives and swamp our fragile psyches should we ever take the life of another human being. I may be horribly hard-hearted or maladjusted, but what I honestly feel about that is, if somebody attacks me, what they get is what they have coming."

"My brethren and I," he said, "would be the last to disparage such a sentiment."

"But I don't take it lightly." I never do, she thought but did not say. "Your little elves were very efficient about scrubbing out the bloodstains on my hardwood floor. No doubt you've got proprietary technology for that, too. The moral stains do not wash out so easily."

"The men who died considered themselves sac-rifices for a holy cause," Millstone said.

"I don't believe in human sacrifice."

"I see. So that is your final answer."

"It is."

He rose. "I regret your choice. I have to say, however, that I greatly respect it. I hope you will re-consider. I wish you good day, Ms. Creed."

7

Annja couldn't let it go. That simply wasn't in her nature.

She went straight home—or straight after taking a few fairly routine detours to ensure Mr. Millstone, or his any of his more hotheaded "brothers" less convinced of Annja's innocence than he, weren't tailing her. She fired up her computer and jumped online.

Blast him, the painfully well-groomed and unctuous Cedric Millstone, with his white wavy hair, had snagged her interest like a rose thorn in white silk stockings. But it was straight down her line—an ancient artifact with strong mythical associations, stolen by men ruthless enough to stage the hijacking of a ship full of three thousand innocents. A bloodbath waiting to happen—just to cover their real crime. That was heavyweight, she thought.

Anyway, she told herself, I feel as if I'm already

caught up in this. She was rationalizing again, she knew—up to a point. When men bust in through your skylight at midnight, it's fair to say you're caught up.

She went first to Google Earth, a delightful resource. She knew its publicly available satellite imaging frequently captured pictures not just of boats but even aircraft in flight. Rumors persisted online and in the coffee shops that some showed less conventional objects moving over the earth, and were quickly suppressed by secret government order. Ridiculous conspiracy theory, so far as Annja was concerned. Her passionate attachment to civil liberties wouldn't let her echo certain fellow skeptics, who demanded such rumor-mongering be outlawed. But she understood where they were coming from.

Having come up with the longitude and latitude of where the hijacking had taken place, she quickly found an image time-stamped not two hours earlier of the *Ocean Venture,* still anchored in place while authorities from at least three nations swarmed over it looking for evidence and endlessly interviewing witnesses. She felt a stab of sympathy for the passengers and crew. Still, there were worse places to be trapped for several days. The liner was stocked with not just necessities but luxuries for a week or more out of contact with land.

The images showed nothing of the hijacking itself. She quickly found an online forum, however, that had sprung up in response to the attack. Through it she was able to locate several archived pictures from different satellite services showing the attack itself. Three big powerboats were moored to the liner's square stern. From them the attackers had apparently fired grapnels over the taffrail and climbed aboard undetected.

The pictures had been snapped at fifteen-minute intervals. Apparently that part of the Caribbean was much photographed. In the third image in the sequence a fourth ship was visible floating alongside the others. It was a bigger vessel, eighty feet long or so, and looked like a power yacht.

By the fourth image it was gone.

Annja sat back and smoothed her hair from her face. Her sound system played Evanescence, just too low to make out Amy Lee's haunting vocals. She considered the situation. After a few moments she got up and went to the kitchen to pour herself a glass of cold water from a bottle in the fridge. Then she returned and sent copies of the pictures of the interloping vessel to several friends, with a carefully worded request.

Two hours later she was roused from reading a geology textbook by the chime announcing she'd received e-mail.

The return address belonged to a Romanian acquaintance of hers in Berlin, although the domain was not a German one. When she saw that she made sure her antivirus library was up-to-date. Just on general principles.

The e-mail had several attachments. Annja ran an antivirus scan on them. When they checked out clean she clicked on the most intriguing, by reason of its extension.

It was a music file, cryptically named "001.mp3." When her media player came up it started playing a song she recognized as being not that much younger than she was. It was an old Van Halen hit.

The song was "Panama."

Frowning, she looked at the other attachments. Then she put the notebook computer aside and sat back to digest what she had learned. By habit she clicked her television on to a news channel.

It showed an oblique helicopter shot of a white-and-blue aircraft broken and burning with billowing orange flames in a marshy-looking area. "Near Kearny, New Jersey," the newsreader was intoning, "where it crashed on takeoff from Newark Liberty International Airport late this afternoon after both engines failed simultaneously. The airplane, a private Gulfstream V jet, was registered to millionaire financier Cedric Millstone of Boston, Massachusetts. The Federal Aviation Administration has just confirmed that Millstone himself was on board the aircraft, as well as an assistant and three flight crew. There were no survivors…."

"HEY, CYRUS! My man," sang out the deep-tanned man with the aloha shirt open to reveal a chestful of grizzled hair with a gaudy gold medallion in the midst of it. He had a New Jersey accent, a shiny brown bald front to his head and a big, hard paunch. His voice echoed over the slight sloshing of water inside the boathouse. "Do I deliver the goods, or do I deliver the goods?"

The man he had addressed as Cyrus allowed himself a thin smile. "I guess that remains to be seen, doesn't it, Marty?"

Marty Mehlman had his whole team, a dozen men, gathered together in the boathouse. Windows set high in the wooden walls spilled an olive-oil colored afternoon light across the water, the plank gangway and the big oceangoing yacht moored to the dock with its mast unstepped and made fast to the deck. The water threw back the light in shifts and surges, playing across the features of the men. Cyrus knew them to be a selection of experienced North American and Central American, mostly Panamanian, hoodlums. They were all pros, all intrinsically small-time—competent, but not the hotshots they thought they were. They had been hired to pull a job. They had done so in workman-like fashion.

Maybe. Cyrus had not gotten where he was by taking things for granted. He happened to be in Panama City, on the Pacific end of the canal.

Marty liked to play up. He made a show of lighting a cigar before answering. Then, puffing a wreath of bluish smoke around his sunburned bean of a face, he said, "What, Cyrus. Don'tcha trust me?"

"You know what they say," Cyrus said in a cold voice. "Trust, but verify."

Marty shrugged. Cyrus had him down as a man who didn't care what you said to him as long as he got paid.

Mehlman circled an upraised finger over his head and whistled to his crew. They used a block-and-tackle arrangement trolleyed from rails along the ceiling of the boathouse to pull a crate from the yacht's hold. It was a big crate, four feet by four feet by eight. Its proportions were suggestive in a morbid sort of way.

Cyrus stood watching as the crate swayed onto the wharf. He wore a white tropical-weight suit and a white straw Panama hat with a garish fuchsia and neon-green tropical-flower band. It was the only hint of color about him, except for the amber of his aviator-style sunglasses. His hair, cut close to his skull, was light blond. His skin was so pale as to make him seem an albino, which he was not.

He was remarkably thin. He was so thin he looked fragile and looked shorter than his actual height, which was only a couple of inches under six feet without the hat. He was so desiccated that his skin had a parchmentlike texture. The combination of gauntness, pallor and dryness gave him the appearance of being both sickly and elderly—even his thin-lipped mouth was wrinkled like an old man's.

Although not young, Cyrus wasn't elderly. As for his skinniness, he had been born with a sense of taste. He simply didn't care for food, so he ate little. He believed that excessive intake of fluids was bad for one's health, so he drank little as well.

He did very little, though, to dispel any impression he might be infirm. He frequently found it useful.

When the long yellow pinewood box thumped on the dock Marty turned and squared himself toward Cyrus. "There," he said, fists on hips. "The goods."

"Give me a break, Marty," Cyrus said. "It's a box."

"Okay. Okay. Louie, bust the crate open."

A big rough-looking American with a broken nose and a blond crew cut came up with a four-foot wrecking bar. "Tell him to be careful," Cyrus said.

"Be careful," Marty said, as if translating.

Louie pried the crate with splitting, squeaking sounds. He pulled the lid off and let it slam down onto the dock.

Cyrus winced. He walked up and peered down. Inside was a lot of strawlike plastic packing material. He brushed at it until he saw a hint of dull gray metal. He touched it. It was cool and smooth to his fingertips.

"Clear it away," he said.

Marty scowled and waved at his men. A couple of dark, spare Panamanians stepped up and scooped handfuls of the packing material out and dropped it on the planks.

"Whoa," Marty said. "It's a coffin."

One of the Panamanians made the sign of the cross.

"Okay," Marty said, puffing like a steamship on his cigar. "Are these the goods, or are they the goods."

"They're the goods," Cyrus said.

"All *right*." Marty slammed his hands together and rubbed his palms.

His lieutenant, Pujols, had light-colored skin and dark blond hair tied in a ponytail. He wore a lightweight white jacket over a black and scarlet shirt. His expression was pinched, his manner nervous. He had been shifting his weight from foot to foot the whole time.

"Just pay us and let us get outta here, okay?" he said in a staccato Puerto Rican accent. His jacket hung open, revealing a big angular hog leg of a government-model Colt autopistol in a holster beneath his left armpit.

Cyrus smiled. "Sure," he said. "Why not? But don't you want a look inside?"

Pujols made an unhappy, impatient sound low in his throat. Marty frowned, looking puzzled more than annoyed. "What?"

"Sure," Cyrus said. "Look inside. You've worked hard for your money. Now why not get a look at what all the fuss is about?"

Marty chuckled. "Sure. Since you put it that way, why not?"

His men tried the lid. It wasn't secured in any way. Though extremely heavy it swung open on hinges that might have been lubricated yesterday, so smooth and soundless were they. A waft of cool air freighted with exotic spices rolled out. Marty and his crew crowded around to peer inside.

Their faces open like flowers of amazement unfolding. "Oh, my God," Marty breathed.

"Say hi to him for me," the man he had called Cyrus said.

At both ends of the boathouse, along the landward wall, doors burst open. Men in street clothes stepped inside. They held MP-5 machine pistols with built-in sound-suppressers to their shoulders. The guns fired with little popping barks, like seals who had lost their voices.

Most of the men fell right down, dead in an instant, killed by surgically precise two-shot bursts to the head. Pujols was fast. Marty was faster than he looked. Both men ducked around on the water side of the opened casket. Pujols drew his big .45.

With barely a ripple and no sound beyond the wavelets slogging endlessly against the yacht's sleek flanks, two heads wearing black wet suits and rebreather masks broke water right behind them. Suppressed MP-5s rose with them. They coughed explosively.

Marty and his nervous lieutenant fell backward into the water.

Cyrus gazed impassively at the bodies slumped on the dock in spreading maroon pools, the corpses bobbing slowly in the water.

"Thanks, boys," he said as the two frogmen clambered up onto the decks and peeled their masks off their heads. The men reloaded their weapons and closed the doors. "Now, if you wouldn't mind giving me a hand getting this sucker closed and picked up on the loader? We've got a boat to get it aboard before it sails," Cyrus said.

"Who's taking delivery?" one of the men who had come in from outside asked, strolling up. He had slung his machine pistol muzzle down behind his right shoulder.

Cyrus laughed like a crow cawing. "You should know better than to ask that, Rushton," he said. "Need to know, amigo. Need to know."

8

The taxi rolling down the wide toll road called the *Corredor Sur* from Tocumen International Airport on the city's eastern edge was white and red faded near pink by the scorching Panamanian sun. It was a Buick, about as old as Annja herself. Its air conditioner wheezed asthmatically and thumped alarmingly without appreciably thinning the humid heat. The cabbie ran it full-on anyway, despite having all the windows rolled down. Its noise and the early-afternoon traffic sounds of downtown Panama City did have the beneficial effect of mostly drowning out the cab's CD player, which was chugging out terrible mid-nineties studio-gangsta rap at a volume that would've rattled the windows had they been up. Annja could feel the beats in her teeth.

They turned off the highway at a downtown exit. As with a lot of Latin American cities everything except the skyscraper-central middle of the business district interspersed shiny looming modern buildings with smaller, more inhabitable-looking older ones. In this case *older* meant mostly a particularly baroque variant of Spanish Colonial that Annja found especially charming.

Looking out the window at the awning-shaded shops and the crowds Annja was struck by a resemblance to New Orleans' Latin Quarter. For all its well-publicized French heritage her hometown owed as much cultural debt to its long period of Spanish occupation as to France.

She did find herself wondering, Does archaeology ever happen anywhere it isn't hot or humid? Although to be fair, she had to admit that she wasn't exactly there to do archaeology. She had archaeological aims, though—to try to make sure an unknown artifact was properly conserved. So maybe that counted.

Her Romanian contact had used what Annja suspected was pirated NSA image-comparison software to sift through terabytes of raw overhead imaging. She had a feeling not all of it was supposed to be publicly available.

Her hotel, the Executive, stood in the midst of Panama City's booming financial district. Annja had picked it because it got good reviews online, its rates were reasonable and also because, to her thoroughly irrational delight, it looked like nothing so much as a tower of giant white Lego. She tipped the driver, a dark taciturn man who had spoken English with a Punjabi accent, and wore a maroon turban.

The Executive staff, perhaps having seen American currency changing hands, leapt forward to help Annja with her bags.

Inside the lobby was cool, bright and clean. There was no line. Panama wasn't exactly a leading summer vacation spot for Northern Hemisphere folk. The neat, compact clerk was cheerful and quite efficient.

Annja walked toward the elevator. A bell-person, a commodore at least, by the splendor of his uniform, trundled a laden luggage cart after her with much creaking of casters. The newspapers for sale in the lobby boxes screamed at her in Spanish and English—Bodies Found in Boathouse.

It was the same message they had imparted with equal stridency at Tocumen, when she had finally cleared customs. It gave her a tight feeling in her gut. She didn't fail to believe in coincidence, exactly. She'd encountered her share, and several other people's, too, she judged. Such as when she found the sword. Of course, if she saw the same vehicle or the same face in the crowd, as she went forth about her business this late morning and afternoon, she'd suspect she was being shadowed. She had been before. and was pretty sure she would be again.

She did not believe that arriving in Panama City in pursuit of a white motor-yacht her friends had tracked through the canal from the Netherlands Antilles by sifting satellite photos to discover a whole bunch of guys had just been gunned down in a boathouse in the old harbor district, came anywhere *near* coincidence.

Her hotel room was clean and fairly comfortable. She clicked on the television, where a local news broadcast quickly confirmed her suspicions. A sixth body had been discovered, bobbing in the harbor. Being Latin American television, it gleefully showed the corpse of a male floating with arms outflung and a seagull perched with its web feet in the salt-and-pepper thatch of his chest.

"And thanks so much for the wonder of zoom lenses," Annja said. She looked away, but left the sound on while she hung her few changes of clothes in the closet.

The authorities, she learned, blamed the massacre on a drug deal gone bad. Next—the sun is expected to set in the West later today, she thought with a grimace.

Still, she told herself, don't be an ingrate. Had it not been for the perpetual war on drugs, and the equally smashing success of the war on terror, she would have found herself facing many more uncomfortable questions about a certain propensity she displayed to turn up in proximity of the freshly dead.

She left the TV running when she cruised out the door. It was a minor security measure to discourage the amateurs—this was the Third World and hence thick with them.

Seven hot, frustrating, increasingly waterlogged hours after setting forth, Annja shoved her weary, footsore way back through the revolving door into the hotel lobby. She had negotiated the Panama City public transit system, labyrinthine and irrational even by Latin American standards, with a combination explorer's instinct and hard-won experience. The sun had dropped into the Pacific in the alarmingly abrupt way it did in the lower latitudes, so that you almost expected it to send a vast boiling tsunami hurtling toward shore. or at the very minimum to make a loud splash. It had left the downtown streets to the neon lights, taillights and loud music and at least as many acres of suntanned skin as there was asphalt.

Annja hadn't found any answers.

She hit the bar in the hotel. She needed to recharge and to come up with a new plan since no one she'd encountered on the waterfront would admit to knowing anything about the mysterious yacht or the bloody massacre.

Her attention was drawn to one end of the bar. Loudly cursing his fate and the television over the bar, a man grumbled to himself about the current newscast and the "nobody-heard-nothin' boathouse massacre."

9

He was a young man, Annja's age, maybe a bit younger. He *looked* as if he might be older. But that was because he was definitely the worse for wear. As was his dark suit and rumpled white shirt, whose collar lay open, like a slack noose. If he had worn a tie it had vanished, like the old-time pirates of the Spanish main. Except it wasn't near as likely to turn up again, either as a signature Disney attraction or in speedboats.

"Damn you," he moaned in Spanish at the devastatingly beautiful female newsreader in the red dress. "Tell the truth for once, can't you?"

"Mind if I sit down?" Annja asked.

He blinked eyes like cocktail onions at her. He had olive skin, light for a local. She guessed he wore a hat and lots of sunscreen outside. He had longish dark hair, almost down to his collar, and a longish sort of face, with brown eyes and charcoal-smudge eyebrows.

"I'd like to ask you a few questions," she said.

"Why not?" he said. "I may despair, but I am neither dead yet, nor blind."

Switching to English, he said, "I am Guillermo Miller. I am a reporter. For a newspaper—a real reporter. I don't just play one on TV."

His smile was even briefer than the joke called for. His lips were loose and purple and moist. They suggested he'd been drinking many beers, as did the array of bottles on the bar before him. The eyes suggested he'd cried into them all.

Annja settled on a stool beside him. They had that end of the bar to themselves. The lounge wasn't particularly crowded. And apparently the existing customers didn't want to listen to his heartfelt moans and groans.

"Why do you bemoan your fate so?" she asked in Spanish.

But he wanted to speak English. He did so with complete fluency, albeit a distinct accent.

"I might, if I were a cautious man," he said, speaking with the exaggerated precision of the well and truly drunk, "suspect you to be from the authorities, come to test my discretion. But I have no such fear. Do you know why?"

"Why?" Annja asked.

"Because I see you are clearly an American. Oh, not by the lightness of your skin—there are Latin women lighter even than you." He turned back to curse the newscast.

Annja could see from watching him that the young Panamanian showed many clear symptoms of being someone who cared, way too deeply, and was wounded by the gashing realization that the world, by and large, didn't.

"Well," she said, a little shakily, "I'm a pretty skeptical person myself."

"Ahhh," he said, drawing it out. "That's too bad."

She felt cold, as if the air-conditioning had suddenly been cranked to rapid glaciation. She was losing him suddenly. What did I say? she wondered.

"It is too bad," Guillermo continued, taking his time until she had to step hard on the impulse to grab him by the throat and shake a few words out of him. "Because people like us, we skeptical rationalists, are prone to disbelieve in conspiracy theory."

He raised a bottle of beer that he almost certainly thought of as *half-empty,* scrutinized it, then drained it. "Because if we actually look closely at the world, we see that conspiracies do not simply exist, they abound. They're all around us."

"You're right," Annja said, a little shortly.

He blinked at her like an owl at a hunter's jacklight. "You agree?"

"Oh, yes."

He nodded. He seemed pleased. His brief reserve had melted away into good-feeling and relief so overt and sloppy she was afraid he'd burst into tears.

"Well then. You might be surprised at what I will tell you, but you may not reject it out of hand,

as I feared a skeptic would. As I would, before I
became a reporter and began to see how the world
really worked."

"Don't tell me anything that's going to endanger
you," she said. It cost some effort to do so. But if I
let my integrity slip I'm no better than those I fight
against, she thought.

He shook his head. "It's already beyond that, dear
lady. Oh, if you went to the authorities, things would
go hard with me. But the greatest risk is knowing
what I know What I dare not say. Because, you see,
I have been *warned*."

"Warned?"

He nodded his head emphatically. Then he
stopped abruptly, as if afraid it might fall off.
"Warned. Warned that if I tried to publish what I had
learned, well—there's always plenty of room in the
broad Pacific Ocean for another body to float in."

"Don't keep a girl in suspense," Annja said.

But he suddenly became coy. "But it is hard to
talk when one's throat is dry," he said.

Part of her, a somewhat cynical side she suspected
she should be ashamed of, actually exulted—a potential informant I don't have to get drunk! That was
always a pain and entailed certain risks. Although
Annja usually found it much easier to get a guy drunk
than a guy would getting *her* drunk. She despised the
sensation of being out of her own control.

But Guillermo was beyond mere drunkenness to
the point where Annja's saying, "Here, will you

finish my beer for me? I hate to see it go to waste," was received, not with instant ice-bath-sobering suspicion, but with a sly sloppy joy, as if he'd somehow, without even trying, put something over on her.

He swigged at it happily and wiped his mouth with the back of his hand. "Better. Much better. Now. I have excited your curiosity, no?"

"Why, yes. Don't be a tease, Guillermo." That was as far into flirtation as she intended to stray. She despised teases, and in general tried not to lie. That said, if lives lay at stake, she would do as she must.

"I know a man," he said. "Not a good man. But one who has no reason to lie. Also he has given me information before which was good as gold.

"He saw what happened at that boathouse. He was watching from an abandoned shop nearby—what he was doing there he did not say, and I did not need to know. Nor do you. He saw only from the outside. But what he saw was armed men who approached the boathouse from cars they had parked some distance away. They suddenly burst inside, as if in response to some signal. And then he heard shouts, and screams, and a *poh-poh-poh,* as if someone was using an air wrench on an automotive tire."

"Oh," Annja said, rearing back. She saw no reason to pretend not to know what a suppressed firearm sounded like.

Guillermo nodded. "He was frightened, as any-

one would be. But he is a curious man. I do not know
if he is brave, so much—he has more curiosity than
sense. Just like a monkey. And we're really all just
monkeys, we humans, are we not?"

"We'll make an anthropologist of you yet," she
said, which seemed to please him. She prodded him
gently back on track. "So what did he see?"

"He saw a large object. Much longer than it was
wide or high. A box. Its shape was, shall we say,
suggestive?" The way he said *suggestive* did not
bring to mind lascivious eye-rolling and hands making violin shapes in the air, but something darker. "A
plain pinewood box. It seemed very heavy. It was
being carried by a front-end loader."

"What happened to it?" Annja said.

"A panel truck backed up. The men shoved it inside
with much grunting and cursing. That was how he
knew how very heavy it must be. And the cursing was
in English. North American English, señorita. My acquaintance, let us say he has frequent contact with
tourists. He can recognize English accents, as some
North Americans can identify Spanish ones—as you
yourself can, if I am not mistaken?"

She bit her lip. I can see why he makes a good
reporter, she thought. Even with his brain sloshing,
he's pretty perceptive. She hoped he wouldn't be too
keen in scrutinizing her.

"I can," she admitted. She knew if he caught her
in a lie he'd glue his lips shut.

"And it was what he heard that was most intri-

guing indeed. What I very most wished to share
with my editors. And which they told me, flat out,
they did not wish to hear."

"Which was?" If he hits me up for another beer
now, I am totally going to smack him, she thought.

He smiled a wide, moist-lipped smile. "Why, the
name of its destination. A freighter, he said."

"What was it?"

He shook his head. "That he would not say. He
wanted money. A substantial sum. More than I had
on hand, shall we say?"

"So you did try to take the story to your editors?"
Annja asked.

"Oh, yes. Yes, indeed. I did try that."

"What did they say?"

He shrugged. "They seemed very…what would
you say? Reserved. Not excited, as they should be
at such a scoop, no?" He picked up a fresh bottle and
cradled it in both hands as if afraid cruel hands might
try to pluck it away. "And then not long thereafter I
received a visit from certain parties. Which I took,
incidentally, to represent in its way the position my
editors had taken on my story."

"Police?" Annja wondered.

Again he shrugged. "Who can say? They made it
clear their visit was official. But off the record—as
they wished my story to remain."

He set the bottle on the bar before him and regarded
it sadly. "I am a young man," he said. "I believed
myself willing to put my life on the line for the truth."

He looked at her, and something like defiance blazed in his bleary eyes. "And perhaps I am. But—" He shrugged and sighed. The fire went out. His shoulders slumped and the muscles of his face, briefly taut with passion, sagged. He seemed to age twenty years right before her eyes.

"It seems not so noble to die for a story that will most certainly be spiked."

She put her hand on his. "This may be little consolation. But I tell you truly, Guillermo—you're right. A brave man does not simply toss his life away. Any dog can die in a ditch."

He gazed at her. "You are most wise, despite your lack of years." He raised the bottle. "I salute you."

She laughed. "Don't be too impressed. It's an old samurai proverb."

"You're a student of the martial arts?" he asked.

"Yes." She saw no harm in imparting that truth.

"Good, good," he said. "They may come in useful when you go to see my man. If of course, you choose to do so. He lives near the old docks, where the shootings took place. In a part of the *Casco Viejo* that is not so quaint. Although it is picturesque in its own way."

He gave her an address, and directions that were likely to be of more use. She memorized them easily.

"Thank you for trusting me," she told him. "You took a great risk, I know. But I will try to justify it."

"I do risk much," he said. "And I hope you can make use of what I have told you.

"But then," he said, and his manner suddenly

seemed more sober, "I know the famous Annja Creed is not a spy for the Panamanian police. Whether she is a spy for her United States Central Intelligence Agency I am willing to risk. Because, I think, who better to make use of information I am denied the use of?"

He stood up. His legs were perfectly steady. So were his eyes as he smiled.

"Many thanks for the drinks," he said and he walked out of the bar—not like a man intoxicated, but rather like one who had just relieved himself of a heavy burden.

Annja stared after him long after he'd vanished into the early subtropical night. Was he setting me up? she wondered. Somehow, she doubted it. His bitter chagrin, and his relief at finding someone who might actually make use of his information, had seemed genuine. Even if his level of inebriation wasn't.

Whether it's a trap or not, you're going to walk into it with your eyes open and trust your reflexes. Because that's what you do. She realized one of the bottles on the bar in front of the young reporter's vacant stool was only half-empty. She realized most of what she had taken for thoroughly dead soldiers were.

She picked up one and drained it. After all that, *she* needed a drink.

10

Annja's hopes of avoiding the bizarre, public transportation system the next day were dashed when her cabbie, a black Panamanian, refused to take her to the barrio where the address she was looking for could be found. He explained in eloquent and vigorous English and Spanish that that was no place for a nice American lady to be.

She thanked him for his concern, paid him off and tipped him well for bringing her from downtown and set off on her own. Two hours later she found herself in what she hoped was the right neighborhood. She could have walked there, she guessed, in about a quarter of that time.

As it was she still had a walk of several blocks past garbage-strewn lots sporting sundry ruins dissolving back into lush subtropical undergrowth, and of desperate government housing blocks, more resembling prisons than apartments, with slab cinder-block walls and razor tape tangles surrounding them. The rusting metal skeletons of derelict cars, some burned out, dotted the cracked and root-heaved streets like casualties of war.

It reminded her of parts of Brooklyn.

Plenty of knots of young men with bodies the consistency and color of tropical hardwood slouched on the corners or perched on car corpses. Without even thinking about it she changed course to avoid them when she could.

Since coming into possession of the sword she had found herself becoming far more solicitous to avoid potential confrontation whenever possible. It was precisely because she possessed such very final means of ending physical attacks. The sword's terrible power, the ease with which it carved human flesh and bone, rubbed her nose in the responsibility of carrying it.

The best way to win a fight, she'd discovered time and again, was to ensure it never started. She had studied the body language of victims—so as to avoid it. She learned to assess her surroundings and who was in them, to recognize potential threats far in advance. For the most part it wasn't particularly challenging—she found it kind of fun, actually. And she religiously did something a lot of people she'd talked to, to her surprise, really resisted. When she identified a potential threat, whether it was a pack of adolescent males or a dark bottleneck with lots of places for muggers and rapists to lurk, she'd go out of her way to avoid it. Many people, it seemed, would rather risk getting robbed at gunpoint, beaten, or worse than be ninety seconds late for work.

Perhaps not too surprisingly, it turned out that *not-a-victim* behaviors were pretty much what she'd done her whole life. That was simply the way she was. She made herself mindful of the habits, and put a little more emphasis on them.

So when she couldn't entirely avoid the rootless young pack predators, since the only way to do that would be stay out of this area completely, she made eye contact, smiled and nodded. It was the same thing she always did with people on the street, even in New York City where the response tended to be hostility or paranoia, if not both. If they continued to look at her hard, she kept smiling—but hardened it a bit, and thought, If you mess with me, you'll wind up bleeding and I'll be inconvenienced. So don't start.

As usual, no one did.

The apartment block where her hoped-for informant lived was one of the dreary many, neither the most desperate nor the most inviting. Once inside she found herself the object of attention by groups of dirty and ragged little kids. She smiled, nodded, said hi. They giggled and ran off.

People watched her from doorways as she climbed up three flights of dingy metal stairs to the third-floor apartment address Guillermo Miller had given her. Their expressions were more suspicious than anything else, except maybe disbelieving. She could hardly have been more out of place if she'd been an alien. Again, she just smiled and nodded.

Abenicio Luján answered the door on the first knock. He was a wiry little guy with a snub nose in the face of a wizened boy, short curly black hair dusted with gray and bandy legs. She saw why Guillermo described him as a monkey. Guillermo had mentioned he lived with "one of his girlfriends." This was more information about his private life than Annja cared to know.

His manner was less suspicious than she had expected. She anticipated Guillermo had called him to warn him to expect a visitor—and to give him a chance to disappear if he feared the contact was risky. She now realized one or more of the young men she'd passed on the stairs had almost certainly called him to warn him she was on the way.

Poor people, she had found, either lived in a war of all against all, or they looked out for each other. Actually, they tended to do both, dividing into factions by neighborhood, apartment block, or extended family. Outsiders tended to dismiss, or dread, such assemblies as *gangs*.

Annja knew, in truth, such groupings were often necessary accommodations to the brutal realities of poverty, especially in places where caste lines or regulation made any kind of economic advancement next to impossible.

Luján, she judged, was probably a marginal type even by the standards of this brutal and ugly place. But he too was part of the net.

Two crisp U.S. twenties were enough to start him talking. He described the scene at the boathouse much as Guillermo had. The curious activity, the men with guns suddenly converging and going inside. The strange sounds. The screams.

He didn't say how he happened to be creeping around the vicinity, undetected by the boathouse killers. Annja didn't ask. She didn't need to know.

"So what happened next?" she asked.

He scratched himself under the left arm and looked as if he were trying to remember. "You get the rest of the money when I get information worth paying for," she told him briskly. "Right now I haven't heard anything to justify what I gave you."

"Look, señorita," he said, his black bright eyes darting up and down the walkway, "I'm putting myself way out on a limb telling you this. Those were some bad men there at the Old Harbor."

"Good men don't usually shoot people down without warning," she said, "even men as bad as the ones who got themselves killed were. Listen, Mr. Luján. You've already said enough to risk becoming a target. I'm making myself one by being here talking to you. So here's the deal—tell me the rest and I'll pay you more. Or you'll be in the same amount of danger *without* having as much spending money in your pocket when you take that little trip for your health."

He laughed. "You're pretty sharp for a gringa, señorita. I bet all the gringos run away scared from you."

"Only when I show my teeth, Señor Luján." If only that were true, she thought.

"Okay. The killers, they come out of the warehouse. They were big men, gringos, too. I don't speak the English good, but I understand it, pretty right. All except one. He was a real skinny guy, dressed all in white, in a white hat and sunglasses. Real pale skin. He was the boss, I could see that. The others, they were all scared of him, even though one of them could twist him in two."

Annja nodded encouragingly.

"And so they backed the truck up, like I said, and moved this big old crate off the front-end loader into the back. They really had to fight with it, you know? And when it went inside, the truck sank down on its springs. It was heavy.

"Then the guy dressed all in white, he says, 'The *Solomon King* ups anchor in two hours. Make sure that's aboard.'"

"The *Solomon King?* Not the *King Solomon?*" Annja asked.

He shook his head. "No. I may not have heard right. But it sounded like that."

She set her mouth. She could sense he wasn't jacking her for more money. The way he was starting to rock and bounce on his toes she could tell he was eager to get this over with and make good his escape.

"Anything else?" she asked.

He shook his head. "Swear to the Virgin, señorita," he said. "They all got in cars and SUVs and drove away. After I was sure they were gone, I got the hell out of there myself. And that was that."

She gave him a fifty and left.

ANNJA MADE IT to the Panama City harbor master's office an hour before closing. Ship departures were public records. She had checked for the date of the boathouse massacre. The offices were brightly lit, well-organized and well run. The canal did too much business, and was feeling too much pressure from potential competition and its own rising passage fees, to be run any other way.

Her heart fell into her now-swollen feet when she found no vessel named either *Solomon King* or *King Solomon*. She took a deep breath and scanned the entries again. This time she spotted the name on a registry—*Solomon Kane*.

Heads turned as she laughed out loud. Apparently the harbor records weren't usually an occasion for hilarity.

"Sorry," she told the inquiring faces. Eyes rolled, then looked studiously away.

IN HER TENTH-FLOOR ROOM in the hotel Annja sat cross-legged on the bed. She had her notebook computer propped on a pillow in front of her so its processor heat wouldn't burn her bare thighs.

She was wearing shorts and a T-shirt and thoroughly enjoying the air-conditioning after the day's exertions.

Somebody's got a sense of humor, she thought, as she sent out inquiries to her contacts around the world. None of whom were her Romanian acquaintance in Berlin. She didn't want to go to that well too often.

Over the music coming in through her iPod earbuds she heard her computer chime. A message popped up in the lower right-hand corner of her screen to let her know she had one new message. She clicked it.

The subject line read *Re: Birthday Party.* The e-mail address belonged to a college nerd friend of hers who now worked for a software development company.

The message read, Picked up an image of a ship sailing from the P-City harbor at the time you gave me. Whoever knew a Robert E. Howard fan would name a Liberian-registered freighter?

"You are such a dork, Frank," she said to the room. "And I'm a total dork, too, for getting the reference."

The bad news, Frank continued, is that it's tricky to track a ship across the big blue Pacific without something like a Keyhole bird targeted specifically on it.

"Great," Annja murmured. She was trying to fend off the despair a few seconds longer. I was this close....

However, the most recent image I can find confirms that, at least for now, your target's on a heading consistent with its self-proclaimed destination of Mati on Mindanao in the Philippines. I think I can keep tabs on it enough to confirm it's continuing to head the right way. As long as there isn't a storm.

"Right," Annja said. "No storms. In the Pacific."

She was going to need luck. Or the artifact for which so many had died—whatever it was—was going to be lost to science.

And into the hands of parties about whom all she could say was that they were *evil*.

11

The sentry walking the foredeck was a small, wiry man in loose, dark pants and shirt. The cloth wound around his head would have been a deep green, had there been any illumination there on the foredeck right by the freighter's blunt prow. The captain and crew kept the *Solomon Kane* dark.

The AKM strapped to the sentry's shoulder was almost as long as he was.

The noise was like a car backfiring halfway down the block. It reached his ears a second before the hollow-tipped 180-grain .45-caliber bullet reached his right temple. He wasn't even curious yet when he died.

Men were already swarming over the railing to either side of the bow. The body did a fast-motion melt to the grubby deck.

The intruders wore black uniforms, with black boonie hats, black boots, black web gear. Their faces were blackened. Their suppressed submachine guns, HK UMP-45s with suppressors screwed on their barrels, were likewise black. The dark hilt of a short sword jutted over each man's shoulder.

Using a variation of the approach that had been used to steal the coffin from them, they had come in motor launches from over the horizon. The *Kane* was not a particularly prepossessing nor well-maintained vessel. If it even had radar it probably wasn't functioning reliably, not that their three small inflatable boats would have been easy to pick up. The freighter's crew seemed a lot more concerned with not being seen than seeing—given the general blackout, no spotlights swept the water.

A fire team of four invaders knelt to cover their comrades with shouldered weapons. Two more quartets ran aft to press themselves against port and starboard ends of the deckhouse.

A man walked sentry on the deck before the bridge. Apparently sensing something amiss, he came forward to the rail to peer into the night. He did not attempt to unlimber his own AKM.

He never got the chance. One of the four men who knelt in the bow fired a single shot from his UMP. The turbaned head jerked. The sentry toppled over the rail to land with a clatter on the main deck.

At once an alarm began to ring from high up on the deckhouse. Muzzle flashes lit the night. As yet no bullets came near the raiders, who were still climbing aboard and moving according to a hastily choreographed but well-rehearsed scheme. As two more fire teams came up, one man from each of the first two quartets to the deckhouse twirled a grappling hook briefly from a black-painted fist and tossed it upward over the rail.

I AM MUCH TOO OLD for this shit, Captain Thorolf Sigurdsson thought, seeing the man on sentry watch vanish over the rail right before his eyes.

Two of the three passengers on the bridge with him and his night-watch crew exchanged alarmed barks in what he believed was Indonesian. Or some accursed language or dialect of that accursed archipelago—there were ten thousand islands to choose from, after all. One hit the switch to sound the ship's alarm. Sigurdsson winced as automatic gunfire snarled immediate response.

"We use radiotelephone," the leader barked at him in English. He alone was bareheaded. He and his aide wore autopistols in flapped holsters. The third man, clearly a mere foot soldier, carried a Kalashnikov slung on his back. All three men wore curve-bladed swords thrust through their sashes, or in the leader's case his web belt. The archaic weapons seemed as much a badge as the racing-green turbans.

In his youth, Thorolf Sigurdsson had been a lusty seaman, eager to live up to the tradition of his Viking forebears who settled his home in Iceland a thousand years before. He studied hard and earned his master's license. He was a master seaman, but never one to be overly concerned with the niceties of maritime law.

In his declining years, that casual attitude had tripped him up, along with a certain propensity to alleviate the boredom of lengthy sea voyages with alcohol. He had not lost his certification…quite. But such was the cloud over his head that he had been lucky to find employment with the somewhat shady holding company, nominally headquartered in Monrovia, who owned the *Solomon Kane*. From scattered hints he gathered the company in turn was owned by someone in the People's Republic of China.

Despite his lapses in judgment, and maybe even morals, he had never stooped to piracy. Nor once considered it. And while he had no more patience or reverence for customs and taxes than he ever had, he drew the line at terrorism.

Unfortunately, it seemed his employers did not.

Cursing the wakefulness that had driven him to this late-night visit to the bridge, Sigurdsson nodded to his own radioman, a diminutive Ghanaian national who insisted on being called Bob. Bob, ebony face sweat-sheened beneath his baseball cap, leapt up from his seat with alacrity. The leader's lieutenant, still standing, picked up the handset.

The front windscreen shattered.

Thunder filled the bridge. The green-turbaned head exploded as if filled with nitroglycerin.

THE VESSEL THAT had dropped off the assault boats kept steaming steadily forward, closing with the *Kane* on a course to pass a few hundred meters to her portside. This was a fairly well-traveled sea-lane; the very immensity of the Pacific made it advisable for ships to ply consistent routes across it, so that help might have a better chance of finding them in a timely way if something went horribly wrong. Worldwide, on average one major ship—freighter to container ship to even oil supertanker—was lost each week. Some were sunk by storms or rogue waves. Others simply vanished from the face of the earth.

For all his high technology, Man was little closer to taming the voracious appetite of the sea than when his ancestors first ventured into the surf on badly trimmed logs.

When the growling whine of the freighter's alarm reached the approaching ship, a freighter no more descript nor reputable-looking than the *Kane,* muzzle flashes blossomed like fireworks from her deck and deck house, and all need for pretense evaporated. Spotlights blazed from the second ship's own deckhouse, turning the *Kane*'s midnight foredeck to day and blinding enemies who happened to be looking that way. Crashing volleys of Kalashnikov fire filled the night with sound and fury. It would have signified more had it been aimed better, or at all. As it was, most of the frenzied full-auto bursts, each dumping an entire magazine, did no more than highlight targets for the men in black to hit with precisely aimed shots.

Fire teams raced back along both sides of the deckhouse. One man fell as a burst from inside an open hatchway ripped across his belly. The man behind him threw a grenade. He and a partner followed its crack and white flash into the passageway. The first man went high and left, the other low and right.

Three green-turbaned men had been crouching just inside the hatch. Two lay on the deck. The third was shot as he leaned against the bulkhead clutching his shattered leg.

He had dropped his AKM. It made no difference. Whatever the outcome of this brief, savage fight, mercy would neither be requested nor extended by either side. This was to the death.

CAPTAIN SIGURDSSON stared with wide, horrified eyes at the headless thing still leaking blood, black in the dim red and amber lights of the bridge, onto his rubberized deck.

The bridge filled with garish, blue-white light. Another vessel, whose approach his radar man had marked just before all hell broke loose about him, had illuminated the *Kane* with spotlights of tremendous candlepower.

His four bridge crew, the radar man, Bob the Ghanaian, the helmsman and the officer of the watch, a Christian Lebanese named Sa'uf who was having a hard time concealing his terror, had all thrown themselves flat. The remaining two terrorists, the leader and the guard crouched behind the captain.

The guard straightened briefly to fire a burst. It took out most of what remained of the front windscreen and made such a hideous, head-shattering noise Sigurdsson was actually amazed all the glass didn't burst out of the radarscope and other instruments on the bridge. The man ducked down again.

The leader, who identified himself as Commander Guntur, had unsnapped the flap of his holster. Now he took out a handgun and, duckwalking over to the prone captain, pointed the weapon at his grizzled crew cut.

"You think you can betray us?" he hissed in his barbarous English. "I kill you first. Then—"

Light filled the bridge and blanked out the captain's senses.

In a moment his vision returned, with a semblance of functional consciousness, although not yet hearing. Or perhaps the fight taking place before Sigurdsson's wide eyes, sporadically seen between big, drifting afterimage patches, really was silent.

Flash-bang, he realized. He was gratified someone cared enough not to throw in a full-strength antipersonnel grenade. Then he realized the attackers might simply be interested in preserving the instrumentation, which, out of date and repair though it was, was needful to operate the ship.

A big man dressed all in black, his face and hands painted black as well, dueled face-to-face with Commander Guntur. His hair was strangely pale. Sigurdsson realized he must have worn a black hat of some sort, now lost in the desperate struggle. Guntur thrust at his largish belly with his saber. The man swept the blade aside with what looked almost like a Roman short sword.

Steel met steel with a faint clang. In that it was slowly coming back, Sigurdsson realized his hearing had gone away, too. It reassured him his eardrums weren't shattered. Both of them, anyway.

As the two men traded blows, sounding like a master chef sharpening his knife on steel, the captain became aware of the third terrorist, the guard, lying on the deck not two meters away staring at the captain with one eye. The other, along with a big part of his head, had evidently been blown off, probably by a burst fired unheard in the wake of the stun grenade. Sigurdsson became aware that the right side of his own head, the one pressed to the deck-mat, was wet with something warm and sticky.

He fought to control the rebellion in his stomach.

Commander Guntur reeled back. His eyes stared like those of a frightened horse from a mask of blood, black in the lurid light from the other vessel. His opponent had slashed him clear across the forehead, unleashing a torrent of blood.

Screaming without any words Sigurdsson could comprehend, the terrorist leader flung himself forward, slashing wildly with his sword. The burly man stepped into him, blocked the stroke forearm to forearm and rammed his blade into Guntur at the notch of his sternum, angled upward to cleave the heart. Guntur's eyes bulged. He gasped, choked. Then he seemed to deflate around the blade.

The big man caught him and eased him down onto his back. Putting a black boot on his chest he wrenched the sword free. Then he wiped it carefully on the dead man's shirt.

He looked over and down at Sigurdsson. "Are you all right, Captain?" he asked. He spoke English with a Dutch accent.

Sigurdsson's throat felt parched, as if he'd wandered the deserts for days without water. "No," he croaked. He hoped he actually made enough sound to be heard over the firefight still cracking on outside. He couldn't hear himself, but then he could still hear little but residual ringing in his ears. "But I do not think I am wounded."

The big man nodded his square head. He reached a big hand down as if to help the captain. Sigurdsson just stared at him.

The black-painted face split in a big white grin. "Don't worry, Captain," he said. "We mean you no harm. Had we done, you would have died with that Sword of the Faith devil, trust me on that."

For a moment the captain looked into those ice-blue eyes. Then he held out a hand and allowed the other man to help him up. Although he was no small man himself, the other hauled him to his feet as if he were a child.

To his surprise the man was clearly—seen closer up—around his own age, no stranger to his fifties. He even showed a bit of a gut, although adipose tissue didn't seem to account for a high percentage of his bulk.

He would have looked ridiculous, with the short beard that framed his broad, square face spiked as if moussed with black paint, had Sigurdsson not just seen him kill a young, fit man in a sword fight.

A sword fight, the captain thought. In the twenty-First Century. And I thought I was the Viking.

The tumult of shots and shouting began to dwindle. The big man got a thoughtful expression. The captain realized he was receiving radio reports through the lightweight headset clamped to one side of his head.

"The ship is almost secure," the intruder told him. "It will be done within minutes, when we flush the last of the rats from the bilges. We will have to confirm against your crew list, but I believe none of your crew has been harmed."

"They're good boys," the captain said hoarsely. Too good for this cursed tub, he thought. "They're too wise to try to play heroes for the profits of another man."

The other laughed. "That is indeed wise. Besides, the heroics are provided free. I don't think this lot would have left witnesses behind once you delivered your cargo, my friend."

It was an easy enough thing to say—calculated to disarm the captain's suspicions. Except Sigurdsson's *real* suspicion was that the mad Dutchman was right.

This wasn't the first time he'd suspected his passengers would shoot them and dump them into the sea when they reached their destination. He'd doubted that was Mindanao, no matter what the charter read.

A second man in black entered the cabin. From the blond crew cut over which his own headset was clamped, to the handsome, boyish face visible beneath the bootblack, Sigurdsson knew he was an All-American Boy before he opened his mouth and confirmed it.

"Ship's secured, Elder Brother," he said, touching finger to forehead in salute. His tone toward the older man was almost reverential.

"Thank you, Brother," the big man said. "Tell the others well done. They have done the Order proud."

"I have to know," Sigurdsson said, his voice as rough as a gale sea, "is that damned box radioactive?"

The big blacked-out Dutchman blinked his sky-blue eyes at him. Then he laughed.

"Only metaphysically, my friend," he said. "Only metaphysically."

12

Annja sat in relative cool beneath the gaudy awning of an outdoor café a few blocks from the hotel. The white buds in her ears and a playlist of Medieval and Renaissance tunes kept the noise of midtown Panama City at bay. There wasn't much to be done about the exhaust smells, especially thick in the heavy, humid air.

The coffee shop served excellent coffee and even better limeade. Annja reckoned she could stay there happily hydrating herself until her bladder gave out. It was all she could do at the moment anyway.

In keeping with Panama City's somewhat self-conscious role as a modern financial center the café offered free wireless access. She was trying to find something online about the bones of a stray "very holy man" turning up—anywhere in history.

Luck had not gone her way so far.

On one Web site she did turn up a brief, tantalizing allusion to a treasure of more than earthly worth that was supposedly unearthed in Jerusalem by an order of knights under the command of the Holy Roman Emperor Frederick II, during the Sixth Crusade in the early 1200s. She had to chuckle at the historical irony of that. The Web site went on for pages about how the Vatican had conspired against the knights—beginning before there actually *was* a Vatican. But Annja knew Emperor Frederick II was a man against whom the Pope genuinely *had* conspired. And not just one pope, but a succession of them, excommunicating him twice and waging relentless war against him.

Regretfully she dismissed the whole thing. Frederick had been something of a rationalist for his day. He had only gone on Crusade when the Pope threatened him with excommunication, and one of the reasons the Pope excommunicated him anyway was that, instead of reconquering Jerusalem with the usual exemplary slaughter, he had simply rented it from his friend, the equally humanist Sultan of Egypt. He was hardly the sort to found a religious order. Much less to set them to searching for holy relics.

She sat back and sipped at her latest limeade. She was coffee'd out. If she drank any more she'd have to throw herself in the ocean and swim to Maui to have a prayer of winding down before next week. She gazed at the unhelpful screen of her notebook computer and sighed.

Why am I even involved? she asked herself. I'm an archaeologist. I'm bound to try to see artifacts properly conserved. Except in this case I'm not even sure there is a relic.

But telling her about the artifact's existence had clearly cost Cedric Millstone his life.

Something had left a trail of dead bodies, including those Garin and Annja had been compelled to kill aboard the *Ocean Venture,* from the time Annja had come within unwitting proximity of it. Abenicio Luján had seen *something*—a crate whose dimensions suggested a casket, a box to contain a coffin—brought out of the boathouse turned charnel house in the Old Harbor district of *Casco Viejo.* So an artifact existed. And it must be of extraordinary value, for people go to such lengths to possess it.

She scratched an eyebrow. A waiter came by to see if she needed anything. She waved him off, aware only that he seemed awfully solicitous of her. He didn't set any threat warnings ringing, so she paid him no mind.

I'm more than just an archaeologist now, though, aren't I? she thought. Whatever lay behind it, the proliferation of dead bodies made it her concern. She was becoming a protector, maybe even an avenger. And there was much to avenge.

She felt a cold certainty that people would continue to be endangered, or even killed, until she tracked the mysterious artifact down. It gave her a sense of urgency, like a pressure inside the chest.

For now she operated on the assumption Millstone had told her the truth. At least as he knew it. Deathbed statements, she knew as a historian, were accorded special weight in the law. While she doubted Cedric Millstone had had specific foreknowledge of his death, he must have known he was squarely in someone's sights. A rival, or rivals, whose identity she couldn't even guess at.

"And if I hadn't been so quick to dismiss the possibility of working with his group," she said aloud, bitterly, "all that knowledge might not have died with him."

"I beg your pardon, señorita?"

It was the handsome waiter again. She looked up and happened to meet his eye. He beamed.

Oh, my God, she thought, he's hitting on me. Why would he do a thing like that?

"No," she said, her own reflex smile curdling. "Thank you. I'll let you know."

His disappointment was clear on his olive features. But he nodded and went about his business.

What's wrong with you, girl? she could almost hear Clarice ask. Why not let your hair down and live a little? You got away from the nuns, remember?

She sighed. "I don't have *time,*" she said aloud, quite peevishly. She returned to her Internet search for clues into the nature of her mysterious objective.

She heard her cell phone's ringtone. She picked it up. The caller ID said *Dale.*

It was the code name for one of her nerd contacts.

Frank wasn't the only one she'd set to trying to track the *Solomon Kane*.

"Hello," she said.

"Hi, Annja," a male voice said. "Something's come up."

"Oh?"

"Your friend's ship has changed course. It happened early this morning, ship's time. If one of my peeps hadn't lucked onto a shot from a French bird of it pointed in a different direction we'd've lost it completely."

She felt an all-too-familiar plummeting sensation inside her. *Too close!* she thought.

"I'm grateful to your friend for tracking it down," she said.

"It, uh—it did cost some money."

She sighed. "I'm good for it." *I'm going to need to take some more of Roux's commissions,* she thought, *even though they smack of pothunting. And they're a devil to reconcile with my work schedule on* Monsters.

Oh, well. Nobody had told her her new life would be easy. Or cheap.

"I know you are, Annja. Just thought I'd say."

Am I painting a big fat target on my back here? she thought, somewhat wildly. *I mean, it's not as if the NSA would ever think of monitoring cell phone traffic here at the Pacific outlet of the Panama Canal or anything.*

"Why are you calling me," she asked, trying to sound casual, "instead of handling this in e-mail?"

"Well…" She could hear his reluctance. "Something's come up."

"What?"

"Well, like I said, we've been pretty lucky so far. But our luck might be about to run out."

"How so?" She felt a passing idle wish she could reach through the airwaves and shake the answer out of him. Nerds loved to dramatize.

"There're some storm systems forming in that part of the world. If the skies cloud over your friend's ship, we can kiss overhead imaging goodbye."

Swell, she thought. "All right," she said. "Can you at least give me a destination?"

"Not with any certainty," her contact said. "They can always change course again. But right now they're pretty clearly heading for the Marquesas, in the South Pacific. As a matter of fact—"

There was one of those pregnant pauses that suggested he was typing busily away on his own keyboard, looking for new data. "They're making right for a particular island. One that has a surprisingly large airfield, from the overhead shots. Apparently there's an astronomical research station there. I'm not sure the island even has a name, but I have a latitude and longitude. I'm e-mailing it to you right now."

"Thanks. We'll settle up later," Annja said.

"Great, Annja. Always fun talking to you."

She hung up and put her cell phone back in its belt holster. Then she surfed to a travel site to start looking for flights to French Polynesia.

13

Annja was arguing in French with the pilot of the small airplane.

It concerned the firefight quite unmistakably taking place on the airstrip of the tiny island they were descending toward.

"I am a charter pilot, not a mercenary," the pilot shouted excitedly over the roar of his two engines. He was a wiry man whom she guessed to be middle-aged, although some of what she took for aging may simply have been the result of years of overexposure to the sun. His blue eyes contrasted madly with skin like old leather. He had a thatch of stiff, straw-colored hair and dark glasses perched on a beaky nose. He wore blue denim shorts, a blue denim shirt, and white deck shoes without socks. He had a gold chain around his right wrist and a big multifunction watch on his left.

The curiously shaped plane, with its twin tail booms and propellers in front of and behind the cabin, wallowed from side to side. Annja wondered whether that was due to winds close to the waves and nearing land, or whether he was that jittery. "I am not paid to land in a war zone!"

"But I've got to get down there," Annja said. She sat in the right-hand seat. She was dressed in a cream-yellow short-sleeved shirt and khaki cargo shorts. Her ponytail was passed out the back of a tan baseball cap. Wraparound amber sunglasses that were unobtrusively also shooting glasses covered her eyes. She had come dressed for trouble.

Evidently she had found it. Earlier than she could possibly have anticipated.

The engines whined as the pilot pulled back on the yoke. He ignored Annja's plea. The island and its black X of landing strip swept by beneath.

"See?" she said. "Nobody's shooting at us."

"That's how I like to keep it!" he shouted.

Of all things a C-130 Hercules sat toward the middle of the strip, which occupied much of the low western end of the island of Le Rêve. The island resembled a kidney bean with its smoothly curved side facing south and a concavity that looked too gradual and shallow to provide much of a harbor on the north. Eastward from the strip the island rose in a series of densely forested hills. On one of them stood the astronomical observatory her contact had mentioned.

The four propellers of the Hercules were spinning

but clearly feathered. The fat cargo plane wasn't moving. Men fought around the aircraft and the nearby cluster of buildings, mostly Quonset-style huts and manufactured-looking wooden structures with pitched roofs. They fired at one another from the ground, around the buildings, over stacks of colorful plastic drums. From the air there was no telling them apart—they all wore sand-colored battle dress. She didn't even have a clue how *many* factions there were. It might be massively multiplayer war down there.

I wonder if some of them were my late-night visitors? Annja thought. Naturally they wouldn't be obtuse enough to wear black uniforms in broad daylight.

"I feel your pain," the pilot said, banking right, to the north. "But if I get shot I'll feel my pain more."

She wanted to tell him no one would shoot at them. That stuck on her tongue. She wasn't at all sure it was true. It was just as likely both sides, or however many, would assume the light plane was reinforcements for the opposition. Then everybody would shoot at them.

"But I came all this way from America!" She had chartered the aircraft on the French-owned island of Nuku Hiva, sixty miles of open water to the northwest. Her informants told her that the *Solomon Kane* had made landfall shortly before dawn that morning.

So challenging had it been to make the proper connections to get there, the slow surface-going vessel had beaten her.

Her pilot shook his head. He continued his bank, turning back toward Nuku Hiva. "You must learn to accept disappointment," he said, leveling the wings. "It is part of life."

She grubbed in her pocket and brought out her wallet. "A thousand dollars if you get me onto the island."

He turned to blink at her through his aviator glasses.

THE WIND BLEW from the west. The airplane came in low over green water from the east, heading into it, so it could slow to the lowest possible ground speed before falling out of the air. Fortunately, the larger of the two runways ran east-west. If the plane had been forced to land in a crosswind the pilot probably wouldn't have done it for any amount of money.

Then again, *landing* wasn't exactly on the agenda. There was a limit to what Annja would get even for a thousand dollars.

The Frenchman cranked down the landing gear as the island approached. The plane rocked and tried to rise as they swept across the foam-flecked beach and hot air flowed upward from the land. Annja swiveled her head left and right. She was looking for combatants.

There were none to be seen. She was pretty sure they were still shooting at one another as energetically as before. But they were doing it from behind cover. Approaching ground level she and the pilot no longer had the height advantage to spot them.

The tires kissed the runway with nervous squeals and a quick kick to the tailbone. Annja unfastened her safety harness. It seemed a pretty foolhardy thing to be doing, under the circumstances.

The airplane vibrated. It was already shaking pretty comprehensively—this felt different.

A hole rimmed in white, as if with frost, appeared in the front windscreen just to the left of the driver's head. A crack filled the cockpit. Annja felt something buffet her lips, like a light tap from someone's fingers.

A hole appeared in the window beside her head. She had felt a bullet's wind of passage.

"That's it!" the pilot screamed in a shrill voice. "I am out of here!"

She reached out and seized the yoke with her left hand. "If you don't do what you promised," she yelled, "I'll crash us."

He glanced at her. What he saw in her expression evidently convinced him she wasn't kidding.

She wasn't. We're on the ground, she thought fiercely. We'd survive. *Probably.*

He kept the aircraft on the ground. He continued to slow. They passed the stationary Hercules on their left. Then they were past the cluster of structures.

"This is it!" he shouted. "You must go now."

She looked out her window, the one with the hole. The airspeed indicator had them going about twenty miles an hour. It still seemed pretty fast.

"This is probably a bad idea," Annja said. She

yanked open her door. Clutching her day-pack to her chest she rolled out.

She hit the hot blacktop, bounced, rolled. Her teeth clacked together. Immediately the airplane's engines howled as the pilot jammed the throttle to the stops so hard he must have bent the handle. The little red-and-white plane scooted away, rapidly picking up speed.

Annja stopped rolling after fifty feet. One of the benefits of her martial arts practice, along with gymnastics training and yoga, was enhanced body awareness. She already knew two things—nothing was broken, and she'd ache for days.

The plane seemed not so much to lift off as run out of island. It just skimmed the waves for a moment, then began to climb. Annja rolled into the ditch beside the runway. She was thankful the pilot had gotten away okay. He really *hadn't* signed on for a hot landing zone.

And he had done what she paid him for—delivered her intact. Mostly, she thought, feeling bruises develop on her hips, buttocks and shoulder.

She let her pack slide to the bottom of the ditch. It was lined with weeds and litter that, she hoped, didn't house anything too venomous that bit. Or anything that bit too hard. She looked back along the runway toward the airfield buildings and the C-130.

The big cargo plane was lumbering into motion, turning onto the runway as if to taxi for a takeoff. She guessed it would have to go all the way to the east end to get a long enough takeoff roll. She knew the Hercules could take off on a fairly short runway—surprising what you learned, when you knocked around the world as much as she did, not to mention got knocked around by it—but it was still a great wallowing beast, and *short* was relative.

Then she saw men running toward her on her side of the runway. Her lips skinned back from her teeth. They were white guys, beefy, not fat like some private military contractors, or overly ripped like 'roid rats. They looked as if their skins were stuffed with muscle like sausages, the way U.S. Army troops in peak training form did. Are they the guys who broke into my loft? she wondered. The odds seemed good they were from Millstone's bunch. Especially when she spotted sword hilts stuck up incongruously from behind their shoulders.

They carried submachine guns or carbines. That put her in a bind. She doubted they intended to kill her. She figured Americans would be conditioned against shooting a white woman without extreme provocation. If they did want her dead, the sensible way to do it was from a distance, by shooting her, that being what guns did and all. But if they wanted to take her prisoner, they could neutralize the advantage of her sword and the surprise factor it gave her just by acting professionally.

Bullets kicked up sand around the men. Two fell. The others dove into the ditch on Annja's side and began returning fire. Someone across the way had ripped them with a light machine gun.

The five survivors forgot totally about Annja for the moment. Taking advantage of the distraction she jumped up out of the ditch and darted for a stand of palms thirty yards or so behind her.

With every step she expected to feel bullets lancing like needles through her back. But the opposition forces, whoever they were, didn't seem interested in her, either. People shooting at them were much more interesting than someone running away from them. She reached the shade of the palms and threw herself down in the pale sand between two of them.

She looked back in time to see the Hercules lumbering down the strip, following the path the smaller aircraft had taken with its touch-and-go. It struck her as dead-brave or at least desperate, to run the gauntlet of fire like that. The machine gun sounded. The burly cargo plane could probably absorb vast numbers of the fast but little bullets. She wasn't so sure about the aircrew.

It was academic. Just before the plane drew even with her she heard a nasty crack, its ultra high-frequency and energy harmonics paining her eardrums from fifty yards away. A white flash and a cloud of debris flew away from the outboard engine on the plane's far side.

A big plume of black smoke immediately streamed back from the stricken engine. The propeller slowed to visibility. The C-130 trundled onwards. Can it take off on three engines? Annja wondered. The pilot seemed determined to try.

The coffin must be aboard, she realized with a shock. They're trying to get it away at any cost.

This time she saw a white comet, blindingly bright, streak from among the buildings on the strip's far side. Someone was firing missiles at the huge airplane. This one hit the undercarriage, blasting half of it to wreckage. The airplane pivoted like a hippo ballerina and went in to the ditch.

Annja scrunched up her face and flattened herself, expecting an orange fireball and a rolling blast-wave. In fact, lots of nothing happened. The aircraft just lay there with its huge tailplane upraised. The propellers of the three surviving engines began to slow to join that of the disabled one, which had completely stopped spinning. The pilot had evidently switched them off.

From Annja's right came the crack of grenades and a fresh outburst of shooting. The men who had started toward Annja gestured that way in evident agitation. Looking, Annja could see explosions on her side of the strip. A wooden outbuilding went up in orange flames and greasy black smoke.

Farther along, the American-looking fighters were laying down their weapons and standing up with their hands behind their heads. Their opponents, their identities still mysterious to Annja, had apparently turned their far flank and gotten in behind them, starting to roll up their line. With their tactical position untenable and the airplane carrying their priceless relic nose-down in the ditch, the Americans had no choice but to surrender.

Dense undergrowth grew down to within forty yards of the palm trees where Annja had taken shelter. Hoping the trees would screen her—and the victors wouldn't look too hard her way—Annja began to speed-crawl on elbows and belly toward the cover of the brush.

14

Annja feared she was about to witness a massacre or worse atrocities. That sort of thing was anything but rare in the Third World, she knew all too well. If the winners were terrorists there was no telling how mindlessly brutal they'd be.

But when they appeared, rising up from cover on the far side of the strip and approaching in a skirmish line from Annja's right, the victors carried themselves and moved like professional soldiers. Dressed in jungle cammies and boonie hats, although of a different pattern than their foes', and carrying assault rifles, they looked a lot like the men they systematically disarmed and herded into a group. They even wore swords of their own slung over their backs, to Annja's amazement. The most visible difference between the groups was that the winners were shorter, darker-skinned and wirier, evidently Asians of some kind. Annja thought they might be Filipinos.

The fight's end brought something akin to anticlimax. The defeated were stoic. But something about their body language at first suggested apprehensiveness to Annja. Although he had never said so, Millstone's words had suggested to her he belonged to some kind of religious sect—if these men indeed belonged to the group he claimed to speak for. If it was true they'd been safeguarding the relic for centuries, they were likely willing enough to give their lives to their holy cause. The issue was just how severe a form their martyrdom was likely to take.

But martyrdom did not seem to be on their captors' agenda. They permitted their captives to tend to their wounded, and even drove out a mule-style utility vehicle to load five men too badly hurt to walk. Meanwhile the crew was ushered out of the disabled Hercules, supporting one of their number who appeared to have broken or sprained an ankle. Otherwise they seemed uninjured. Annja had no way of knowing if any had been left inside the airplane dead.

The victors marched the prisoners at gunpoint into a small Quonset-style building a quarter mile from where Annja hid, back by the airfield's main buildings. She took a pair of very compact binoculars from her pack to watch. The half-cylinder corrugated-steel structure had bars over the windows, she saw, evidently to fend off pilferage. The Asian-looking men wheeled over a few handcarts loaded with cases of water, left them inside for the prisoners and locked them in.

On the whole, it was more as if a sporting event had ended than a brief, bloody battle. In fact Annja couldn't remember watching a sporting event whose participants had been so calm and well-behaved when it was over. Although she'd never been much for spectator sports.

She transferred her attention back to the C-130. A big bulldozer came clanking out from among the airfield buildings and hauled the monster airplane out of the ditch on a chain affixed to its undercarriage. She was startled that the dozer could budge it.

The aircraft's tail ramp was let down. As Annja watched in an agony of growing frustration, a gang of men pushed the yellow pine casket containing the relic down the ramp. Annja was startled to see just how large it was. With much loud grunting and what Annja was pretty sure was cursing—even if it was in no language known to her—they wrestled it onto another one of the low, small flatbed mules.

A dock stood on the shore south of the airfield. Annja expected them to trundle the artifact straightaway there, load it onto a ship and sail away across the horizon, beyond her grasp forever. The storms her informant had warned her of still hovered west and north of the island, but if the vessel headed that way it would vanish from sight of the ever-vigilant satellites within a couple of hundred miles.

She almost wept with relief when instead of turn-

ing off toward the beach the mule carrying the casket
kept heading down the runway toward a Quonset
hangar. She recalled that she had seen no vessels of
any size at this end of the island when they flew over
it, only some small craft pulled up on a couple of
beaches, fishing or pleasure craft. Clearly, the
victors had no means at hand of moving their prize
off the island.

Annja watched as the mystery men drove the
utility truck inside the hangar and then came back
out, locking the artifact away. Then she started
trying to judge how close she could work her way
to the buildings under cover of the brush and trees.

THE ANSWER WAS, not close enough.

She was able to work her way to within perhaps
five hundred yards of the hangar south of the runway
where the artifact was locked up. She spent the next
several hours in frustration and increasing appre-
hension that whatever mode of transport the Asian
fighters were waiting for would arrive at any moment
and whisk the coffin away. She'd carefully nursed a
couple of bottles of water she'd packed in her pack,
all the time wishing she had some of the water the
victors had supplied the vanquished. And she played
all-you-can-eat buffet to all the island's mosquitoes.
She hoped this wasn't a malaria zone.

The bulk of the victorious forces retreated to what
she guessed was the little airfield's lounge, such as it
was. Pairs of watchful men patrolled the buildings on

foot. Two stood guard before each of the structures where the relic and its would-be protectors were secured. She wasn't certain just whom they were supposed to be guarding *against*. She saw no sign of any local inhabitants. They were smart enough to stay out of the way of all these heavily armed men. Likewise the local French-colonial officials.

The sun set. As usual in the South Pacific, the sunset, though adequately breathtaking in terms of splashes and bands of orange and gold and scarlet, was not a drawn-out affair. The sun went away, it got dark. Even more bugs came out, or at least more vocal ones.

Keeping to the undergrowth, Annja worked her way around to the west of the main buildings. If the winning team had night-vision equipment she was sunk. But if they did they didn't seem to be using it. She wondered if victory had made them overconfident.

They are, she thought grimly, if I have anything to say about it.

The field was not particularly well-lit. There was no illumination around the runways. There was probably no budget to keep them lit at night unless there were planes landing or taking off. The blank rears of the two locked buildings were unguarded.

She timed the foot patrols. They came her way about every fifteen minutes. When she was sure of this she slipped in among the buildings. She then hid behind some crates while the next patrol passed.

When they were out of the way Annja moved

quickly to the rear of the hangar where the relic was. It had huge double doors and a person-sized door to the side. The walls were thin metal. She could see through the barred windows that the interior was mostly dark.

She frowned at the metal end wall. Whatever you do, she thought, do it quickly.

She summoned the sword. Reversing her grip and taking the hilt in both hands she pressed its tip against the slightly rusty wall to the right of the door. She pressed hard.

The blade punched through the metal with a slight squeal, like cutting up a can with tin snips, with a bit of musical saw thrown in. The noise sounded loud as a cannon to her. She realized, after she calmed herself with a few deep abdominal breaths, that for anyone farther than ten feet away it wouldn't have been audible above the saw and chirp and trill of the nocturnal insects.

She pulled down. The sword cut the thin wall easily, like a box-cutter through not particularly stout cardboard. The metal squealed protest, but as long as she kept the cutting slow, it didn't do so too loudly.

Annja cut from the level of her head to the ground. Withdrawing the sword, she turned its blade horizontal and pierced the wall again at the top of the first cut she had made. She sliced right to left for about three feet. Skin beginning to crawl for fear of guards happening by she made another similar cut a couple of inches from the ground. Then she released the sword.

She pushed on the metal door she had cut. The steel bent with a louder noise than cutting it had made. She went rigid. No shouts or shots came her way.

As quietly as she could she pushed the flap open far enough to squeeze through. Then she pushed it back roughly into place. The hangar's rear was dark and the patrolling guards had shown no particular interest in it. She hoped they'd see nothing amiss.

Apart from some worktables, shelves and metal cabinets along the walls, the hangar was empty except for the mule with the casket loaded onto it. She went to it, examined it. There were no markings on the outside of the big box except some tool-marks, indicating it had been jimmied open and then resealed.

Climbing up on the open-topped vehicle's seat Annja checked the crate's lid. It was nailed down. Calling back the sword, she slipped the blade into the crack between the lid and the crate's end. Leaning on it and working it around a little—but gently, to avoid warping the wood and making it evident it had been tampered with again—she got a foot of the blade inside. Then she levered up the corner with a groan.

She bit her lip. She burned to look inside, even though she suspected all she would see was the coffin. Or, more likely, whatever packing material was used to protect it and keep it from banging around inside the crate.

But that would entail getting the lid all the way off. She doubted she'd have time.

As if to make her mind up for her she heard voices. Men were approaching the front of the warehouse, hailing the guards. Again, she could not understand or identify the language they spoke.

She reached into a cargo pocket of her shorts. From it she took out a small circular object—surprisingly small, considering its function. She pried up the corner just enough to glimpse strawlike plastic packing material inside and a glint of gray metal. Slipping the circular object inside, she tamped it with her fingers so it slid down between the packing-stuff and the wood of the crate, safely out of view. Then, jumping up to put all her weight on the corner of the lid, she pushed it back in place.

A loud rattling told her the padlock was being removed from the big front doors. Annja rabbited toward the shadows at the hangar's rear. Stabbing the sword through the metal flap, she quickly levered it open far enough to slip through. She gasped as a ragged edge cut her left forearm.

Then she was through. With a squealing rumble the double front doors began to open. Annja slipped the sword into the cut from outside and torqued the flap closed again.

She darted to another building nearby. Crouching there, panting more from stress than exertion, she checked her watch. If the patrols kept to their schedule one must have gone past thirteen minutes ago. She had less than two minutes to get clear.

A quick check of her arm showed her the cut

wasn't bad. But she didn't want to leave a blood trail. She quickly whipped off her shirt, leaving her torso bare but for a sports bra to the tender mercies of the biting night bugs. She tied it quickly around her arm as a makeshift bandage. Then she sprinted back for the shelter of the woods.

Just in time she dropped on her belly in the shadows. This time she panted because she was legitimately winded. It had been a close race. The two guards passed as she glanced back.

More lights showed on the hangar's far end as the mule and its precious cargo were driven out into the night. Evidently the transport had arrived. The coffin was slipping through Annja's grasp again.

She had known that might happen. It was the most likely outcome. After all, the little charter plane she'd flown on couldn't have held the crate, much less carried it away from the island. She couldn't even lift the thing by herself.

Disciplining herself to breathe through her nose deeply into her abdomen, Annja could not help grinning with triumph. She had come prepared.

This time, when the coffin in its crate was loaded onto the ship, it would carry with it the compact GPS transmitter she had slipped inside.

15

There were worse places to be stuck than on the beach in Tahiti.

Lying on her towel on Maeva Beach, with a colorful sarong wrapped around her waist and the island of Moorea rising picturesquely across the turquoise waters of the lagoon like a cinder cone covered in lush tropical vegetation, Annja chafed at paradise. The coffin and its mysterious contents were slowly making their way across the Pacific to the Philippines. And there was nothing she could do but think.

When, sometime before midnight, the inhabitants of Le Rêve had crept out of the hiding places they had so prudently found when the crazy foreigners started shooting up their island, Annja had pitched her best hysterical American tourist act for them. The French-speaking locals, both native Polynesians and colonial expats, were sympathetic. They

were pretty shaken up too, although both sides of the
firefight had treated the few inhabitants they dealt
with—the ones who hadn't successfully scampered
off into the scrub—with scrupulous politeness. It
was like a War of the Gentlemen.

Annja would've loved to interview some of the
gentlemen, whom the locals saw fit to continue to
hold captive in the Quonset warehouse, although
they replenished their supply of beverages and gave
them food besides. No opportunity presented itself.
The islanders were twitchy, understandably, and
Annja did not want to call any unwanted attention
to herself by pushing too hard to talk to a bunch of
captured mercenaries, which the inhabitants believed the American fighters were.

The locals treated Annja in very friendly fashion.
She soon relaxed, especially once she realized no
one gave much thought to who she was or where she
had come from. Since they couldn't fit her in their
minds with either set of combatants, they took for
granted she was who and what she said she was, and
had arrived by charter plane—and awful luck—
shortly after the white guys took over the airfield.

A large and cheerful native family had taken her
in. The husband was a machinist who made replace-
ments for cars, boats, aircraft and just about anything
else with metal parts that broke for the islanders. It
was a lot cheaper than having them shipped there,
not to mention quicker. The wife ran a taxi and tour
service. The kids, who ranged from toddlers to teens

and whose numbers Annja was never sure of, especially since she was pretty sure neighbor kids cir-
culated freely in and out, bombarded her with
questions about America in French. She'd at last
gotten to sleep in the wee hours of the morning.

Morning brought a French gunboat. It also
brought final ruination of Annja's plans to talk to the
prisoners from the previous day's battle royal. During the night they'd got the hinges off a personnel
door and escaped. They left behind the Hercules
crew, including the guy with the busted ankle, who
were a mixed bag of Americans and Australians and
claimed innocence. The French colonial police kept
them secluded, but the airfield manager, a fat, cheerful French expatriate from Lyon with an imposing
walrus moustache, told Annja the flight crew
claimed to be a charter, hired to pick up a cargo and
fly it to the United States. They believed the plane
could be made airworthy, although how long that
would take and how much it was going to cost
worried them. The authorities, while not notably
sympathetic, seemed inclined to believe them.

More to the point, the authorities believed
Annja, especially when she brought out the hysterical American-woman tourist routine again. Age
of global paranoia or not, Le Rêve didn't have
much by way of entrance and exit controls at the
best of times. The airstrip barely had radar for the
roughest-and-readiest form of air-traffic control.
She expanded on what she had told the locals. The

light charter flight had arrived after the initial takeover but before the Asian dudes attacked. The charter pilot flew away and left her, mainly because he could. She ran off into the weeds and hid until the shooting stopped and the bad men went away. The end.

The colonial cops, if anything, seemed less interested than the locals did. They barely bothered to glance at her passport, which was real. Her story was at once both plausible and impossible either to prove or disprove. Nor could they see her having anything to do with the mysterious firefight, either. After cursory questioning they cut Annja loose.

She had the impression the authorities were simply going to throw their hands in the air on this one and cross their fingers no reports of the battle found their way on to the Internet. Nobody local had gotten dinged, particularly no one from the French-run observatory. As mere astronomers, Annja knew they rated—if possible—lower than archaeologists in the world power structure, but their university would be sure to emit colossal clouds of stench had anything befallen them. No dead bodies were left behind to clutter things up. The property damage could be ascribed to the frequent tropical storms, including the one bearing down on the island even as Annja flew off to Tahiti, southwest of Le Rêve.

So here she was, lying out on the white sand near the Sofitel Maeva Beach Hotel, which was a curious step-design resembling a section cut out of the middle of a Meso-American temple. It was pleasant enough and also relatively cheap, by Tahiti's ruinous tourist-trap standards, anyway.

She had spent the last two days snorkeling in the lagoon to admire the coral and the brightly colored fish. That and fending off amorous advances from French and American tourists, trying not to get sunburned and slowly going crazy.

Thanks to some software, probably only mildly heinous and illegal, provided by her go-to geeks, Annja could actually track the ship now carrying the coffin in real time. And wasn't *that* exciting, she thought. Even watching a jetliner cross the Pacific live would have been like watching nothing happening at all, actually, since on a fifteen-inch laptop screen it would move about an inch an hour. It would look like a still photo. And the ship moved *much* slower than that.

She took a certain gloomy satisfaction that she couldn't see it anyway. The long-promised storm system had swallowed the western Pacific, so far as satellite imaging in visible wavelengths was concerned. She was not about to pay the costs of trying to get more close-up pictures of the ship. She hadn't even gotten to see what it looked like, although she rather guessed it had a sort of pointy end, a sort of flat end, and was longer than it was wide.

Annja fervently hoped that, wherever they were going, the mysterious Asian fighters were seasick every nautical foot of the way. She still wasn't sure who was playing in the coffin sweepstakes, nor how many players there even were. But she was in no doubt that they were all mightily pissing her off.

She made herself close the laptop. She laid it aside beneath a towel so the sun wouldn't fry its electronic brain, which without any help ran hot enough to scorch her legs if she got careless about using it on her lap. She spent a fruitless while trying to get in to the book she'd grabbed on a whim at the hotel shop, a novel about the romantic adventures of an intrepid, globe-trotting female archaeologist, the intrigues she got up to and the beautiful, exotic men she got up to them with. She was totally unable to suspend disbelief. These writers have no clue, she thought.

With a sigh she shut the paperback, dropped it back in the string bag she'd bought, tempted as she was to chuck it into the surf. She followed it with the computer. Picking up the bag with one hand and the folded rental chair with the other, and ignoring the odd wolf whistle she trudged back to the hotel.

The lobby was like the inside of a cave, cool and dark—at least after hours of the dazzle of South Sea sun on white sand. Annja had returned the chair at the rental kiosk outside by the pool.

"Ms. Creed?" a male voice said.

The voice sounded unfamiliar. Warily she turned. "Yes?"

Two men stood in the lobby among the potted

palms. One was a handsome young blond guy, built like a linebacker, with a fresh gray-eyed face and short blond hair. The other was heavyset, but in a way suggesting more muscle than body fat, with gray-shot dark-blond hair and beard cropped close to square head and jaw. His eyes were brilliant blue. Both wore standard tropical tourist drag—T-shirts, shorts, sandals.

Annja's eyes narrowed. To her recollection she had never seen either man's face before. Yet both seemed somehow familiar.

"May I help you?" she said in neutral tones.

"We need to speak with you confidentially, concerning a highly urgent matter," said the older man. He had a European accent—Dutch, she thought.

"With all respect, I'm not sure what that could possibly be. I don't know either of you gentlemen."

"You did know our associate, Mr. Cedric Millstone, though, didn't you?" the young man asked.

"Our late associate," his partner added.

She looked from one to the other. The young man seemed to be trying hard to keep his dead-serious manner. The older man seemed quietly amused.

She didn't bother asking how they'd found her. If they'd been able to punch through Garin Braden's wall of obfuscation and mount an operation to crash through her skylight in Brooklyn inside of forty-eight hours, tracking her to Tahiti's capital Papeete in a similar period of time was no great stretch.

Especially when those people had resources sufficient for little errands like capturing ships in the mid-Pacific, and dispatching small armies to distant Polynesian islands.

"My room," she said. "Five minutes."

She was amused to see the younger man give a look to the elder that was nearly panic-stricken. She had little concern about her physical safety, and if possible less about what an island of total strangers would think of her. Besides, it amused her to fantasize what would happen if word ever filtered back to the television studio in Manhattan that she'd entertained two men in her hotel room in Tahiti. Clarice and Mindy would crack open a bottle of champagne and exchange high fives.

Annja firmly dislodged the speculation from her mind. It reminded her all too acutely of what she was missing.

SHE WAS DRESSED conservatively, long khaki pants and cream cotton blouse, when the brief authoritative knock sounded on her door five minutes later. She admitted the pair.

"I am Hevelin," the burly, bearded man told her when she had shut the door behind them. "My associate is Mr. Sharshak. It is good of you to consent to meet with us like this, Ms. Creed."

"You might as well call me Annja," she said, walking back to sit on the orange bedspread with its white tropical-flower designs. She intended to make herself as comfortable as possible physically, no matter how uncomfortable the interview turned out to be otherwise.

She looked challengingly up at them. "So. Are you going to report me to the French authorities?" If they were going to try strong-arming her, she wanted those cards on the table right away.

Young Sharshak looked positively pained. "By no means, Ms. Creed," Hevelin said. "Your secret is safe with us. And we ask you, if we may, please, for similar discretion."

"Fair enough. How did you boys get out of that metal hut, anyway?"

"It wasn't easy," Sharshak said with a grin.

She smiled and nodded appreciatively. She had him pegged for a terribly earnest young warrior-hero-jock type. It was nice to see him flash a little humor.

Hevelin took the easy chair by the window. Sharshak sat in the wooden chair at the desk. The floor-to-ceiling curtain stood open next to the Dutchman. For once Annja had lucked in to a great view—over the beach and the lagoon, with Moorea green and black in the background. As opposed to the usual view she got, of the restaurant roof and the garbage containers.

"Ms. Creed," Hevelin said, "we belong to an ancient order of knights—the Knights of the Risen Savior, founded in Jerusalem in 1228 by the Emperor Frederick the Second."

She raised an eyebrow. "I've never heard of any

order called the Knights of the Risen Savior," she said. "And I find it hard to believe the man they called *stupor mundi,* the Wonder of the World, would found any such order. He had far more of a reputation as a patron of the arts and sciences, and a humanist for the time, than for his piety. That's putting it mildly, given what a major thorn he was in the Vatican's side."

"You know your history, I see," Hevelin said.

"I'm a professional. The Middle Ages and Renaissance are my specialty."

"The Emperor, if the accounts of our Brotherhood are to be believed, was a complex man. He did found a new militant knightly order—a secret order. At the risk of sounding disrespectful of our patron, I suspect the prospect amused him. He would have his very own equivalents to the Templars and the Hospitallers. He was, as you must know, an avid collector of curiosities."

"It wasn't so much what he founded," Sharshak said, all earnestness again, "but what we *found.*"

"The coffin," Annja said.

The young man blinked blankly. Hevelin smiled. "You describe the container. We are accustomed to thinking in terms of the contents."

"I've no idea what the contents are," Annja said, "although Millstone suggested it was the bones of a very holy man. Whoever that might be. I blew him off at the time. Which, yes, I regret very much."

"You mean you spent all that time on the island

with the holy relic and never got a look at it?" Sharshak asked.

Annja sighed deeply. "I hope the French colonial police aren't as efficient as you are. Or worse yet, the DGSE."

"Neither the police nor *La Direction Générale de la Sécurité Extérieure* has the motivation we do," Hevelin said. "Indeed it's in their interests if this whole matter simply goes away. No one likes doing unnecessary paperwork. Even intelligence agents. Perhaps especially them."

"Anyway, the answer's no. I only got a peek inside the crate. I didn't see much but packing material," Annja admitted.

"You would have seen little in any event," Hevelin said. "We resealed the coffin itself, as you call it, after we recovered it. We try to keep moisture from damaging the contents, which are very precious."

He leaned forward, knitting his big square hands together between his hairy knees. "What our order found in Jerusalem had an enormous effect on the Emperor. Whether it produced some intense religious reaction within him, only he and our Lord can know. But his actions indicated he took the discovery most seriously indeed.

"He charged us with guarding the relic. And preserving thereby the order of the world."

She raised a skeptical brow. "The order—"

"Of the world, yes. The sealed metal coffin, or rather its contents, were believed to threaten the very fabric of society in some way. Despite, or perhaps because of, its holiness."

"Hoo," Annja said.

"Among other things the Emperor Frederick richly endowed us with funds and properties." Hevelin shrugged his massive shoulders. "Over the centuries we have added to that initial endowment, amassing substantial financial holdings over eight centuries."

"So how did you avoid the fate of the Knights Templar?"

"Well, as you point out, Ms. Creed," Sharshak said, "you've never heard of us, have you? Our Elder Brothers saw early on how the Templars' wealth and prominence earned them as much resentment as admiration. And we didn't lend money to princes."

"Prudent of you. So. What's really in the coffin?" Annja asked.

The men looked at each other. Hevelin's lips were rather thick within his beard. He moistened them with his tongue before he spoke.

"It is a very powerful relic," he said.

"Powerful how?" she asked. "In the sense of the ability to perform miracles?"

"Maybe it can," Sharshak said, eyes shining.

"And maybe I don't buy any such mystical explanation," she said.

"It must have *some* power," the young man insisted. "To have made that kind of impression on a man with a temperament like the Emperor Frederick's."

"All of us make mistakes," she said. "Even old Fritz. And I doubt I need to remind you how big a cathedral you might have built out of all the frag-ments of the 'True Cross' scattered through churches all over Europe."

"Let us say, at the least," Hevelin said, "that the contents possess enormous symbolic significance. Their mere possession confers great status and propaganda value. Such that, in the wrong hands, they could cause irreparable harm. One might almost say, unimaginable."

She frowned. "I am still having a hard time fitting my mind around concepts like an eight-hundred-year-old secret somehow threatening the modern world. Such an item causing *unimaginable* harm strikes me as well, unimaginable."

"We're in a race with evil Muslim fanatics for possession of the holy relic," Sharshak said. "That must tell you how important it is."

She sighed. "Well, a lot of people have been willing to die for it, and a whole lot more to kill for it. So thinking about it I'd have to say it's having a pretty malign influence on the world."

"That has much to do with why we were convey-ing it to our newly built chapter house in North America," Hevelin said, "where it could be kept safe from the eyes of the world. And the hands of profaners."

"Speaking of profaners—if you mean those men you fought on Le Rêve, they sure didn't act like

Muslim fanatics. They fought as if they knew what they were doing—both sides did. But after they got the drop on you, they seemed to treat you pretty well."

"That's the honor of fighting men," Sharshak said. "We'd've done the same for them."

"Maybe. Okay, forgive that—I'm sure you would. But when I think evil religious fanatics, I think, burning people at the stake, flying airliners into buildings full of people, that sort of thing. Not this chivalrous treatment of defeated enemies. That wasn't even common in Medieval times, as you've got to know. Chivalry was more a creation of popular culture than any widespread reality."

"Yet the Saracen king Saladin was noted for treating his defeated foes decently," Hevelin said.

A lot better than the Crusaders treated Jerusalem's Muslims and Jews, Annja thought, not to mention Greek Christians when they sacked Byzantium.

She shook her head. "Well, maybe we'll have to disagree on the nature of fanaticism. Who were they, anyway? The same people you took the relic back from in midocean? A pretty slick trick, by the way."

Sharshak grinned. "Thanks."

"They were not," Hevelin said.

"So who were *they?* People who would arrange the hijacking of a cruise liner full of innocents just to cover a theft—and then turn around and murder the thieves they hired to pull off the heist—" She didn't know for sure that was what happened, but it fit the evidence better than any other explanation she could think of. "Well, I've got no trouble calling people like that evil. No trouble at all."

"Let us say this is a multisided struggle," Hevelin said. "There are evil men who will stop at nothing to get their hands on this most holy artifact. We are its rightful guardians."

Sharshak leaned forward, eyes gleaming. "We'd like you to help us recover it, Ms. Creed."

"Well, here's the problem," Annja said. "Whatever the details, we're dealing with a priceless archaeological artifact that should go back to its rightful owners."

"That's us," Sharshak said.

"That's not really clear to me," she said. She passed her hands over her face and smoothed back her hair. "It seems to me the proper authorities should decide."

Hevelin laughed. "And who might they be, in this instance, Ms. Creed?"

"I don't really know," she said. "Okay? I admit it. I'm pretty sure these Muslim commando-types aren't the rightful owners. Maybe if they were Arabs, but they clearly aren't. But until I have a better idea of the real rights and wrongs of the situation, I can't help you."

Sharshak looked as if he wanted to argue. Actually, he looked as if he wanted to cry. But Hevelin stood up.

"Very well, Ms. Creed," he said. "We respect your reservations. However, I urge you to consider carefully that others will not."

"Are you threatening me, Mr. Hevelin?"

"You have nothing to fear from us. You have my word on that. But I cannot speak for the other parties involved in this affair. Good afternoon, Ms. Creed."

16

Night was falling on the harbor of Mati with its usual abruptness. Annja tried to focus her compact binoculars on the freighter before the light failed her completely.

Mati, on the southerly Philippine island of Mindanao, was to her possibly jaundiced perception a typical depressing tropical tramp-steamer port. It had scraggly palm trees, ugly urbo-mechanical encrustations around the waterfront, all scented with untreated sewage, dead fish and spilled diesel fuel.

Aside from a few lights burning in the superstructure, the *Ozymandias* was blacked out. The dry-cargo tramp ship was registered in Denmark, of all places. Her dark-painted hull rode high in the water, indicating she wasn't carrying much cargo.

But what she did carry was extremely valuable.

For several minutes Annja stood in what she

hoped was the shelter of a cargo container on the dock. The area she had chosen for her lookout was apparently little used, and poorly lit at night. Of course, if anyone on the ship used night-vision equipment, they'd spot her the instant they glanced her way.

If this ship was what she thought it was—and the GPS transmitter assured her that it was—those aboard no doubt possessed night-vision goggles and were quite proficient in their use. What she gambled was that they had no particular reason to be sweeping the dock with them right at that moment.

Dockside idlers, most of whom spoke English and if not, Spanish, had told her the vessel had put in for engine repairs. Annja had even talked to a boatman who had ferried engine-repair parts out to the stumpy little freighter. She suspected that was true, not just a cover. Why else put in here? she thought. They haven't transferred the coffin. Evidently, the commando-types who had most recently seized the artifact valued stealth over speed.

She lowered the binoculars and sighed. It had taken her two days to get to the somewhat grungy seaport, on the southerly coast of Mindanao. The whole time she feared she wouldn't arrive in time.

Now here she was. Here was her quarry. Where it would go next she had no clue. But she had the strong impression it would only get harder for her from here on in even to get close to her objective.

"When there are no more good alternatives," she

said softly to herself, "sometimes the only thing to do is pick something full-on crazy and just go with it."

ROWING WAS HARDER WORK than it looked.

The little two-stroke engine on the craft she'd rented that afternoon had gotten her within a couple hundred yards of the anchored freighter's stern. There she killed it. She didn't want to risk alerting the ship's occupants by making a noisy approach to their craft.

Muscles on fire she felt the small boat's sharp bow bump gently against the ship's stern, beside the rudder. "Finally," she said under her breath.

She laid the oars down and glanced up. No faces peered over the aft rail down at her. Of course, there was no way for her to know if the commandos aboard were lined up clean across the stern like an outsized firing squad, just waiting for her to clamber up over the railing and into their sights. But then, if that was the case, there was nothing she could do about it.

It had taken the good offices of Federal Express to get the special set of climbing magnets. It had also required her to enter the Philippines as herself, Annja Creed. She'd been reluctant to do so because the last time she visited the islands terrorists had blown up the cab she was riding in. It had killed her hapless and blameless cabby, for which she still felt responsible. The authorities had accepted it as a case of wrong-place/wrong-time. It wasn't as if such attacks were rare in the Philippines, unfortunately.

She knew she was running the risk of being found in the proximity of dead bodies yet again by Philippine cops. If that happened, they were liable to ask her a lot more pointed questions, and keep asking them until she gave answers she really didn't want to.

She reckoned, however, that should some alert customs official notice what was being delivered to her, and local security types decided to ask her why she wanted electromagnetic climbing-grippers, she'd have a much easier time convincing them she didn't intend anything too controversial as Annja Creed, the globally if not exactly well-known archaeological consultant on *Chasing History's Monsters*. The show was known, after all, for its somewhat show-boating explorations all over the world.

She wasn't sure what lie she'd tell that would explain why climbing sheer ferrous surfaces might further the pursuit of monsters. But she felt a lot more confident of coming up with an explanation that might conceivably be swallowed than if she traveled under the guise, of, say, a vacationing Realtor from Poughkeepsie.

And now, barring the inopportune arrival of a random harbor patrol boat, the Philippine officials were officially the least of her worries.

Before setting out she had strapped the two larger disks to her knees. She wanted to do the least possible thrashing and contorting in the boat, not to mention spend the least possible amount of time sitting there right under the stern of the ship. Now she quickly strapped the smaller magnets to her hands. Then with the slosh of the water against the hull in her ears and her nose full of the smells of salt water and rusting metal she peered up at the ship's stern.

It looked approximately eight feet lower than the summit of Mount Everest. It occurred to her, rather forcibly, that she'd never actually *done* this before.

"That's the trouble with this whole sword of Joan of Arc thing," she muttered. "It's nothing but on-the-job training, all the time."

She set off and, fit and agile, made it to the top without difficulty. She rolled over the railing onto the shadowed deck. Crouching, she took stock of her situation.

Ozymandias was an older carrier, elderly in fact, if Annja was any judge. Her experience and knowledge of full-sized ships, especially oceangoing craft, was largely restricted to watching them pass from the levees, up and down the Mississippi. But the ship showed obvious signs of aging—flaking paint and patches of roughness that hinted at much painted-over rust. It had a certain feel, a certain smell, as of layers of stale remnants of cargo and passengers and crew. Also the ship's design struck her as outmoded. Its superstructure, which spanned the vessel from beam to beam, rose like an island amidship, instead of at the stern as was more common today. She was obviously designed to carry most of her cargo in the holds below decks, not riding stacked on the open deck, as many modern carriers did it.

Annja slipped forward. She was playing it by ear. Relatively small as *Ozymandias* was, it was still a cargo ship—a mostly empty one. There were likely to be plenty of shadowed, little-frequented places to hide out. With her light pack stuffed with bottled water and beef jerky, she knew she could survive for days. The ship was probably nearing its destination anyway. Hevelin and Sharshak had played it cagey as to who their opponents had been, but she suspected they probably hailed from Indonesia, Malaysia or the Philippines themselves.

Of course, the odds were she'd be caught, and sooner rather than later. She had plans for that contingency, too.

What she didn't see herself as having was a choice.

Several yards ahead she saw a hatch cover. She crept up to it, tried the handle. It lifted.

She opened the hatch. Blackness lay below. She risked a quick flash from a penlight she carried in her right hand. The intense but localized LED gleam showed steel rungs leading down into indeterminate darkness. The warm heavy air that wafted up into her face smelled musty and vaguely oily. Slipping the light into her pocket, she got onto the ladder and climbed carefully down.

A tentatively extended corrugated rubber sole touched bare metal deck. Annja relaxed slightly. She'd had no way of knowing in advance whether it would be awash with unspeakably nasty bilge water. It wasn't.

She got both feet down and turned away from the ladder. She reached for her shirt pocket again. She'd need the light to risk moving in the hold. It was black as the inside of a giant animal's belly.

A sudden blue-white light stabbed into her eyes, jacklighting her like a deer.

THE LIEUTENANT, who had introduced himself as Mahmoud, looked at Annja across the table in the little galley with his smooth-skinned forehead rumpled in a frown more of puzzlement than anger. He was relatively tall, not much shorter than Annja, with large brown eyes and a bald spot blazing a trail through the curly black hair on his head. He wore a khaki uniform without badges of rank or nationality.

"Why do you spy on us, Ms. Creed?" he asked in English. They had relieved her of her possessions, including her passport. Mahmoud had it on the table before him. He tapped its jacket with his fingertips.

She could imagine Roux sighing exaggeratedly and rolling his eyes. Americans! she could hear him say in exasperation. Must you always lead with your chins? *Discretion* is not a four-letter word, you know!

"I'm not a spy," she said, leaning forward and looking the lieutenant in the eye. "I'm an archaeologist."

"We know," said a commando who stood behind her. He was one of the squad who had apprehended her in the hold. "I am a very big fan of *Chasing*

History's Monsters on the satellite. Might I have your autograph later?"

Annja raised an eyebrow. "If you were planning on intimidating me, it looks as if you just weakened your cause, there," she said.

Mahmoud sighed. "Bima, restrain your enthusiasm. These men really are professionals, Ms. Creed, no matter how starstruck some of the younger ones may be. Now, what might your being an archaeologist have to do with your sneaking aboard our vessel? Is trespassing a usual part of the repertoire of the archaeologist?"

She smiled thinly. "Sometimes the circumstances call for extreme measures," she said. "Such as when we learn of illegal trafficking in stolen antiquities."

That caused a murmur among the half-dozen commandos in the galley with the lieutenant and her. Evidently they all understood English. Or at least, several of them did, and were translating for the others.

Mahmoud leaned back. "Why do you suggest we are doing such a thing?"

"You have on board a crate," she said. "A large crate of yellow pine wood. It contains a metal coffin. The coffin and its contents may be a relic discovered in the Holy Land some eight centuries ago. That's one of the things I'm determined to find out."

He stared. "What leads you to believe we carry any such thing?"

She took a chance. "I saw you bring it aboard this vessel from the island of Le Rêve, after a very nasty firefight."

"You were there?" He seemed thunderstruck.

"That airplane!" another commando exclaimed. "The strange aircraft with propellers in front and back that touched down briefly toward the end. She must have come in on that."

"But the aircraft didn't *land*," someone else said.

She shrugged. She tried to make it look more casual than she felt. She was still far from sure what payoff her gamble would receive. She dared not betray any uncertainty. That could guarantee disaster.

"I was on a cruise liner when it was hijacked off the coast of the Netherlands Antilles last week," she said. Mahmoud blinked his big mahogany eyes at the apparent non sequitur but said nothing. "Innocent lives were put at risk. Lives were lost—fortunately, only those of some hijackers. But it was all a ruse, meant to cover the theft of the coffin now in your ship's cargo hold."

She heard multiple intakes of breath around her in the half-lit galley. It was close and smelled of old coffee grounds and some strong cleanser. And sweat.

"Since then the crate has left behind it quite a trail of dead bodies. That in itself has kept me in pursuit of it."

"Exactly what is your intention in relation to this relic?" the lieutenant asked.

"As an archaeologist, it's my professional responsibility to do whatever I can to ensure the relic is returned to its rightful owners."

"A laudable aim," Mahmoud said. "But whom might these rightful owners be?"

She shrugged. "I don't know yet. I don't even know for sure what the relic is. It will require investigation, once I've determined the nature of the artifact, and gleaned what clues I can about its origin."

She hesitated. "The Knights of the Risen Savior claim to be the rightful owners."

She heard someone hiss. "Dangerous fanatics," a commando said in distaste.

"Do you not know that these Knights you speak of consider themselves modern-day Crusaders who believe the time is overdue for Jesus to judge the world in fire?" Mahmoud asked. "And who do their best to bring it about? They would use the relic to bring down Armageddon on us all."

She looked at him hard. He seemed sincere.

"That doesn't square with my experience of the Knights," she said. "For that matter, your actions don't bear much resemblance to the claims the Knights made about you. They say you're the dangerous fanatics, Islamists who intend to use the relic to further your *jihad*."

Mahmoud drew his head back. "Islamists? We are Muslims. That is true. But fanatics—no. In fact, as soldiers it is our primary mission to fight *against* Islamists. Our nation is torn by a brutal insurrection, led by madmen who call themselves Sword of the Faith. They hate and fear our Sultan Wira for his reforms."

Annja tried to digest all that. "Has anyone considered that there might be a legitimate misunderstanding going on here?" she asked.

Mahmoud looked at her a moment in return. He shook his head.

"In any event we might argue in turn that the artifact was stolen from Islam. And that we might return it to our brothers, the real rightful owners. In fact such decisions are not ours to make. Our duty is to return the relic to our homeland. And to keep it from the hands of any and all irresponsible parties."

He leaned forward onto his elbows. "Now, tell me, please. What made you think you could escape discovery?"

"What makes you think I thought I could?" she said.

"Wouldn't it be polite to let me ask the questions, Ms. Creed? You sneaked over our stern railing like a common thief. Didn't you think we would be on our guard?"

She shrugged. "I hoped you wouldn't be. But it wasn't vital to my plans."

"Oh, no? Weren't you afraid of the consequences of being discovered?"

"No," she said with more confidence than she actually felt.

"Why not? Weren't you afraid we might be terrorists, as your friends the Knights told you? Or at least ruthless enough to slit your throat and drop you overboard?"

"No," she said. "I saw how you treated the Knights who surrendered to you on Le Rêve. You behaved like civilized men. Chivalrous, even. And the Knights are not my friends, by the way. They contacted me to ask me to help them get the coffin back."

"Did they, now?" She felt a certain tension come into the room. "And what did you tell them?"

"What I told you—that I would do whatever I could to see the relic in the hands of the rightful owners. Whomever they turn out to be."

Mahmoud sat back. He looked around at his men, who seemed to be very carefully keeping their dark faces impassive.

"Ms. Creed," he said, shaking his head, "you are a remarkable woman."

"Tell my producers," she said. "Maybe they'll give me a raise."

She felt, more than heard, an almost subliminal rumble. Vibration rattled through the deck, up through the soles of her walking shoes and her tailbone on the chair. She sensed motion.

"Hey!" she exclaimed. "We're getting under way!"

"Yes," Mahmoud said. "We have completed repairs on our engine. We've an appointment to keep."

He stood. "Bima, find a cabin to secure Ms. Creed in until we are well out to sea. And best make it a comfortable one. Otherwise you'll have no chance of ever getting your autograph."

"What are you going to do with me?" Annja asked.

"Turn you loose," Mahmoud said, "as soon as we land. Until that time, we want to keep you out of further mischief."

Then with a smile he said, "It's gratifying to be able to surprise you for a change, Ms. Creed. I hope you will enjoy your journey to the Sultanate of Rimba Perak."

TRUE TO THE lieutenant's word, the door to her cabin was unlocked several hours later. At the slight metallic sound she snapped awake where she lay on her bunk, fully clothed atop the taut blanket. Just in case.

She waited tensely in the dark. The door did not open.

She rose, walked to the door, listened. She heard nothing. She yanked the door open.

The gangway outside was lit by dim and dingy bulbs. It was empty.

Annja stood a moment, looking up and down the corridor. Then she turned and went back into the cabin, closing the door behind her. She stripped to her panties, put on a T-shirt from her pack and got into the bed. She fell at once into a deep untroubled sleep.

ALMOST ANTICLIMACTICALLY, the Rimba Perak commandos proved as good as their word. The next morning was overcast, with squalls walking all around the ship and sometimes swirling them in sheets of rain. Her door remained unlocked. No one tried to stop her going up on deck.

A guard in a rain slicker paced the deck with an assault rifle. He nodded and greeted Annja politely. She returned the greeting.

She found the galley empty. The larder was amply, if not particularly imaginatively supplied. She made herself a breakfast of sorts out of ramen noodles heated in the microwave and corned beef from a can. It would never be a favorite, but it wasn't rotten and it wasn't moving. She was hungry, and ate with her usual appetite.

She spent the day exercising, which seemed to intrigue the commandos, and talking with them. They were surprised but pleased when she showed interest in their weapons. The rifles were called SAR-21s, 5.56 mm NATO weapons made by Singapore Technologies Kinetics. The machine guns also came from ST Kinetics, also in 5.56 mm. They were called Ultimax 100, after the hundred-round box magazines they used. The commandos seemed especially fascinated at how knowledgeably Annja handled the firearms, although she had never seen these particular designs before.

She was with a half dozen of the commandos, sheltering from the wind and spray on the aft deck close behind the superstructure. "We buy much of our equipment from Singapore," said Bima, who seemed to have appointed himself her guide and watchdog. He had been absurdly pleased when she'd signed the promised autograph for him after he showed her to her cabin the night before. "It is very good. Most modern."

He had a cheerful-puppy air to him. His eager youth reminded her of the American-born Knight, Sharshak, although Sharshak was a good deal more earnest. She harbored a vagrant wish the two might meet each other.

Maybe each one would see the other isn't really an ogre after all, she thought.

"What about the swords?" she asked.

They looked at one another nervously. Then Bima unslung his scabbarded weapon from his back. Holding the scabbard, he presented its curved hilt to her. Slipping her fingers inside the slim knuckle-bow, she drew it out.

A curved weapon with a single edge, it resembled a scimitar. The blade, about two feet in length, widened steadily from guard to angled tip. Its balance was clearly intended for slashing. To her surprise the hilt was neoprene. The sword felt good to Annja's experienced hand.

"It is the *parang nabur,*" Bima said. "It is the traditional weapon for Borneo." Borneo, she had learned, was the island where the Sultanate of Rimba Perak was located. The Sultanate had broken away from Indonesia about a decade before.

She turned the weapon in her hand, then rolled her wrists, doing a slow-motion sort of figure-eight pattern favored for stick or sword play. The small, hard, smooth-faced men looked on with wide, appreciative eyes.

"A fine weapon," she said. "A weapon for a warrior." She slipped it back into the scabbard, still held in Bima's hand, at a single smooth try.

"Ee!" the commandos cried. They grinned and laughed and slapped him on the back.

SHE ATE DINNER with several of the men, including Mahmoud and the inevitable Bima. Mahmoud told her he had a wife and two daughters. He wanted to take them to Disneyland in California. He was a pleasant, if somewhat harried, man in his early thirties. The commandos treated him with affectionate respect, but without much conventional military rigmarole.

From the ex-SAS man who had first taught her combat pistol craft, Annja had learned that was frequently the way of elite soldiers—they were easygoing, almost lax, behind the lines, but razor-sharp in battle. She had seen as much in her own later observations. She hadn't had opportunity to confirm or deny his flip-side contention, that all too often soldiers who looked sharp in barracks and on the parade-ground proved limp in combat.

After they had finished a meal—much better than her self-made breakfast—of steamed fish and rice, with peanut sauce and fierce red chiles, prepared by one of their number, Annja entertained them with stories about shooting *Chasing History's*

Monsters in exotic locales. She excused herself early and went to bed.

She was surprisingly tired, given how little she had done. But she'd had a tense couple of weeks. The enforced ocean cruise—that seemed to be a theme in her life, these days—actually gave her a welcome respite. It took her no time to fall into a comfortable sleep.

IT SEEMED SHE had just closed her eyes when a pounding at her door awakened her.

"Annja!" a muffled voice shouted through the door. "Ms. Creed!" It was Bima's voice.

She clicked on the light. Pausing to pull on clothes and walking shoes, she went and opened the door.

The young commando stood in the gangway holding his SAR-21 by the pistol grip. His eyes were wild.

"Annja Creed, you must come with me. We are under atta—"

From down the corridor to her left a burst of gunfire erupted in noise and flickering light.

17

Bima grunted and sagged against Annja. Her left arm went around him. She felt wetness on her palm on his back.

She pulled him quickly into her small cabin, sat him gently on the deck, then lowered him to his back. He resisted briefly when she tried to pull the rifle away from him. She twisted it free, took hold of the pistol grip herself. She snapped off the safety as her new friends had shown her how that afternoon.

A man appeared in the door. He was smaller even than Bima and wore a dirty yellow rag tied around his head. He held a Kalashnikov leveled from the hip.

Instinctively she fired a burst into his chest. He fell over backward.

Holding the SAR-21 toward the open door she quickly knelt to examine Bima. The lower left front of his khaki uniform was maroon with blood. She guessed the slug had hit him in the lower back on that side and punched out through his belly. The good news was there was a distinct, small hole visible in the blood-soaked cloth. The bullet hadn't tumbled through his viscera like a miniature circular saw.

If it had nicked his kidney, he'd probably be dead before he could get any kind of treatment that would do him any good. If it hadn't, and if he was very lucky, he *might* not bleed to death.

First things first, she told herself. He was moaning and stirring feebly. She straightened, went to the door, took two quick looks around the door-frame, left and right down the corridor. She made sure to poke her head out at a different level in case somebody had spotted her the first time.

She saw no one. She heard plenty, though. Shouting and shooting.

A lot of shooting.

She grabbed the dead man by a foot clad in a filthy tennis shoe and dragged him inside. The dark rubber runner on the deck might hide the blood trail and it might not. A body lying right outside the doorway would be a dead giveaway. It was a slim hope. But from the sound of things, *slim hope* was the best she could wish for.

She shut the door and locked it from the inside. It would certainly not stop bullets, nor probably repeated kicking. But she had reflexively pulled Bima out of line with the doorway, and thus a probing burst fired blind through the door. And any attempt to break the door down would make enough noise for Annja to prepare a lethal reception.

Again it was a thin advantage. Better than none.

A nasty crack vibrated through the deck and bulkheads, a sharp sound scarcely muffled by distance. She guessed somebody had just laid into the vessel with an RPG. She knew it was the favored weapon of the modern terrorist.

Or the twenty-first century pirate.

She went quickly to the porthole. She could not see the main deck fore or aft. The superstructure spanned the hull from beam to beam. What she did see was blinding yellow-white and blue light beams stabbing the *Ozymandias* from several directions. She ducked back just as one swept across the port.

Pirates, she thought. A flotilla of South China Sea pirates. The only terrorists she knew of who boasted a navy that size were the Liberation Tigers of Tamil Eelam, but their home island of Sri Lanka lay as far away as Australia. And terrorists seldom mounted an operation as large as this one had to be.

As she thought, she acted. She summoned the sword. Bima was semiconscious. With luck he, or anybody he'd talk to, would pass off Annja's suddenly plucking of a broadsword from the air to delirium. What mattered was surviving long enough for that to become an issue.

She slashed wildly at her bunk. Pirate gangs had been growing in number, size and ferocity for years. She knew it was one of the world's great unknown stories. So many people around the Pacific Rim were so desperately poor, and the rewards from taking even a small freighter so large, that piracy was a definite growth industry.

She took a handful of linen strips back to Bima. She made a pad and quickly tied it around his middle. Blood instantly began to seep through it, a spreading stain. She had to hope the crude pressure bandage would staunch the blood loss so he had a chance of not bleeding out.

There was nothing she could do about the internal bleeding.

"What are you doing?" he croaked at her. His eyelids fluttered.

"Getting out of here," she said. "I'm taking you with me."

He shook his head violently. For a moment she was afraid he'd do himself damage. "Can't! Must stay—"

"Hear that noise? There have to be a hundred pirates swarming this ship. They have automatic weapons, RPGs. You guys are hard-core, but you can't hold out against odds like that."

"But we fight to death," he gasped.

She grimaced. "I know," she said. "That's why I'm taking you with me."

She laced one of his arms around her neck and stood, in effect dead lifting him in an unbalanced kind of way. Fortunately he was slight, although with the density of his wire-hard muscles he probably weighed little less than she did, and *she* was muscular. He did help push with his legs, so at least he wasn't dead weight.

He didn't fight her. But he still shook his head. He wasn't bleeding from the mouth, but the sweat flew off his face and short hair like rainwater.

"Must stay," he said.

She had let the sword go. When she straightened, hauling the injured man upright, she had threaded the sling of his assault rifle around her right arm, her free arm. Carrying it, she guided him to the door and yanked it open.

"Must go," she said, reeling the weapon up. She risked two more looks out, left and right. There was no one in sight—which was lucky, because she couldn't change head-height this time. She urged Bima out into the corridor and aft. The ship's stern was closer and seemed to offer the best chance of escape. If there's any chance at all, she thought.

"We have to get out alive," she said. "Otherwise your Sultan will never know what happened here."

She didn't know if Bima bought that. But he quit arguing, anyway. They staggered along the gangway like a dying horse.

A hatchway burst open before them. A pair of commandos in their black night uniforms sprang in and spun back. Their scimitarlike *parangs* flashed in their hands.

Pirates surged in toward them. They fought with swords, too, and fat-bladed bolos. The two Rimba Perak commandos were clearly their masters, but disparate numbers would soon tell. The pirates went down spurting blood and howling. The commandos gave way toward Bima and Annja.

At the outburst of clanging and cursing in half a dozen languages, Bima snapped his head up. "See?" he said. "We still fight. Let me go. I have to—"

The metal of the outer bulkhead to Annja's right began to ring as if a jackhammer was going at it. Lances of light stabbed into the gangway behind the battling men. They seemed to walk forward.

As Bima fought to pull away, Annja rocked her weight back slightly. Then she bent forward, hard, bringing her stiffened leg at an angle across his shins. At the same time she threw her weight down and right. They went down in a judo sacrifice throw. She twisted so he'd land on top of her to minimize the extra damage the fall did to him. She grunted as her tailbone cracked the hard deck through the runner.

In the dim yellow gangway lights and the floodlights streaming in through the marching holes, men came apart in sprays of blood. The hammering went on and on, growing louder.

Bima cried out. Annja wrapped her arms around him and closed her eyes. The impacts grew horribly loud as they passed above. She smelled salt air and spilled blood.

The hammering stopped. She opened her eyes.

A line of holes passed a good three feet above Bima's back, which heaved convulsively as he breathed.

She rolled him off her so she could stand. Then she helped him up. His eyes were huge in his dark face.

He was too stunned to resist or protest as she tottered them forward, refusing to look down, no matter how they slipped and slid on the wet wreckage the .50-caliber machine gun, raking the doomed ship at random, had made of seven men.

Somehow she got him down the metal steps. The main afterdeck was surprisingly dark. Most of the attacking vessels lay lower in the water, and aimed their searchlights upward at the *Ozymandias,* concentrating on her superstructure. The sounds of combat still emerged from inside, but they grew faint.

Annja and Bima stumbled toward the stern. They made it almost halfway before the hatch to her right, which led down to the hold where she had been captured, opened up. Three pirates with rags wrapped around their heads scrambled out.

Chattering among themselves they did not notice the curious four-legged beast lurching at them from the shadows. Annja screamed and fired Bima's assault rifle from the hip, one-handed.

Her first burst raked one man's legs. He yelled and went down. It also struck the head of the last while he was still on the ladder. He disappeared without a sound.

The two pirates on deck had slung their Kalashnikovs to scale the ladder. The one still on his feet struggled frenetically to get his weapon off his back and into action. The sling seemed to wrap him like sticky tape.

Annja had no mercy. She charged toward him as fast as she could totter. She pumped burst after burst at him. The weapon's recoil was relatively light. It wasn't hard to keep the muzzle from climbing.

It wasn't accurate shooting. But accurate enough. The pirate spun down to the deck in a whirl of blood.

The third man rolled around moaning and clutching at shattered legs. He didn't seem to pose much threat. From the amount of blood he'd already lost he was likely to be none at all, soon.

Annja let the empty SAR-21 drop and hauled Bima to the rail. His legs gave out on him as they reached it. Easing him to the deck, she looked down.

Her heart soared as she saw a twenty-foot motor launch bobbing there, tied on by a line to the rail.

Then it plummeted as she realized it had six pirates aboard, bristling with weapons.

THE HOLD WAS an echoing black cavern. Some trouble lights clamped to stanchions shone on a large oblong crate held by bungees to grommets in the very center of it. The pale yellow wood seemed to glow in the lights.

Three men stood around it, facing outwards. Their firearms, with no more magazines to feed them, had been thrown down and kicked away to leave their feet clear. They held their distinctive Malay swords in their hands.

"No shooting," Eddie Cao Cao commanded, striding forward. His own curve-bladed Chinese broadsword sang clear of the sheath he had thrust through his belt. "It might damage the goods."

Around him a dozen men from half as many countries drew steel or clubs. Eager to impress the most powerful pirate chieftain in the South China Sea, they surged past him like a scruffy tide.

At the first echoing exchange four of the pirates went down. Eddie Cao Cao frowned. This was turning out to be an expensive operation. On the one hand, that meant more shares of loot for the survivors, including obviously the captain's share. On the other, it didn't make it easy to recruit new bravos.

The man who faced him was taller than the others, almost as tall as Eddie himself, who stood six feet tall…or anyway, no one said he didn't. Something about him suggested he commanded. He was prominently balding and wore a resigned look. Eddie was not deceived—the man had cut down three of the pirates with remarkable speed.

Eddie strode purposefully forward. The man turned to face him, right foot advanced. As the pirate leader drew near he lunged.

With his sword hand he feinted a high attack, then whipped his blade down to his left, then back in a slash at Eddie's legs. Eddie stepped away with his right foot. His curved blade whistled down to meet the other's in a ringing clash.

As his two remaining men were swarmed over

and hacked down he launched a desperate whirlwind attack. Eddie found himself forced to give ground. That was a surprise in itself. He was a fanatic about swordsmanship.

His men began to crowd near. Some shouted encouragement. Others seemed poised to move in and intervene to score points with the boss.

Eddie had no intention of letting that happen. This man had made him give ground. He must be seen to fall by Eddie Cao Cao's hand, and his alone. A good pirate leader did not rule exclusively by fear. Just by a *large measure* of fear.

After pulling back for a brief, panting breather, the Rimba Perak commander came on again. This time Eddie gave way deliberately. Then as he stepped back with his right foot his boot slipped out from under him, as if he'd come to a patch of spilled oil—or some other fluid.

He turned to his right as he went down. Still silent, the commando raised his sword and closed for the kill.

Still turning, Eddie Cao Cao lashed out with his left leg. He was a powerful man and it was a power shot. Both his attacker's legs were swept from beneath him.

Like a tiger Eddie sprang. As he came up he reversed his grip on his big sword. With both hands he thrust downward into his opponent's sternum. His momentum drove the blade through his chest until the tip grated on the deck.

Eddie Cao Cao leaned on the blade until it bent.
The other man glared up at him. For a wild moment
Eddie feared the man would simply swarm up the
sword at him like a speared boar and take him with
him into death.

Then the eyes glazed. The man relaxed. His head
fell to the side.

Shaking his head, Eddie Cao Cao straightened.
He almost hated to put his boot on the dead man's
chest to give him leverage to pull his weapon free.
But it played well—his men cheered and shook their
weapons in the air.

He cleared blood from the weapon by snapping
it down and right. Scabbarding it, he stalked forward
to the crate.

"Open it," he commanded.

The bungee cords were quickly removed. Instead
of bothering to go for pry bars, the pirates swarmed
over it, wedging in their blades, levering at the lid
with clubs. It came free with a screeching of nails
and fell to the deck.

Inside was a mass of tan fibrous packing-filler.
"Clear it away," Eddie said. Pirates jumped in and
began to pitch the stuff out as if bailing a boat with
their hands.

In a moment they had revealed the top of a
metal coffin.

Eddie Cao Cao frowned. A tip from one of his
carefully suborned contacts, this one in the Sultanate
of Rimba Perak, had told him this ship carried cargo

valuable beyond measure. Yet this coffin was the only cargo.

"Is this a joke?" he rumbled. He rubbed his wide jaw, which was fringed with blue-black beard. "If it is, then someone is going to spend a long time begging to be allowed to die."

"Shall we open it?" one of the pirates asked. His teeth were stained red from chewing betel nut. Eddie Cao Cao found the practice revolting. But he couldn't ban it without losing too many men. Some of the best pirates in the business wouldn't stay if they couldn't chew.

He looked at the coffin. His square, handsome face furrowed. He felt a strange sense of unease in the pit of his belly.

Eddie Cao Cao was not a superstitious man. But he had learned to trust his gut.

"Not now," he said. "Put the packing back and seal it."

He turned and strode toward the ladder. It was time to get the captured freighter under way. He had contacts or better in every level of government of every state in the region. But if such a concentration of the Red Hand fleet were spotted, by surface craft, air patrol or satellite, those contacts might not be able to forestall a fast and violent retributive strike.

For every friend, ally or hireling Eddie Cao Cao had in the South China Sea, he had a thousand enemies.

THE PIRATES HAD TIED a blue-and-white nylon rope to the taffrail to secure their boat to the bigger vessel's stern. With only a heartbeat's hesitation Annja went right down it feet-first.

It was a scary climb. The boat bobbed in a considerable swell. The rope jounced all around, threatening to smash her against the hull, or simply shake her loose and drop her into the black waves to drown.

The men below were preoccupied playing some kind of game in the boat. She knew she was spotted when she heard a surprised cry. Encouraging hoots followed. The pirates couldn't believe their luck.

She kept sliding downward with her legs wrapped around the line. The last thing six heavily armed and murder-hardened thugs were going to feel by a lone woman was threatened. Even if she was probably taller than any of them. In fact they were probably focusing on nothing but the long legs and muscle-rounded rump descending toward them.

The wolf whistles rose. Annja let rope play through her hands. The nylon was relatively smooth but still tore at her palms. All she needed was for it not to tear her hands up too badly to *grip*.

The waves tossed the boat. As she got lower she began to time the essentially chaotic motions.

The catcalls reached a joyfully predatory crescendo. A couple of pirates stood and clapped their hands. Though Annja couldn't understand their exclamations their tone alone would have chilled her blood to the point of congealing.

Except she—and she alone—knew what was really about to happen.

About eight feet from the boat the line snapped taut. Anticipating that, Annja had turned away and braced. She used the springlike action to leap directly into the crowd.

Abruptly her reception committee got more than they had bargained for. The hard rubber cleats of one hiking shoe took one man in the chest and slammed another in his shoulder. Both went down beneath her, cushioning her landing. The man whose shoulder she struck clutched the man behind him as he fell, taking them both into the rough water in a tangle of limbs.

By this time the sword was in her hands. She was as a wolf among a flock of chickens.

One man, shrieking now in terror, got a knife cocked over his shoulder for a desperate overhand stroke but Annja lunged and knocked the man over the gunwales into the sea. Most of his crewmates did no more than raise their hands defensively and howl for mercy.

Annja cut them down with fury. It was a measure of vengeance for the brave, cheerful, courteous young men who had been butchered aboard the *Ozymandias*. And her only hope of escaping with the lone survivor.

The wounded men, recognizing defeat, threw

themselves into the sea. They were swallowed by the rough water almost instantly.

One last man, pumping blood from his severed forearm, fell backward in the stern of the launch by the small outboard engine. With his remaining hand he brought up a double-barreled shotgun.

Annja lunged across the muck and jumble that filled the bottom of the boat. The sword pierced his throat. His eyes bulged toward her, then rolled up in his head.

She let the sword go. It vanished as the dead man seemed to melt into the bottom of the boat.

Annja rolled the dead man overboard. Then, wiping her hands clean on her shirt as best she could and trying not to fret about the blood of strangers mingling with her own in her torn-up palms, she began the tortuous climb back up the mooring rope.

The wind was rising. Spray lashed her. Adrenaline and sheer determination gave her strength to persevere.

On deck she found Bima conscious, if muzzy and weak. He lacked the strength to climb down unaided. Near exhaustion herself she was almost foolishly grateful to find a metal locker nearby with a safety rope coiled inside. She cinched the wounded man to the mooring line, eased him over the rail and onto it. She took a couple turns around her waist, looped the safety line over the rail and climbed over to join him on the thicker cable. Then with her legs wrapped about the cable and playing out the safety line through her already painfully abraded palms, she lowered them both toward the launch.

The trip was a particular annex of hell. But no matter how it felt, it wasn't eternal. And Annja's body might fail her, but she refused to let her determination do so.

They made it down. Annja had to go in the water to get to the launch. It was colder than she'd expected. But she got into the craft without capsizing it, though her arms came within an ace of failing her, and got Bima in safely as well. As soon as she had her feet beneath her she summoned the sword and cut the ropes free.

The launch's engine was idling. She fired it up and turned the prow away from the looming, bobbing stern. As she did, the water began to churn greenish-white as the freighter's big screws began to turn.

The squall was their shield. Annja accelerated into it. The freighter, and its cargo, were quickly lost to sight.

18

An hour after the sun passed the zenith an orange-and-white Sea Knight chopper appeared, headed roughly toward them. The sky had cleared, leaving Annja and Bima exposed to the mercies of the sun. She did her best to shade the now-delirious man with her rapidly sunburning body.

Rather irrationally Annja stood up in the launch and waved. The chopper was clearly looking for the *Ozymandias* or survivors, and there was nothing else on the sea from horizon to horizon. The big helicopter swept two hundred feet overhead. Faces surrounded by helmets peered in amazement from the open side of the hatch at the spectacle of a tall woman wearing a sports bra and cargo pants hopping up and down, waving her arms and shouting like a fool. She recognized the insignia of the Republic of the Philippines armed forces.

Within ten minutes she had been winched up from the launch and hauled inside the Sea Knight by crewmen. A medic attended to Bima, still alive but barely, strapped to a stretcher on the deck. She had insisted he be taken aboard first.

The helicopter had already dropped its snout and accelerated forward with a rising growl of its twin turbine engines. The launch was left behind to the mercies of the sea.

There was nothing to suggest any men had lost their lives on the small craft. Annja had bailed out as much blood as she could, for hygienic purposes rather than to hide forensic evidence, although after the fact she realized that was a helpful side effect. As for the blood that soaked her pants and Bima's uniform, that was assumed to have leaked from the wounded soldier.

Of course, if the rescue crew realized she had killed any South China Sea pirates in the boat, it wasn't likely to lower her esteem in their eyes. But she didn't want people *talking*. If the wrong officials heard talk like that, they were going to ask those inconvenient questions she was always so concerned with.

As it was, she spent much of the next two days in the port city of Zamboanga answering questions. They weren't terribly pointed. Some of the circum-spection came from her carrying a U.S. passport, she realized. She'd had it, along with her wallet and credit cards, in a buttoned pocket of her pants. She claimed she had been aboard a freighter bound for Rimba Perak, doing research for a *Chasing History's*

Monsters episode she intended to pitch on modern-day pirates.

Her ever-pleasant interrogator frowned at that as if he didn't quite get it. He spoke English well. Middle-aged, with gray liberally dusting the tightly curled black hair that surrounded his large head like a cloud, he had a round belly on a slight frame, wrapped in an indifferently tailored suit. He had thick horn-rims in an inside pocket of his jacket, which he took out to read things. "I thought the show concerned, well, monsters," he said, taking a sip from a bottle of pink lemonade.

Annja just looked at him. After a moment he laughed, softly and sadly. "I have investigated dozens of these attacks," he said. "I see what you mean."

Mostly she played Hysterical American Woman again, claiming to remember few details of the experience. The sudden night attack, shooting, shouting. A badly wounded guard who heroically helped her escape.

That she was too freaked out to give a clear account was neither implausible nor unexpected. The horrors of a pirate attack were too well-known to the Philippine authorities. She hated to foster that particular stereotype about females but she knew it would play into the perception that Western women were pampered and impractical. Her interrogators would have regarded her fighting back against the attacking pirates as unbelievable as if she'd told them about the sword.

Annja did have a couple of uncomfortable

moments the second day, when kindly Mr. Baxa, the lead investigator, actually got her dossier from Manila and learned she had narrowly escaped a terrorist attack before.

She shook her head and sobbed—hating herself, but hating the consequences of having the Philippine government wonder about her a whole lot more. "It's my *job*," she explained tearfully. "It—it takes me places where trouble can happen."

She hated herself even more because Mr. Baxa seemed horribly upset by how upset he had made her. He ended up giving her a whole box of tissues and apologizing effusively.

He also answered her questions about Bima. She was terribly afraid that cheerful, brave young man would die from a combination of the wound, blood loss and dehydration, even though there had been bottles of drinking water in the boat.

She was also concerned about what the injured commando might tell the Philippine authorities. There had been no opportunity to coordinate stories with him. In the launch, Bima had alternated between delirium and unconsciousness, blessedly mostly the latter.

"His condition had stabilized," Mr. Baxa told her, leafing through the documents on the table in front of him, "when last I heard about him." Something about the way he said that puzzled her. She asked him what he meant.

"He was flown out aboard a Rimba Perak armed

forces air transport this morning," Mr. Baxa said. "The Sultanate's government made urgent representation to mine to repatriate him as soon as possible. They have promised a full transcript of any information he is able to give them, provided he survives. It appears he will do so."

He frowned. "I suspect," he said, polishing his glasses with a handkerchief and sounding disapproving, "that my government hoped first, to spare themselves the expense of keeping him in intensive care any longer than they had already, and also to escape the onus should he die. There could be an incident. In any event—" he put the glasses back on "—he was able to tell us nothing. And both the *Ozymandias* and the pirates who took her have vanished, as though from the surface of the earth. It is also a depressingly common story."

He sighed, reached over and turned off the little cassette tape recorder. "Ms. Creed," he said, "I trust you will forgive me if I tell you that all my investigator's instincts tell me that much of what you have told us is a tissue of fabrications. Shocking, but there it is."

She let herself stare at him wide-eyed, as was her natural reaction. It's what an innocent person would do, she told herself.

"However," he said, "the evidence is overwhelming that, whatever the particulars, you are an innocent victim of a particularly vicious attack. Whatever knowledge you might be withholding from us, my instincts also tell me, is by no means guilty knowledge. Indeed, something tells me you played a far more active role in the escape than that poor sailor. It's a miracle he could walk any distance, much less fight off South China Sea pirates.

"In any event, I frankly doubt that any additional information you could give me would be of any practical use. Even if we knew exactly who was responsible, that would not be the same thing as being able to do anything about it. Such pirates as these have protection, and I don't just mean their sometimes frighteningly complete arsenals."

He rose. "You are free to go, Ms. Creed. I hope that I have not wronged you. And I hope, for both your sake and that of my republic, that your business does not bring you back to our archipelago again for a good long time."

NEXT MORNING a Philippines Airlines 737 deposited her at the Sultan Rashid International Airport in Meriahpuri, capital and principle seaport of Rimba Perak.

Mr. Baxa had kindly arranged to have Annja's backpack, including her cell phone and notebook computer, brought from her hotel room in Mati. With so little luggage, and ever-helpful *Chasing History's Monsters* credentials, she cleared customs with surprising quickness. The process was efficient, featuring neither the hinting and grubbing for bribes characteristic of the Third World, nor the rudeness and suspicion that characterized the First.

Shouldering her pack, she turned toward the exit

of the smallish but new and blindingly modern airport. The light outside was so dazzling through polarized windows that she put on her sunglasses before striding toward the doors.

Two men materialized out of the crowd before her. One, bearded and broad-shouldered, stood taller than she, leaving aside his turban. He looked Indian to her, probably Sikh. The other was a small, exceedingly neat man, bareheaded, with receding, black, slicked-back hair. Both wore conservative suits and ties.

"Ms. Annja Creed?" asked the small one in English.

"Yes," she said, trying not to sound as glum as she felt. Secret police? she did not ask.

He showed her a shield in a leather carrier. It might have identified him as a bubblegum quality-control inspector. She didn't feel inclined to scrutinize it too closely.

"We are from the Sultanate of Rimba Perak's Department of Public Safety," the neat little man said. "We must request that you accompany us, please, Ms. Creed."

She showed them a big smile. "Of course," she said. Mostly because she knew she had no choice, so there was no point in antagonizing them. Of course, it might not make much difference.

Do I hope they're who they say they are? she wondered, as they took up station to either side of her and escorted her out into the slamming hot molten-silver sunlight. Or do I hope they're not?

"Sultan," the lean man in the white suit said in his New England–accented English, "everybody admires what you're doing here with this little country of yours. You've done a great job bringing your Sultanate back from the tsunami. The whole world knows it.

"But now it's time to get serious. Serious about the war on terror. And that means getting with the program with the United States of America. No holding back. It's crunch time."

And how well has the United States done rebuilding its own Gulf Coast, after the 2005 hurricane? Sultan Wira wondered. He knew the answer full well. He chose not to say it. It would be ungracious. Sultan Wira was a young man who believed in being polite.

When at all possible.

His visitor was a tall, middle-aged man with nearly white-blond hair cut close to a narrow head beneath the brim of the white Panama hat he never took off. The color of his pale eyes remained indeterminate behind his equally perpetual sunglasses, and he wore an expression suggesting he smelled something unpleasant you stepped in. His U.S. diplomatic credentials identified him as Cyrus St. Clair.

Sultan Wira took neither name nor status altogether literally. He had ruled his small breakaway nation for a decade. He had not done so by being naive, nor slow on the uptake. Nonetheless, his capable intelligence service assured him that his guest did officially represent the United States.

"You yourself have suffered personal loss at the

hands of terrorists," St. Clair said, as if Wira might be unaware of the fact. "After all, you were thrust into rulership of the Sultanate at the tender age of fifteen, back when reconquest by Indonesia was a very real possibility, after your father was assassinated by terrorists. May God rest his soul."

"I appreciate your solicitude, Mr. St. Clair," he said. He had a rich baritone voice. It had cost him hours of practice, and some expensive speech coaches, to overcome the hormone-driven tendency of his voice to crack when he spoke, right after he ascended to the throne. He had gone on to develop his voice as best as hours of practice and tutoring could make it. He knew it would be an asset and he needed all the advantages he could get.

"As well as that of your government," Wira said. "I would point out, however, that despite the best efforts of the Sword of the Faith movement, my government and I have survived. And even made some progress in modernizing this country, despite the tsunami."

St. Clair nodded. He looked like a schoolmaster trying to hide impatience at being interrupted by a pupil. "Yeah, yeah. Sure. We know that. But the world has changed. Everything's changed. I know the concept of nonalignment plays well with the national-pride crowd. But the threat is out there, and it's growing. A small country like this one can't go it alone. It's brave, sure. But, realistically, not a chance."

Wira smiled. They sat in the scented shade of a

flowering jasmine tree on a terrace overlooking the palace gardens. A pitcher of iced green tea sat on the round white table between them. St. Clair's glass was conspicuously untouched. No doubt he would have preferred something harder.

Wira was mildly surprised St. Clair hadn't asked for alcohol, to emphasize his authority as an emissary of the world's only superpower over a pissant rag-head potentate. And Wira would have obliged him, as hospitality demanded. Although he drank no spirits himself, the palace stocked them in abundance for its nonobservant visitors. Wira had worked hard to secularize his country's government while honoring its majority Islamic faith—and others as well. That he was succeeding was shown by just how vigorously the Sword of the Faith kept trying to put him away for good.

"It amazes me," he said mildly, "how many offers of partnership Rimba Perak and I have received since rich new oil reserves were discovered beneath our soil and territorial waters. The Australians, the Filipinos, the Chinese, the Indians, the Japanese—even the Russians and the French. Everyone seems so eager to be Rimba Perak's friend—and protector."

St. Clair clamped his lips to a bloodless line, draining away the little color they had. He said nothing.

"I am not so overwhelmed by this multinational display of generosity," the Sultan said, "that I fail to wonder what strings might come attached to it."

"Surely you don't suspect the U.S. of ulterior motives?"

"Naturally not. I do find it in the interests of my people, as well as myself, to pay close attention to the desires expressed by my near neighbors as well as benign but distant great powers. Give-and-take with the community, if you will."

"Well, just remember what our president said," St. Clair replied from behind a patently false smile. "If you're not with us, you're against us."

Wira laughed delightedly. "Your president says so many amazing things," he murmured.

St. Clair stood up. The interview was clearly over. He clearly felt it was his decision, and not that of a mere head of state. "And when the commander in chief of the free world talks, the wise listen."

"I assure you I always listen most attentively, Mr. St. Clair. I bid you good-day."

19

Wira sat several minutes on the veranda, sipping his lemonade, enjoying the shade and the perfume of his garden. He found few pretexts for relaxation. Now he was giving his visitor a decent interval in which to leave. He almost felt gratitude to the man, despite having seen quite enough of him for one day. If not longer.

At last, unable to postpone any further, he rose and went into the palace. The foyer was cool, with high, white walls. Fragrant floral sprays sprang from vases in niches in the walls. Potted plants of various sizes were everywhere. He had inherited his father's love for greenery.

As he walked down a corridor a man materialized at his side. He was small, even for a Malay, wiry, of indeterminate but plainly advanced age. His head was shaved. He was dressed in a traditional sarong. Wira nodded at him.

"Krisna," he said. "I perceive you're going to nag me."

"Someone must guide my Sultan when his feet stray from the path of wisdom," his Grand Vizier said.

A simile occurred to the Sultan, concerning a sheepdog. He smiled to himself and left it unsaid. Despite his name—which meant "wisdom" in Malay, and was common among islanders of all faiths and also belonged to a Hindu god—the Grand Vizier was a devoutly traditional Muslim. Comparing him to a dog, an unclean animal, would have insulted him, which Wira did not intend. As Sultan, Wira had to make many unpleasant decisions, take many harsh actions. He hated to act unkindly unless necessity forced it. And Krisna had been his loyal adviser and friend since boyhood.

"I appreciate your solicitude, as always," he contented himself with saying.

"You must take care to placate Mr. St. Clair," the Grand Vizier said.

"Why?" Wira asked. "Because he's CIA?"

"Oh, no, my Sultan." Krisna shook his hairless head. "He is most assuredly not CIA. I suspect he belongs to some other, more secret arm of the U.S. government. One which by reason of flying below the radar enjoys more latitude than the CIA, you see."

Wira waved a dismissive hand. "I don't care about details. I dislike playing games. There's so much work to be done. I want to help our people educate themselves, to develop a strong economy—without allowing ourselves to become addicted to our own oil, a prisoner of monoculture, as it were, like the Saudis."

"The United States of America is hardly a *detail,* Excellency," Krisna said stiffly.

"Neither are the other powers who pretend such avid friendship. At the very least, let them buffer one another. Play games undermining each other—and meddle in our affairs the less. In particular, Krisna, I have no desire to serve the U.S. as a torturer-by-proxy. Nor do I intend to suffer being deposed by some kind of color-coded people's revolution, bought and paid for with U.S. dollars."

They came to the foot of a broad stairway sweeping up to the palace's second floor. Wira glanced down at his smaller companion and sighed. "Please forgive my vehemence, old friend."

"There is nothing to forgive, Excellency. I only advise that you take care not to give the Americans anything to forgive, either. They're not good at it."

"Noted," the Sultan said. He sprang up the stairs.

At the top a female aide in a stiff tan tunic awaited. "We have received word from the security forces," she told him. "They have picked up the American archaeologist Annja Creed at Meriahpuri Airport, as you instructed."

He chuckled softly. "I wish I'd bet old Krisna," he said. "He thought she'd be discouraged and go home. I told him it takes determination to be the lone skeptic on a television series such as *Chasing History's Monsters*. Excellent, Miri. Tell them to bring her to the palace at once, please."

"They are on the way."

"Thank you."

He went into the antechamber to the office. It was spacious, well-lit and elegantly appointed, with a fine Bokhara carpet on the floor and spiky palms in planters. On a broad white divan lounged a strikingly beautiful woman with her legs tucked up beneath her. A green band held a gleaming mass of black, wavy hair back from her face. As was her custom her whole outfit was the same rich hue—the wrap around her upper body, leaving one shoulder bare, the sarong about her hips. An emerald winked from a gold setting in her navel, seeming to glow against her cinnamon-colored skin. It was an ambivalent sort of outfit—green was the color of Islam, yet the ensemble showed so much skin as to aggravate if not outrage the more puritanical traditionalists. But then, that was a Sufi all over.

He raised an eyebrow at her. "Are you waiting to lecture me as well, Lestari?"

She smiled coolly. She looked no older than he. He suspected she was, though, possibly a good deal. Or is that mere superstition? Sufis enjoyed a reputation for all manner of mysterious powers, although they disavowed mysticism themselves. He tried hard for a very Western kind of rationalism, himself.

"I wanted to counterbalance that old hen, Krisna,

presuming he'd counsel you to leap into bed with the Americans with both feet," the woman said.

"Krisna is an old and valued counselor, Lestari," the Sultan said. "He served my father before me. I'd never have survived without him. He may be prone to notions and to worrying. But he's very wise."

"The wise are often the worst fools," she said.

He cocked a brow at her. "Another of your contradictory Sufi sayings? Your *impacts* are worse than Zen *koans*." He was tweaking her—Sufis tended to bristle at having their Path compared to other forms of Eastern esoterica.

But Lestari laughed. She was a hard woman to read. That was refreshing in itself. Most women he encountered, as a young, rich, athletic Sultan, were as transparently easy to read as Cyrus St. Clair. And had much the same motivation.

"It seems no more than an obvious observation," she said, "based on experience. And I'd advise you most urgently against considering Mr. St. Clair transparent. He is a man who is happy to play up those aspects of his motivation which his circumstances make apparent. There's nothing so subtle as the proper kind of obviousness."

"Another observation? You Sufis are inordinately fond of apparent contradictions, in all events." His expression hardened slightly. "And I refuse to believe you're reading my mind. I am a committed skeptic."

She shrugged. "It is the Sultan's privilege to believe what he desires," she said, "and as for most self-professed skeptics, commitment would suit them well. You can attribute my occasional flash of insight to training in the Western discipline of reading body language, if you want."

He raised a brow. "You give the West that much credit?"

She shrugged an elegantly bare shoulder. "Remember, my Sultan—we Sufis did not invent the motor car, but we still ride in them."

"What I'll remember is not to try sparring mentally with you," he said ruefully. "It makes my poor head ring like a gong."

"It does not," she said matter-of-factly. "You are young, and thus intellectually lazy. So you seek convenient excuses."

He glared at her. She returned his gaze calmly, her slightly squarish chin uplifted. He laughed.

"You've no more respect for authority than my cat," he said.

"True." She stretched, perhaps to emphasize the resemblance. "But as a perceptive cat person, you've noticed that despite what most people believe, cats are exceedingly loyal—in their own way."

"Yes. And now, if you'll excuse me—"

"Do I bore my Sultan? Then let me be brief—be careful of the American."

"St. Clair? Always."

"He's one," she said. "I had in mind the woman. The very ingénue archaeologist. She's trouble."

"Lestari," he said, in tones of exaggerated exasperation, "you're too young to be my mother. Give me a break. *All* Americans are trouble. And at the risk of sounding sexist, so are most women."

"*Most?* Indeed, my Sultan has yet much to learn."

ONCE ALONE IN THE sanctum of his office, Wira checked the palace network for the special digest of local information and intelligence reports, constantly updated by his intelligence service. If anything urgent happened, he'd be alerted at once. But he liked to keep a finger on Rimba Perak's pulse. Next he skimmed the headlines at several external sites for world events. He felt they gave him an insight into how the ever-mercurial Americans were thinking.

Then, having assured himself no crisis, local or global, was any more likely to loom up and swat his little kingdom than usual, he went to the Web site for *Chasing History's Monsters.* He gazed at the lovely image of Annja Creed.

TO ANNJA'S surprise the Sultan sprang up from behind his mahogany desk and strode forward to meet her, smiling with teeth bright white in his dark face, his hand extended.

"Ms. Creed!" he said in excellent English with a slight British accent. "Such a pleasure to meet you. I'm a big fan of your work on *Chasing History's Monsters.*"

She shook his hand. His grip was warm and dry.

It was also like taking hold of a carved cypress root. Apparently the job of Sultan of Rimba Perak didn't entail lounging on cushions all day eating grapes and being fanned. Unless that somehow gave you a grip like a vise. He didn't exert any more than the polite degree of pressure—it was just obvious how much he held back.

What really surprised her was how young he was. And how handsome.

He wore dark blue trousers with a stiff-looking white tunic and a modest white turban. He was nearly as tall as Annja, trim, with the grace of a stalking tiger. His face was lean, with pronounced cheek-bones and large brown eyes. The youthfulness of his appearance and carriage didn't quite square up with the way he spoke, which suggested an older man.

"Do you usually have your favorite celebrities arrested the moment they enter the country?" she asked. "If that's the case, I'm afraid you can pretty much kiss any prospects of developing a movie industry goodbye."

The Sultan laughed. "I'm afraid I have yet to entertain a sufficient number of celebrities to develop a proper protocol. Perhaps you will be kind enough to assist me. Please, sit down."

The office likewise took her off guard. It was spacious and well-lit, like everything she had seen of the Sultan's palace as her two guards escorted her through it politely and with professional briskness. There were the plants in terra-cotta planters and a

ceiling fan turning overhead, a lot more quietly than
the one in Mr. Baxa's interrogation room.

She was surprised how modest the office was.
The desk, though a beautiful piece of furniture that
gleamed as if it had been polished by several straight
generations of artisans, was simple and clearly not
designed to intimidate. Nor was the office set up
with a huge expanse of open floor to be crossed to
approach the Presence, nor little dinky or altogether
absent chairs. Instead comfortable-looking chairs
upholstered in batiklike designs awaited. With the
shelves full of books and the sliding doors that led
onto a balcony with palm fronds waving over it, it
looked like a thoughtful man's study, instead of
the office of an absolute potentate barely halfway
through his twenties.

The chairs *were* comfortable, she found as she sat
in one. Wira went behind the desk and seated himself.

His brown eyes met Annja's. For a moment, they
simply held gazes.

She looked away. Her cheeks felt unaccountably
warm.

"I apologize for the rather abrupt way I had you
brought here," he said. "But you have, after all,
involved yourself in the affairs of this country."

"True," Annja said. "But your country seems to
have involved itself in trafficking in stolen antiquities."

His lips pressed together. After a moment he put
his hands on the desktop and stood. "Would you care
to walk with me in the garden?" he asked.

20

The palace occupied a bluff inland from the bustle of Meriahpuri, where it was washed both by breezes from the sea and from the not particularly high but quite steep mountains inland. The shade of tall trees spaced carefully throughout the garden helped the breeze cool the air. It was still midday in the tropics. Annja was glad for her sunglasses.

Wira walked beside her with hands clasped behind his wedge-shaped back. He carried himself with a distinctly military bearing.

"You mentioned stolen antiquities," he said. "I'd point out that most recently the artifact presumably in question was stolen from *us*."

"Yes," Annja said. "But only after you stole it from the Knights of the Risen Savior. There were a couple of other thefts along the line, culminating in their stealing it back. But ultimately, they claim it rightly belongs to them."

"The question is, is that true? To whom does this relic rightfully belong?" Wira asked.

"That's my question. Certainly, whoever it belongs to, it isn't a murderous gang of South Sea pirates. They'd have a pretty tough time documenting a claim, anyway."

Wira stopped and turned toward her. She halted, too. "Before we go further, what happened to my men? The Philippine government was kind enough to send along transcripts of your interviews with their investigators, although I've no way of knowing how accurate they may be. But they leave out a few details. Such as how twenty-four of this land's finest warriors set out on that ship, but only one returned!" His dark eyes blazed with passion.

"Don't hold it against Bima, please, that he survived," Annja said. "I persuaded him that our escaping was the only way for his superiors—for you—to learn what really happened. He never would have agreed to leave his comrades had he not been in shock from his wound. And he was concerned about me, although I don't think that swayed him from his duty."

"Do you know what his name means? Bima?" She shook her head. "It means *brave*. His comrades often teased him about that, did you know?"

She smiled wanly. "Not really. If they teased him when I was around, they did it in Malay."

"I am satisfied he lived up to his name, Ms. Creed. And I am more pleased than I can say that he at least survived. Losing one man would be unacceptable. Losing so many—"

He shook his head and looked carefully away. For a moment he looked even younger than his age, and quite vulnerable.

"It may not be fashionable to say so," he said, "but I will avenge them." His voice was thick with emotion.

"It may not be fashionable to say so," she said, "but I agree. Revenge can get out of hand, don't get me wrong. But the men who did this are evil men. They've earned your vengeance."

He nodded. They walked on, between rose bushes buzzing with bees. "You are an exceptional woman, Ms. Creed. The Filipino investigator, a Mr. Baxa, mentioned as much in his annotations to the transcripts."

"He didn't say the whole thing was a tissue of lies, did he?"

"He said that to you?"

"Well—not in those words. Exactly. But of course, it was. As you're well aware."

"I am. Will you please tell me, succinctly, what happened? I would appreciate it greatly if you would also agree to give a full account to my intelligence staff. It will help to bring the murderers to justice."

"I'll be glad to," she said. It wasn't entirely the truth—given her life as it was, she never felt comfortable talking to authorities about anything in any detail. And she had the depressing certainty Sultan

Wira's intelligence service would be distressingly competent. But she would willingly endure their scrutiny, if it might bring justice to the pirates who had slaughtered all those valiant, laughing young men. And win back the relic.

She gave the Sultan a quick account of events. It consisted mostly of details she hadn't told the Filipinos. She edited out all mention of the sword, as well as the fact she had shot several pirates. In her version, Bima did the shooting needed to get them clear in spite of his agonizing wound. Annja also claimed that once out of the superstructure they encountered no more pirates, and that they stole an unattended boat while the pirate crew infiltrated the ship like maggots, mopping up defenders and looking for treasure.

"You didn't hear anyone talk about what they intended to find?" he asked.

"Not in any language I could understand," she said.

He nodded. His brow was furrowed thoughtfully. "They must have gotten some hint as to what the ship had aboard," he said. "Even as bold as pirates have become these days, it's no small thing for them to mount an operation of such size. It was overkill for a normal freighter. They knew they'd meet resistance. Otherwise they would have fled."

Annja had no idea how many casualties the commandos had inflicted on the pirates. The only actual fighting she had seen, as opposed to done by herself, had ended with both Rimba Perak warriors and the marauders indiscriminately chopped to pieces by the pirate heavy machine gun, probably firing blind. But I saw the commandos in action against the Knights, she reminded herself. I can't believe they didn't give better than they got.

"The pirates seemed awfully determined," she said. "I know even a small ship like that, with cargo, is worth an awful lot of money. Especially to people who come from grinding poverty. But those men seemed to feel something really extraordinary was at stake."

She looked at him hard. "And speaking of which, Sultan, what really is at stake here? What is it that so many people are willing to kill or die for?"

A white gazebo rose ahead of them. He gestured to it. "Let's sit in the shade and have something to drink. I'll tell you what I know."

They sat in the small white structure's shade and sipped lemonade served by a tall silent servant in khaki tunic and blue turban. "You have a lot of staff who don't look ethnically Malay, if you don't mind my saying so," Annja said.

Wira nodded and grinned. It made him look even younger. "We're pretty much a melting pot. The Pacific Rim's always been like that, you know. My father, and my grandfather before him, took in a great many ethnically Indian refugees, Hindu and Muslim alike, fleeing persecution. What would today be called ethnic cleansing, in the sub-Saharan African states following the collapse of colonialism.

The last wave of it, anyway. My mother was Indian. A Rajput—and a Hindu."

Annja nodded. "You have a reputation as being very liberal, politically and religiously," she said.

"I like to think of myself as liberal in the classical sense," he said. "The modern usage seems to have acquired a lot of excess baggage. Of course that fits up pretty strangely with being a despot, no matter how hard I try to be an enlightened one. Those are the circumstances in which I find myself, however."

He seemed at ease, sitting back with one long leg crossed over the other. He had a way about him that suggested he could snap into action like coiled spring from full relaxation, like a cat. Annja knew about that—it described her pretty well, too.

"I told your men on the *Ozymandias*," she said, reluctant to wander back to potentially touchy subjects, "that they, and now you, don't match up with the picture the Knights of the Risen Savior paint of you."

His young face hardened as he sipped his lemonade. "You should be careful of them, Ms. Creed. They are dangerous men. Zealots, fanatics who long to bring back the days of the Crusades and help the gentle Issa, a holy man to Muslims as to Christians, to judge the world in fire."

"Well, now, Your Excellency, that's the thing," she said. She was thinking, He probably won't have an American television celebrity, even a very minor one, publicly beheaded or caned or anything for effrontery. "They don't match your image of them any more than you match their image of you."

"With all respect, people's true motivations can be hidden by a winning nature and a smile." He laughed. "As my own might well be, of course. At least, I try for a winning nature. Being confrontational causes more friction than it's worth, I find. Especially when the nation one rules is the size, if not of a stamp, of only a largish postcard. Fortunately, I've studied a book on that very subject by a most wise man."

"Jalal-ad-din Rumi?" she asked.

"Dale Carnegie," the Sultan said. *"How to Win Friends and Influence People."*

She laughed. He shrugged. "It works," he said. "Although sometimes I admit I have trouble behaving myself."

He emptied his glass, set it down, and gazed at Annja for a moment. She tried hard not to think about other possible meanings of his words. She found herself more than a little drawn to him.

"I have set scholars to researching the relic's history," he said. "They come up with a great deal more speculation than solid information. There are persistent stories of some kind of relic being found in Jerusalem during the Sixth Crusade, long after the alleged True Cross was discovered. It has been alleged to be a coffin containing the remains of a very holy man."

"That squares with what the Knights told me,"

Annja said. "Also, I can confirm that the object in the crate appears to be a coffin."

He blinked at her. "You can?"

"I got a glimpse of it on the island of Le Rêve," she said. "After your people took it away from the Knights and stashed it in a warehouse. Waiting for the *Ozymandias*, I suppose."

"Quite," the Sultan said. "You're very resourceful, Ms. Creed. As well as most determined."

"Thank you."

He shrugged. "I myself am skeptical. At least, in terms of any sort of power belonging to such an object, although the Sufis assure me it might contain great *baraka,* which might be translated as 'blessings.'" He paused a moment as if in thought.

"I do believe the coffin possesses, at the least, enormous symbolic significance. Enough to incite all manner of passions, in the wrong hands. That's why I am determined to keep it from both our domestic extremists and present-day Crusaders."

"I'm certainly behind you on that. Although I have to admit I don't agree with you that the Knights are Crusader wanna-bes. Their own founder, the Emperor Frederick the Second, had to be excommunicated to get him even to go on Crusade. But that's not my main motivation."

He drummed fingers on the tabletop. "You do seem highly motivated. You've followed the coffin halfway around the world. Are you sure you don't believe it has miraculous powers yourself?"

She shook her head. "I'm sure that I don't," she said. "My interest is to see the relic—which, regardless of its specific nature, is an archaeological relic of incalculable value to the world—properly conserved, and entrusted into the proper hands."

"And whose hands might they be?"

She laughed without much humor. "That's the question, isn't it? I'll give you my stock answer—I don't know. I need more evidence to decide."

"Will you help us recover the relic, then?"

She felt her lips compress. *I need to choose my words very carefully, here.*

The Sultan leaned forward intently. "I'm willing to have the matter adjudicated," he said. "In fact, I'm willing for you to participate in the process. I'd like that. You seem to be impartially interested. You can call upon whatever experts and authorities you desire. I will pay for the procedure."

"Well, since you put it that way—" She regarded him carefully. "One thing you must understand. I will not under any circumstances turn the artifact over to anyone I believe will use it for destructive ends."

"That seems fair enough—if one accepts the premise that this object actually has that kind of power. But I guess it's not too far-fetched that it might cause social upheaval, by overturning long-cherished beliefs."

Annja drew in a deep breath, shaking her head. "Given all the blood spilled over it in just the last few days, there's no denying its power to cause mayhem."

She studied the Sultan closely. He seemed sincere, even ingenuous. All the same, sincerity wasn't hard to fake—as he himself had pointed out.

"What's your interest in the artifact?" she asked.

"I'm fascinated by history, and both personally and, as you might say, professionally interested in the question of reconciling people of different faiths. I decided to involve my people when I discovered that it had been stolen from the Knights who had held it for centuries, and that in some way the Sword of the Faith, the Islamist terrorist movement that afflicts this country, had gotten involved. My intelligence indicates it was from those terrorists that the Knights recovered the artifact in midocean."

Annja blinked. "How did they get involved in all this?"

"I've no idea. My security advisers suggest they may want it to serve as a rallying point for a violent *jihad.*"

"Against you?"

"First," he said.

She waited for him to say more. He didn't. "I see your point," she said. "But how about the allegation that you want to use the relic to further your own expansionist aims?"

He laughed. He sounded incredulous. He stood up and paced a few steps behind his chair.

"Only because our near neighbors the Malaysian Federation so quickly recognized our secession, leading to other nations of the world following suit, have we been able to resist being forcibly rejoined to Indonesia," he said. "It's an open question whether the pool of oil it has recently been learned we float upon will provide us sufficient means to prevent its being taken away from us by violence. If I am deranged enough to dream of conquest, won't that be a self-correcting problem? Inasmuch as it will ensure I'm overthrown and killed, either by outsiders or my own people?"

"Good point," she said. "Still, you could have powerful friends."

He laughed again. "Representatives of various world powers have flocked to Meriahpuri proffering just such friendship," he said. "Are they less to be feared than my declared enemies? I wonder."

21

The Sultan's palace walls were gleaming white stone, fifteen feet high and topped with black wrought-iron spear points that served substantially the same purpose as knife-wire—which Annja had gotten more than her fill of, in recent months—but made the place look less like a penitentiary.

The guards were trim little Malays in crisp khaki uniforms, with royal-blue turbans that were more head-wrappings than what Sikhs wore. They carried wavy-bladed *kris* daggers thrust through their web belts and SAR-21 machine carbines slung. They looked more spit-and-polish than the easygoing but fiercely, and fatally, brave commandos she had met on the *Ozymanaias*. She guessed that was necessary. They formed part of the public persona of the Sultan, as it were. She suspected they would fight capably enough, if necessary, to protect their Sultan.

She hoped it wouldn't be. She found she quite liked young Wira, the half-enthusiastic post-adolescent, half-seasoned elder statesman. He was remarkably handsome and charismatic. Maybe too much so, for her peace of mind. Developing a crush on a head of state was not a good move, in her mind. As friendly as he was, she was after all a foreign woman, of no great status.

The gate guards did not halt her or inspect ID. Instead they snapped to attention as the tall wrought-iron gates rolled open as of their own accord. After a brief hesitation Annja drove through, with a big smile and cheerful wave for both guards. It seemed the polite thing to do. She didn't want to try returning their salutes, for fear of it being taken as mockery. She wasn't hugely impressed with military ritual, but she did respect people doing their jobs.

"Hmm," she said aloud as she drove up a long, broad, gently winding road up an emerald-grassy slope toward the gleaming Mughal-looking jumble of the palace itself. "That's interesting."

She had called down to the desk of the Rimba Perak Hilton that morning to ask for suggestions on a car rental. That would not be necessary, the cheerful young woman responded. A pearl-gray Lexus awaited her, compliments of the Sultan.

She guessed it carried a kind of transmitter that alerted the gate guards to her imminent arrival. Realizing that, she wondered if the car also had a means of monitoring how many passengers it actually carried,

even who they might be. She knew all kinds of scary
spy devices existed and were widely available. She
also knew that the Pentagon's rosy conviction that the
U.S. had an insurmountable technological lead over
the rest of the world was fiction—if it was even a
footnote. She'd seen evidence of that herself.

And Rimba Perak's near neighbors and guardian
angels were Singapore and Malaysia, both self-
conscious high-tech wonderlands, at least at their
cores. Sultan Wira had a lot of money and was known
to be a full-bore modernist. The sky could well be
the limit.

Annja disapproved of that sort of thing. A full-
surveillance society wasn't compatible with liberty,
so far as she could see. Still, she felt a degree of reassurance that it was deployed by what was shaping up
to be her side. She had a feeling things could get ugly.

She also felt more than a passing twinge of guilt
at being reassured by that. Am I willing to give up
freedom for supposed security?

She shook her head. She had plenty to have mis-
givings about. To start with, playing ball with an
absolute despot, no matter how personable, or apparently liberal.

To Annja's surprise, after the afternoon chat in the
gazebo the Sultan had told her she was free to go.
He requested she return the next day to begin helping
with the recovery of the artifact from the South
China Sea pirates. They agreed that was a priority.

He told her a room had been reserved for her at the Hilton in Meriahpuri. She was to be the guest of the Sultanate. Indeed, as of now, she was an official consultant to his government. Contracts were being drawn up. If she found that satisfactory?

Given that she had come in a car with a huge, silent Sikh secret policeman sitting next to her, and no particular reassurance that she'd ever be leaving again, that was more than fine with her. Her knees had gotten shaky with relief.

Once Annja checked into her hotel she found Wira hadn't been entirely candid with her. Her luggage was already in her room when an official Sultanate car dropped her off, the desk told her. Except it wasn't a room. It was a penthouse suite, with a glorious view of the crescent-shaped natural harbor and city of Meriahpuri.

The contracts were slipped under her door while she soothed herself in a long bubble bath in the swimming-pool-size tub, complete with water jets and gilded fixtures. All that was needed was a handsome, well-muscled male attendant. Or even two. Except she was afraid to say anything about it within hearing of the hotel staff, even in jest. She'd be totally mortified if they actually showed up.

The contracts were lucrative. She might not have to take a commission from Roux after all. So far she'd gone into this on a flyer, and her special accounts had taken a pretty large hit. Island-hopping in the Pacific, especially on the shortest possible

notice, wasn't a cheap proposition. Even without
having to bribe a pilot to do a touch-and-go drop-
off through the middle of a firefight. But if this deal
came across she was going to see a hefty increase
in her balances.

Provided she survived, of course.

APPROACHING THE PALACE Annja noticed weird
cement protrusions to either side of the road. They
were overgrown with vines and had planters atop
them. But each also had a funny little metal disk in
the face pointed toward the road.

She guessed they were self-forging projectile
launchers. Those little five-inch copper plates could
turn in a microsecond or two into a sort of spear-
head, at the tip of a jet of incandescent gas, courtesy
of a shaped explosive charge. They could punch
through a light armored vehicle like a blowtorch
through butter, even kill a main battle tank from the
right aspect.

She knew insurgents in Iraq had been using them
against the occupation for years. She had actually
known about them for years, courtesy of some of the
special-ops buddies she had made even before she
found the sword, or it found her. They all learned
how to make them early on. The U.S. government
had even published manuals explaining it all in easy-
to-understand terms, with diagrams, for use by
civilian guerrilla fighters.

But clearly these emplacements were anything

but *improvised* explosive devices. She guessed they were intended primarily to discourage truck bombs. But Sultanate security, clearly, believed in taking no chances.

It was understandable, given that Sultan Rahim, Wira's father, had been assassinated ten years earlier. Annja had done some research online the night before. She was pretty sure the hotel wireless net monitored her Internet activity, whether or not the hotel actually knew about it. It hadn't slowed her much. She figured Wira, bright boy that he was, expected her to do her homework. Especially for what he was paying her.

There was one little thing she hadn't done. Not yet. Nor had she made up her mind how to play it.

Her suspicions about the truck bomb defenses seemed confirmed by the odd insets in the pavement, just before the road curved under the gleaming white portico of the palace entrance. Her tires rattled ever so slightly as they passed over them. Pop-up cement barriers, she thought. Blast shields. And I have my suspicions about what lies beneath those neat linear flower beds, in front of the portico and along the whole front wall.

A solemn Sikh man with a sidearm in a flapped holster helped her out of the driver's seat. Her place was taken at once by a skinny little adolescent in Sultanate livery, who grinned at her toothily, as if she'd just given him the gleaming luxury car as a birthday present. He wouldn't have been her choice to trust for valet service. Then again, it wasn't her car. And possibly even a teenager would think twice about putting his Sultan's paint job at risk.

"Your car will await you on departure, Ms. Creed," the Sikh said in crisp English. He had the air of someone who could face down a horde of howling foes with just his *kirpan* dagger and that ferociously splendid beard. "Will there be anything you require from it in the meantime?"

She shouldered her new daypack. "No. This is all I'll need, thank you."

The car engine revved. The Sikh gave the driver a pointed look.

The car purred off at about five miles an hour. Laughing silently, Annja followed the guard inside.

A tiny, neat man in a green-and-brown sarong stood waiting for her. His head was shaved. It was hard to read his exact age. He was clearly not young, to judge by the lines around eyes and mouth. He had the look of a statue carved of dark wood come to life.

"You are Dr. Annja Creed?" he said in accented but clear English.

"Yes," she said. "Just Ms. though, or Annja. I haven't finished a doctorate."

He smiled and nodded. "Very well. I am Krisna. It is my honor and pleasure to serve our Sultan Wira as Grand Vizier, as I served his father before him."

"Pleased to meet you, Your Excellency," she said. If that was what one called a Grand Vizier. He was her first.

"I understand you have an appointment with the Sultan," the small man said. Annja nodded. "Come, walk with me this way."

Annja agreed. "You are American, I believe?" he asked, smiling broadly, as they moved into the palace.

"Yes."

"You consider yourself a good citizen, yes?"

"Yes," she said. "That doesn't mean I agree with every action taken by the government of the United States. I don't have much say in that." Like any U.S. citizen abroad she had grown somewhat defensive on the subject.

"Ah, but is the U.S. not a famous democracy?"

"Sure," she said. "And that gives me about a one-three-hundred-millionth of a voice in government affairs. That doesn't add up to a lot of influence."

"Ah," he said again. They walked in silence for several steps through a cool hallway well-lit by tall narrow windows. "Well. What counts is your patriotism. Not that I would ever dream of questioning it. What I must ask is that you use your influence with the Sultan to encourage him to accommodate the United States to the greatest extent possible."

"My influence?" She stopped and looked at him. "I'm a private citizen, a foreign national, and I just met the Sultan yesterday. He seems interested in engaging my professional services as an archaeologist, which is flattering. To derive any kind of influence from that seems pretty far-fetched, with all due respect. Except purely in the line of my profession, and even there it remains to be seen how much I can affect his decisions."

The Grand Vizier smiled and bobbed his head. "To be sure. To be sure. Come, let us proceed. I have no wish to make you late for your appointment. It is only that the Sultan is a young man, for all that his experiences and circumstances have aged him far beyond his years. I had a role in that, I fear—the cruel murder of his father forced him to forgo much of his childhood.

"But he is still young, and still a man. And while I understand it might be considered politically incorrect in the West to do so, honesty compels me to point out that you are a young woman of considerable attractiveness."

"Thank you," she said as neutrally as possible. She tended to react defensively to perceived flattery. She was sure somebody with the title of Grand Vizier wouldn't exactly be above manipulating people. It was like expecting an archaeologist to live totally in the present, with no interest in old things or bygone days.

He nodded as if she'd said something inestimably wise. "So it may be that you enjoy more influence with his Majesty than you might imagine. Not, of course, that I suggest you would ever do anything improper."

"Of course not," Annja said, a bit edgily. "If I might ask, why are you so interested in advancing the United States' interests, Mr. Krisna?"

He laughed gaily. "Ah, although I have the greatest

of respect and affection for your very great country, my interests are focused solely upon the welfare of Rimba Perak, her ruler and her people, who are, of course, as one. It is simply a matter of geometry."

"Geometry?" Annja asked.

He laughed again. "Consider the map of the world, Ms. Creed," he said. "Rimba Perak is a mere speck, oh, so hard to see. And America is large. These are frightening times. The small need all the help they can get to avoid being crushed. It is the mutual interest of our nations and peoples which I ask you to bear in mind."

"I'll certainly try," she said.

He beamed and nodded. "Very well. I thank you, Ms. Creed."

He stopped at the foot of a broad white stairway that curved up to the second floor. "I must leave you now. Just beyond the top of these stairs you will find the Sultan waiting in his office for you. I trust you will enjoy your stay in Rimba Perak."

"I certainly hope so," she said.

At the top of the stairs she found the antechamber with the potted plants and white leather sofa, just as it had been the previous day. But now a gorgeous dark-haired woman dressed in red was half-reclining on it. Beyond her stood the closed door of dark-stained native hardwood.

"The Sultan has no receptionist, if that's what you're thinking," the woman said in a throaty alto voice. She rose. She did so as gracefully as a dancer. Or a serpent. "Those who are unexpected do not get this far."

"I'm sure," Annja said. "And I didn't think you were a receptionist, for what that's worth." She was trying hard to step on an upsurge of jealousy concerning what she did think. Or suspect.

The woman smiled. She had olive skin, her hair was black, her eyes rimmed with what might be a bit much kohl for Annja's taste. She was not fleshy by any means, but she carried a bit more body fat than most of the islanders Annja had seen, who generally had the wiry look of authentic poverty. That was emphasized by the fact that so much of her flesh was on display. She wore an off-the-shoulder top and a slit sarong that showed a lot of long, smooth-muscled leg and left her stomach bare. She had a ruby in her navel.

She extended a hand to Annja. Annja took it and shook. The woman's grip was firm and surprisingly strong.

"I am Lestari," the woman said. "I am a special adviser to Sultan Wira."

Expression neutral, Annja ordered herself sharply. It evidently didn't work. Letting go of her hand, the woman laughed from deep in her throat.

"Not the kind you may be suspecting," she said. She may have had a tinge of regret to her voice, Annja thought

Annja had a hard time believing she couldn't be the kind of "consultant" Annja had reflexively suspected her of being, if she wanted to. She exuded a sort of smoldering sexuality that would have men swooning at her feet. Yet something about her suggested she possessed a deep and devious intelligence. And, just possibly, a subdued deadliness. Annja was reminded of an exotic serpent, its scales glittering like jewels in the tropical sun.

"I'm Annja Creed," she said.

"I know," Lestari said. Annja couldn't entirely repress a sensation the entire contents of her brain had been downloaded into the woman's through their briefly linked hands.

"What exactly do you do here, Ms. Lestari?" she asked.

"Many things," the woman said. "Most of which concern looking out for the welfare of our young Sultan. He has before him a great destiny. He also has a choice—to use that destiny to work good, or ill."

"Don't we all possess such a choice, Ms. Lestari?" Annja asked, feeling unsettled.

The woman laughed softly. "Yes, we do. Not all of us have the potential to act on it that Sultan Wira does." Did her eyes bore into Annja's a little too long, a little too knowingly?

"You have unusual potential too, Ms. Creed," she said. "I can read it in your aura."

"Are you of a mystic turn of mind, Ms. Lestari?" Annja asked.

"Not at all," she said. "I am a Sufi."

"I thought Sufism was the Islamic mystic tradition?"

"Even a student of history and cultures as learned as yourself can harbor certain misconceptions, Ms. Creed. So much is human. We might discuss the matter more at another time."

"You want to warn me, too, don't you?" Annja asked.

Lestari smiled. "Of course. First, I will watch you most carefully. I say this not as a threat, since I do not as yet perceive any threat in you. Second, others will be watching you as well, and far from all with such neutral intent."

"I figured that," Annja said. "You seemed to leave that hanging. What's three?"

Lestari laughed again. "You do have a certain skill at perception," she said. "So few Americans do—or make use of it, anyway. Third, and most important, watch yourself at all times, Annja Creed. Especially your back."

INSIDE HIS OFFICE Wira stood looking at a large high-density television screen. Annja realized she had taken it for a painting of a tiger hunt on her last visit. With him were another Sikh and a small wiry man in jeans and black T-shirt.

"Annja Creed," the Sultan said, turning toward her as she opened the door. "So happy you could join us!"

His teeth were very bright in his dark face as he came to squire her forward with a hand behind her shoulder—chivalrously not quite touching her, yet somehow impelling her gently forward, as though by sheer personal magnetism. "I'd like you to meet Colonel Ranjit Singh, commander of our armed forces, and Mr. Purnoma, my chief of intelligence."

The Sikh nodded gravely. Purnoma grinned. "Hi." He had crew-cut black hair with a hint of gray at the temples and wore black Converse All-Stars. Ranjit Singh had a glass eye. Annja wasn't sure whether that was a good sign or not. It probably indicated he had extensive combat experience. It might also mean he was just unlucky.

"A pleasure," Annja said.

"Purnoma tells me," Wira said, turning back to the display, which showed a map of Rimba Perak and environs, "that we have discerned the pirate gang responsible for the attack was the one known as the Red Hand."

"It is a bad sign," Ranjit Singh said. "Eddie Cao Cao is the most ruthless pirate leader in the South China Sea, possibly all Asia. He is also the smartest. The Red Hand is large, and very powerful."

"And its tentacles extend into every government of the region," Purnoma said. "To a high level, I might add."

"Including yours?" Annja asked the Sultan.

Purnoma looked to him. The Sultan's chocolate eyes never left Annja's. She felt a thrill at that soul-deep scrutiny and fought sternly to suppress it.

Wira seemed to sigh and looked away. "We have

to presume so," he said. "It is no reflection upon my security forces, but rather on the fallen nature of humans."

Both advisers began to protest. He held up a hand. "I'm not excusing it, my friends. Allowing oneself to be suborned by a creature like Eddie Cao Cao is tantamount to treason, and I intend to treat it as such when it's uncovered. I just have to face the fact of the enormous leverage he can bring to bear—not just bribery, but blackmail and extortion. We are speaking of a man who routinely sets his packs of human jackals loose on boats full of refugees or immigrants, to plunder and rape as they like, and then scuttle their boats beneath them—or simply fling them over the rail, should he find their vessels worth stealing."

Annja felt her internal temperature drop a few degrees. It's not as if I didn't know such men existed, she thought. But I don't think I'll ever get used to being reminded of the fact.

"What can we do?" she asked.

"Well, I would like to have you see what further research you can do into the nature and real provenance of the coffin," Wira said.

"Meanwhile," he went on, and she flushed to realize he was scanning her face extra intently, having read some kind of reaction there, "we shall continue our efforts to pin down precisely where among the tens of thousands of islands in the immediate vicinity the Red Hand are hiding their newest acquisition."

She looked at him a minute, considering quickly. Then she drew in a deep breath and sighed it out.

"I think I can help you with that," she said.

22

There suddenly seemed to be more than twice as many eyes in the room than heads. All were staring at her, saucer-sized.

"You what, young lady?" Colonel Singh demanded.

Annja shrugged. "I slipped a miniature GPS transmitter inside the crate on Le Rêve when I peeked in at the coffin," she said. "I knew before I went to the island I probably wasn't going to be able to physically reclaim the artifact—I couldn't even lift it by myself. And it was mostly by sheer luck I was able to trace it that far. So I decided to at least make sure I could follow it wherever it went from there."

Wira laughed. His advisers stared at him.

"But this is splendid!" he exclaimed. "Why the long faces, gentlemen? It simplifies our task immensely. Admit it." He turned to Annja. "Excellent,

Ms. Creed! You continue to amaze me. I must say I'm pleased you're on our side."

Annja felt a twinge of guilt. Am I on your side? she asked herself. Is that good if I am? Or have I sold my principles for a handsome stipend and a handsome smile?

The Sikh scowled, his face clouding like an approaching typhoon. "Why did you not tell us this before, young woman?" he asked.

She shrugged. "I wasn't sure how much I trusted you," she said. "And I didn't want to show all my cards at once."

The Sikh drew himself up to his full height, which was considerable. He looked outraged.

Wira laughed. "I take it that means you've decided to trust us, then, Ms. Creed?"

"I guess it does," she said.

ANNJA ALMOST CRINGED at the volley of camera flashes that greeted her as she entered the lobby of the Meri-ahpuri Hilton. The relative obscurity in which she labored as frequent talking head on *Chasing History's Monsters* had actually suited her just fine.

Now that comforting anonymity seemed to be getting stripped away. She had acquired her own swarm of paparazzi. All because of a perceived romantic connection with one of the world's most eligible bachelors, the young, handsome, charismatic, fabulously wealthy Sultan of Rimba Perak.

"There's nothing to it," she muttered between

clenched teeth as hotel security men, mostly big Sikhs in dark suits with wires coming out of their ears, formed a cordon to hold the photographers back. She spoke low, not to be heard by her tormentors. After all, she thought bitterly, nothing is ever confirmed until it's officially denied.

"Ms. Creed!" A pudgy Japanese man in a rumpled suit, with his necktie tossed over one shoulder, pushed his way clear of the Sikhs to run to her side. "Please. You have to use your influence to convince the Sultan to see me!"

She shook her head. "You and ten thousand others." All were seeking investments, grants, stipends, appointments, all the fruits and vegetables and nuts of government largesse.

The elevator door opened. A pair of small but teak-hard Malay house detectives in plainclothes materialized from the potted palms to pin the supplicant's arms and keep him out of the car. "Obviously you don't care about the suffering poor, Annja Creed!" the man shouted, his glasses askew, his sweat-sheened face distorted with passions she couldn't even guess at. "You're just like the rest! You want to deny the world the benefits of abundant energy—free energy!"

She looked him in the eye. "My best advice to you, sir," she said, "is don't even open that can of worms. Or you'll have worse problems than Sultan Wira to worry about."

The elevator doors closed. She sighed. It took a

major exertion of will to keep from just folding with that sigh, as if her whole body deflated. She laid her forehead against the cool brass-colored doors and squeezed her eyes shut.

What's happening to me? she wondered. I'm trying to do the right thing, and the world is trying to make me the latest nine days' wonder, as if I'm a calf born with two heads or a cloned sheep.

Plus, people were trying to kill her. Two attempts had been made in the last two days. *That*, at least, she could handle. Nothing new about it at all.

THE FIRST TIME, a little boxy blue Nissan subcompact slowed alongside her as she walked along a busy street a few blocks from her hotel. She was feeling good. She had eluded the paparazzi already sniffing around her, and may have even outdistanced her unseen internal-security escorts. Their very existence was notional, but she suspected Wira's secret police would shadow her with or without the Sultan's command, or even his knowledge.

The street was full of expensive stores, reflecting both the success the Meriahpuris had had in bringing themselves back from the devastation left by the tsunami and the increasing global interest in Rimba Perak's abundant mineral wealth, already a major prize before oil was discovered. Annja, who liked nice things as much as the next woman, although she had never been much for shopping—probably because she'd never had much money to shop with—

had been admiring the expensive watches, the fancy handbags she'd never carry, the designer shoes. Even though her feet still twinged in sympathy when she saw stiletto heels.

Experience had drawn Annja's reflexes to hair-trigger tautness where her survival was concerned. When the faded blue Nissan began to brake she automatically launched herself for the cover of the base of a light standard, basically a truncated cement cone a yard across at the base, two feet at the top and four feet tall. It should stop most things that might be shot out of a car at her. And if nothing was, if the car really was slowing down right next to her for a harmless if not immediately obvious reason, she could always pick herself up, dust herself off and walk away. The locals all knew Western women were crazy. The tourists all knew Americans were crazy. Even the American ones.

In the corner of her eye she saw a reflection in the window of the fashionable boutique she was walking past—the unmistakable shape of a Kalashnikov rifle being wrestled out the open window of the little sedan. Noise exploded. The boutique window burst in a whirlwind of glass shards. Bullets and glass shrapnel shredded a little blue dress of some shiny material. The pink mannequin that wore it pirouetted madly away from the force of the burst.

Annja got her shoulder down, hit the ground hard and rolled behind the cement cone. Another burst clanged ineffectually off the cast-iron standard itself. Then with a petulant mosquito whine the Nissan accelerated away into traffic. It vanished from view in seconds as sirens began to wail.

THE SECOND ATTEMPT had come the previous morning as she sat in a sidewalk café near the hotel, finishing her light breakfast and coffee before heading to the palace for a day of research. A pair of young men approached. Something about the purposeful way they crossed the street through traffic straight for her put her on guard. One was a young man with long swept-back dark blond hair, who wore a beige jacket over an orange shirt and blue jeans. The other looked as if he might be a local. Like his partner he was around six feet tall. He had a dark, round face, and a cap of wild black hair. He wore a loose ill-fitting blue suit over a blue shirt with no tie, buttoned to the collar. The two walked up to the low ornamental wrought-iron rail around the outdoor eating area.

Annja saw them reach inside their jackets. Once again her survival reflexes kicked in. She hurled her half-full coffee cup at the blond man's face. He flinched, discharging a handgun in the air as he raised his hand to ward off the cup. The dark young man extended his arm and fired deliberately.

His bullets cut the air where Annja sat a heartbeat before. It passed over her metal chair, which she had knocked on its back as she vacated it, and ricocheted from the base of the café's brick facade. Annja scrambled on all fours to the door. More shots cracked behind her.

A stout man in a green tunic and a Nehru cap opened the door from the inside, emerging with a cardboard carrier full of cups of coffee. "Get down!" she shouted, as she dove past him into the café. She managed to avoid knocking him over, but he was so startled he shied like a horse, throwing his cardboard tray in the air.

Not looking back Annja rolled to her feet and sprinted toward the back, into the utility passageway, past the kitchen, past startled employees, out a door into a narrow evil-smelling alley. There she stood with her back to the wall and her sword upraised in her hand, breathing hard.

She heard more shots from the far side of the building. Glancing toward the mouth of the alley she saw people running.

The door opened. She tensed to swing—then opened her hand.

The face of a waiter turned toward her in astonishment a heartbeat after the sword vanished.

Within moments the alley filled up with armed Sultanate security men. They scooped Annja up and whisked her off to the palace, where a worried Krisna had plied her with green tea and disconnected bits of advice. She learned that internal security had in fact been tailing her. They had quickly converged on the scene, opening fire and killing the blond man as he tried to turn his weapon on them. The local-looking shooter had escaped into the crowd.

Fortunately, and amazingly, Annja escaped both times without any bystanders being hurt. She felt chagrined to have done nothing more than duck and flee. But with the Sultan's internal-security types keeping close tabs on her she was glad not to have used the sword. She had no idea how Wira would react if he found out about it. She didn't want to learn.

The rest of the day she had been left to her own devices, to use the palace's extensive library and high-speed Internet connections for research. The Sultan himself stayed occupied in other business of state—as urgently as he treated the problem of the stolen artifact, it was only one of many confronting his small nation, some of them of far more overtly threatening nature. But he turned up to check on her, as if to confirm to himself that she had come through intact.

NOW, IN THE hotel elevator, Annja remembered the way Wira had looked into her eyes and took her by the upper arms. "I'm pleased you escaped harm, Annja," he'd told her. "May the Gods continue to keep you safe." She remembered it very well indeed.

She felt hot liquid on her cheeks, realized her eyes were leaking tears. "Oh, for God's sake!" she exclaimed. She snapped her head up, stood bolt upright, throwing her shoulders defiantly back. Her eyes blazed.

"What's *wrong* with you? Crying because the paparazzi are snapping their silly cameras at you? Or because every escaped doorknob with a cause or an itch for unearned wealth is running at you with his palm out? Suck it up."

The elevator doors opened. A maid in a black-and-white uniform stood waiting patiently with a cart laden with fresh linens and cleaning supplies. The tiny birdlike woman cringed, her dark eyes wide in utter terror at the spectacle of Annja, a foot taller than she, standing there looking ferocious. She couldn't have looked more overtly terrified had Annja held the sword raised in her hand.

Annja didn't smile. She just nodded and said, "Sorry. I'm not mad at you," and then strode rapidly past, to clear the unfortunate woman's personal space as quickly as possible.

Great, she thought, now you're scaring the life out of people, too What's next, kicking puppies?

She opened the door to her designated office and stormed in. Two men rose from the comfortable settee in the sitting-area to greet her.

"You!" she shouted. "Out!"

"But Ms. Creed," Sharshak began. His eyes were wide.

The other man, Hevelin, older and steadier, smiled slightly through his grizzled beard. "Aren't you even going to ask how we got in?"

"The first time I met you people you kicked in my skylight and dropped through it shooting at me," she raged. "I'm way past caring about your means of ingress. It's your egress I'm interested in seeing right now. Out. Out!"

"But won't you at least tell us why you've betrayed us to the Sultan?" Sharshak almost wailed.

Annja glared at him through slitted eyes. Then she crossed to a leather-covered chair and fell into it with the grace of a sandbag.

"Let's get some things straight," she said, glowering at each man in turn. "First, I don't owe you anything. *Nothing*. I refused Cedric Millstone's attempts to hire me. I turned away yours."

Hevelin rubbed his bristly cheek. "Still," he said in his deep voice, "you did assure us you would not help our enemies to take possession of the relic."

"And I'm not doing that," Annja stated clearly.

"But aren't you working with the Sultan?" Sharshak asked.

"I've agreed to help him recover the coffin from the pirates who stole it most recently," she said. "They murdered two dozen of his men for it. They almost murdered one other commando. And me. They've murdered hundreds if not thousands of people over the years."

She smiled unpleasantly. "Surely you don't think it should be left in their hands, gentlemen," she said. "Nor disagree with the idea of visiting a little old-fashioned retribution on them in the process. Unless you believe that vengeance belongs solely to the Lord?"

"We'd make a poor military order if we did,

Ms. Creed," Hevelin said, sitting back down and clasping his hands over his knees.

"What about these reports in the media," Sharshak said, his voice high and agitated, "that you're—that you're dating the Sultan?"

Annja raised an eyebrow.

Hevelin flapped a hand at his young partner, who was practically vibrating. "Sit. You make me nervous. You generate more heat than light, like that."

Sharshak sat.

"Listen to me," Annja said. "I am becoming friends with Sultan Wira. Nothing more than that, no matter what the gossip columnists say. I'm just an archaeologist, a minor cable TV celebrity, if you can even call me that. He's a Sultan, for goodness' sake. Nothing's going to develop between us. Things like that don't happen in the real world."

"And the fact that you are an extremely attractive young woman doesn't enter into it, I suppose?" Hevelin said.

"Right," Annja said sarcastically. "Like the Sultan can't have supermodels throwing themselves at him anytime he cares to snap his fingers. They can't *all* be dating ballplayers and drug-addled rock stars. And even if we are friendly that doesn't mean I've agreed to let him keep the coffin once it's recovered from the pirates."

"You think he'll hand it over to you," Sharshak asked in apparent disbelief, "just like that?"

"He's agreed to," she said. "Yes."

"And you believe he will honor such an undertaking?" Hevelin asked, arching a skeptical eyebrow of his own.

"I do. He appears to take honor as painfully seriously as—as you people do. As his commandos do, those who died facing you on that island, and who died—except for one man, badly wounded, whom I more or less kidnapped—to protect the relic."

"Is that honor or fanaticism?" Hevelin asked.

"Where's the fanaticism? The Sword of the Faith killed Wira's father. They've spent the last ten years trying to kill him. It's precisely because he *won't* agree to turn the Sultanate over to them—especially with all this oil money pouring in.

"Meanwhile he had this equally silly notion of you as Christian nuts who want to help bring Jesus back to judge the world in fire."

"Us?" Hevelin laughed. "Frederick the Second was our founder and patron. What would he have said to such a project?"

"He probably wouldn't care for it any more than I do," Annja said.

"He charged us with preserving the order of the world," Sharshak said. "Isn't that the opposite of bringing on a new Crusade? Much less Armageddon."

"We are men of faith," Hevelin said. "We are also men of science, and the modern world, after the spirit of our founder."

"And that description perfectly fits what I've seen of the Sultan," Annja informed them.

"And whom do you believe then, Ms. Creed?"

She rose. "Both of you. You boys need to get together and talk. What could be more in the spirit of your founder? He was best buds with the Sultan of Egypt."

"Be that as it may," Hevelin said, pushing himself to his feet, "we must regain possession of the relic. It is our holy quest. It is our penance for our sins."

"When we have the coffin back," she said, "I will arrange to have appropriate archaeological authorities adjudicate its proper ownership. The Sultan has already agreed to this. When that happens, you can put forward your claims. I'll ensure they receive a fair hearing."

"But—" Sharshak began.

"Peace, boy," Hevelin said. "We are dealing with a woman of principle and of character. Contrary character, perhaps, but character. Hectoring her will only make matters worse."

"Thank you," Annja said.

"I only hope your judgment is the equal of your resolution," Hevelin said. "The fate of the whole world could ride upon it."

23

"We've received a communication from the Red Hand," Lestari said. They walked together through darkened palace corridors. Lamps at the bases of the walls cast amber fans of light upward, past the plants in their copper pots and shadowed niches. Tonight the Sufi woman wore royal-blue, with a sapphire in her navel.

"What did they say?" Annja asked.

"I'll leave that for His Majesty to tell you," the woman said in her usual manner, which somehow contrived to be at once sultry and deadpan. Annja could never shake the impression the woman was laughing at her on the inside. She felt a strange, nerdish urge to find some way to let her know she was in on the joke. But she could not. Especially since she wasn't.

At the foot of the stairs Lestari paused and draped

a bare arm over a banister. Everything she did looked as if she was posing for a classic Greek sculpture. Her ability to exude sexiness without apparently trying. like her air of superiority, infuriated Annja.

"You'll find the Sultan awaiting you in his study," Lestari said in her throaty contralto. "It's to your left at the top of the stairs, down two doors. I leave you here. But before I do, I have a question. What do you intend in regard to the Sultan?"

Annja felt her stomach lurch. Her nostrils flared like an angry horse's. "I really don't see what business that is of yours," she said.

"It may be and it may not," the woman said with a smile. "That remains to be seen. I did not ask the question in order for you to answer it to me. I asked it in order for you to answer it for yourself. Good evening."

She turned and glided past Annja, back along the amber-lit hallway. She moved silently, as if her slippered feet did not touch the floor tiles.

Shaking her head, Annja trotted up the stairs. "The worst thing," she muttered under her breath, "is that she's right. I need to ask myself that."

She had spent a lot of time in the Sultan's company the last few days. Even if most of it entailed little more than sitting in his office, leafing fruitlessly through volumes from the palace's vast libraries, or flipping through endless pages of Internet printouts while he read reports off the thin plasma screen that rose up out of his desktop on his command. He also muttered earnestly on his phone, issuing the occasional command, questioning constantly.

She could never help feeling his presence, like a warm stove in a cold room. Even away from the palace, walking clean streets between whitewashed downtown walls, past construction sites where the last of the tsunami damage was being repaired, or sitting in her room reading her e-mail, she kept seeing his face. Even doing her workouts his face or voice popped into her mind, to her aggravation.

I'm just a commoner, she reminded herself sternly as she set off down the second-floor corridor. She hated thinking of herself in those terms. Yet like most Americans she found herself fascinated by the concept of royalty and nobility, even though as an antiquarian she knew better than most the foibles of the high-born. Why would he be interested in me?

She blushed, slightly embarrassed by her own thought.

"Ms. Creed!" the Sultan exclaimed. "What a pleasure to see you."

She looked around. She saw no one.

"Up here," he called. She had stepped into a room with a high-domed ceiling, patterned with intricate looping knots and interlocked rectangles, like the floor tiles. The walls were lined with bookshelves. An old-fashioned mobile ladder on casters stood to her right, attached to a rail that ran around the top of the wall. Wira, dressed in green trousers and a loose white shirt with the sleeves rolled up his hard brown forearms, perched at the top of it.

He climbed down. "Are you all right?" he asked. "Your cheeks—you aren't feverish, are you?"

She shook her head quickly. "Just a touch of sun. That's all."

He gave her a stern look. "Be careful," he said. "Our tropical sun can be hard on fair skin such as yours."

Then he laughed. "Listen to me! I sound like Krisna. Who sounds just like Polonius, most of the time. As if you, the globe-trotting adventurer, needs me to warn you about the sun!"

"Your concern is always appreciated, Your Majesty."

He came toward her holding out both hands. "There's a time for formality, I know," he said. "But I hope that time has passed for us. I dare to think we have become colleagues, and may be on our way to becoming friends. I'd be honored if you'd simply call me Wira. Except when Krisna is around—it'll make him crazy."

She laughed. "You? Honored? The honor's mine—Wira." She took his hands. "But please call me Annja, your— Wira."

He smiled and squeezed her hand. For a wild heart-pounding moment she was sure he was about to lean forward and kiss her.

Instead he let go of her hands and raised his head. "Gentlemen," he said in a sharper tone. "Our guest has arrived. Please join me in the study."

She looked at him, puzzled. Inside she was trying to sort out whether she was disappointed or relieved. Or maybe why she was both.

He caught her eye, grinned and shrugged.

"Your people bug your own quarters?" she asked.

"Palace security," he said. "They'll do it no matter how sternly I order them not to. So I make use of it. It's handier than an intercom, and I hate walking around with a headset on all the time, or something stuck in my ear."

Purnoma and Colonel Singh came in, the Sikh looking tall and grave and splendid as always, with his beard oiled and up-curled at the bottom, and Purnoma dressed as if he was either a cat burglar or heading out for a little midnight basketball when they were done. She wouldn't put either past him.

They returned her greeting in their usual ways, Singh nodding gravely and Purnoma with his usual grin. Whereas Wira looked and acted, when he wasn't being prematurely middle-aged and serious and head-of-state, like a young man scarcely past adolescence, Purnoma looked and moved like a fifty-year-old kid. He seemed genuinely likable. At the same time Annja suspected that the flashing grin and those glittering obsidian eyes, if he was seriously interrogating you, would be far more terrifying than any bellowing or bluster.

I'm glad he's on my side. For now, she thought.

"We've heard from the pirates," Wira said. "Through an intermediary. The usual channels through which ransom demands are delivered, you understand."

Annja nodded. "I have some idea of how business is done in such cases."

Singh's stern expression, which usually looked chiseled in place, actually hardened. "Everyone speaks of never negotiating with these pirate scum," he said. "But everyone does it. Even ourselves."

"Speaking of terrorists," Annja said, "I've been wondering—could the pirates be working with the Sword of the Faith?"

Wira shook his head. "If anything, they hate each other more than they hate us," he said. "Like any purists, Sword of the Faith are prudes, deeply conservative. And like many terrorist movements around the world they try to gain popular support by crushing more conventional criminals."

"So the pirates want to sell the relic to you?" Annja asked.

Wira nodded. "They're giving us an exclusive opportunity to bid before they put it up for open auction."

"Including to Sword of the Faith," Purnoma said. "Greed makes strange bedfellows. Just like fanaticism."

"Where are the pirates now?" Annja asked. For some inexplicable reason she was starting to get a cold, creeping sensation in the muscles of her cheeks and down her lower spine.

The domed room was dominated by a large, low table with eight sides. Its top surface gleamed like polished mahogany, causing Annja to suspect it was a reading table, or perhaps for gaming. Wira did something with his right hand. The tabletop revealed itself as a circular high-definition screen showing a map.

"Nice techno-toy," Annja said.

"Useful, too," Wira said. He was a bit of gadget geek, she had noticed. Still, if you were as rich as Croesus and had high-tech haven Singapore as a near neighbor and patron, why not? He did seem to make good use of his toys.

"Thanks to your giving us the frequency for your GPS tracker, Ms. Creed," Purnoma said, "we've located them in the Sulu Sea. Overhead imaging shows a substantial junk fleet gathered there at anchor."

"Aren't they making a conspicuous target of themselves?" Annja asked.

"They are, unfortunately, in Philippine territorial waters," Singh said.

"And you can't strike at them without causing a nasty international incident," she said.

"And there you have it," Wira said.

Annja frowned down at the map. A set of little red ship figures showed the pirate fleet's location. "I don't suppose you could get the Philippine government's permission to hit them?"

The Sultan's young cheeks bunched in a grimace. "We don't dare," he said.

"Eddie Cao Cao would get the request before the Philippine Foreign Minister did," Purnoma said, "courtesy of his paid traitors."

"Who plague us in abundance," Singh rumbled.

"Minister Purnoma is highly effective at rooting them out," Wira said quickly.

"And it does precisely no good," the boyish internal-security chief said. "They're like roaches. They just keep breeding, in dark, moist, smelly places." He shrugged. "Maybe I'm just confessing to my own incompetence."

"Not at all," Wira said. "We have to face reality, no matter how unpleasant."

Annja looked from face to face. "That's my cue," she said deliberately, "to ask why you gentlemen have invited me here to tell me this. I don't have such an exalted opinion of myself to think you'd seriously consult me concerning Rimba Perak affairs of state."

"Don't sell yourself short, Annja," Wira said earnestly. "You've displayed remarkable gifts."

"Listen, Ms. Creed," Purnoma said, "speaking of roaches, you seem to have a gift for turning up whether you're wanted or not, and being pretty hard to kill. Apologies for implicitly comparing you to pirates. What I'm saying is, if you're not an operator, you should be. I'd offer you a job." His eyes crinkled in amusement. "Consider it done."

"I'm flattered, Mr. Purnoma," she said. "But surely you don't believe I'm somebody's intelligence agent?" If he does, she thought, I'll be leaving in a van with no windows. If at all.

"*I* don't," Wira said hurriedly.

Purnoma was looking at her with his head tipped

to one side like a curious bird. "I don't know what you are, exactly," he said. "But I don't think you're a threat to the Sultan or the State. And everything else is just idle curiosity."

"I don't want to be rude," Annja said, "but I still wonder why you took the trouble to call me here tonight. I have a feeling it's important."

The three men traded glances. She had the impression they were uneasy in her presence. That was odd, for three such powerful men—and in this small nation, their power was functionally absolute. As warmly friendly as Wira was, as cheerful as Purnoma was, as unfailingly polite as Singh was, the Sultan was an absolute ruler, and the others were his left hand and his right. They were hard hands indeed, Annja had no doubt.

Wira actually cleared his throat like a schoolboy admitting he put the frog in the teacher's desk. "I have come to a decision," he said. "It pertains to your area of expertise, and your own involvement in this affair. My advisers concur."

"What's the bad news, then? You don't mean—"

"Whatever the nature of this relic the Red Hand's stolen," Wira said, "we all agree it has enormous potential to do harm—as a symbol of enormous power, if nothing else. Even your Knights admitted it could contain a secret that might conceivably overturn the order of the world."

"That's highly speculative—" Annja began.

"Yes," Wira said, nodding. He was all elder-statesmen now, old beyond his years. "But the order of the world, such as it is, is already balanced on a dagger's tip. Tensions run high. Rivalries between great powers, that once seemed extinguished forever, are now at least flickering alight again. And no one knows for sure who might have nuclear weapons, nor where. We cannot afford to let the coffin fall into the wrong hands. Nor, for that matter, to permit it to stay long in the hands of Eddie Cao Cao."

She gasped. "You can't!"

"We hope not to," Wira said.

"As a last resort, Ms. Creed," Singh said, making things explicit, "we are prepared to sink the entire pirate fleet, and send the relic to the bottom of the sea. If not blow it to pieces."

She turned away. "I can't believe you're even thinking of this."

She felt Wira approach. Sensed a hand reach for her shoulder then stop short.

"We only consider it," he said softly, "because the alternative might be even more unthinkable."

"Relax, Ms. Creed," Purnoma said, with a little laugh. "We're not launching yet. You were about to remind us we couldn't attack the pirates in Philippine waters anyway, am I right? And as the Colonel says, it's a last resort. Somebody as clever as you are ought to be able to help us find a way to avoid it coming to that."

She turned. "You really think so?"

"We do," Wira said. "You not only got onto one

of my ships, you got off it again, bringing with you a badly wounded man, in the midst of a pirate attack. That was quite an achievement."

She still wanted to rage, to demand, to plead, to force them to promise to preserve the coffin at all costs. She knew how much good it would do. Her shoulders rose and fell as she drew in a deep breath and let it go.

"All right," she said. "I'll come up with something. Thanks for giving me the chance." She turned to go.

"Ah—one more thing," Wira said. He actually sounded embarrassed.

She turned back.

"In light of the fact that the Red Hand have made their first move," Wira went on, "and in light of the two attempts on your life—"

"You know about both? The drive-by, too?"

Purnoma laughed. This time it grated a bit. "Give me some credit, Ms. Creed," he said. "Maybe terrorist attacks in the city are more common than we like, but people don't blow out the windows of our finer boutiques in the shopping district with machine guns every day. It'd play hell on tourism. And we did scrape that one shooter off the sidewalk by that café. Allah knows who he was working for, because I sure don't."

"But why didn't you—"

Purnoma laughed. "What? Bring you in after the first attempt? Question you? What were you going to tell us we didn't know? Somebody tried to kill you?

Noticed that, check. You have a pretty good idea why people might want to? So do we." He smiled wider. "I hope that if you have any possibly pertinent information, you'd make sure to share it with us."

So you let bad guys take a couple of cracks at me, she thought, to make sure I was telling you everything. You cagey little son of a—

She shook her head. "You're thorough at your job, Mr. Purnoma."

For the first time since she'd met him he looked something other than cheerful. His youthful face suddenly looked its age and more with obvious worry. "I hope I'm thorough enough, Ms. Creed."

"With those attempts on your life in mind," Wira said, with what she thought was a reproachful glance at his security chief, "I have decided to move you into the palace for the duration of our contract. I've taken the liberty of having your possessions transferred from your hotel. I trust you'll find your quarters here satisfactory. If not I'm sure we can find a way to accommodate you."

Why, you arrogant, high-handed...*Sultan,* she thought. She forced a smile.

"I'm sure I've been in worse places," she said brittlely. "Thanks for your concern, Your Majesty."

24

"You're still mad at me," the Sultan said. He raised a glass pitcher half-full of orange liquid. "More juice?"

"No thank you," Annja said. "And only a bit."

Wira shrugged and poured himself another glass. "I admit it was a bit high-handed arbitrarily transferring you here to the palace," he said. "Are you comfortable here, by the way?"

"Yes," she said, a little curtly. A gilded cage is still a cage, she thought. It reminded her uncomfortably of the last time she felt that way. This whole bizarre adventure had started then, in the ballroom aboard the *Ocean Venture*.

She made herself smile. She didn't want to get on bad terms with Wira this morning. Aside from the fact it could have unpleasant side effects, she had thought of something during the night that might help get them the coffin back. But she was none too sure how it would be received, coming from a mere woman, and a foreigner at that. Wira didn't seem to have any trouble taking her seriously—but that was in her own area of expertise. This suggestion came from far afield.

"Your majordomo, Krisna, keeps fluttering around like a mother bird, making sure my every wish is tended to," she said. "He really is a sweet man."

Wira smiled. "He does worry," he said. "But really, Annja, it was much too risky to leave you at large in the capital. You obviously have a gift for survival, but there is such a thing as pressing one's luck."

"I suppose it's a good thing you're so solicitous of your contractors' welfare," she said. She didn't want him to dwell too long on her peculiar "gift of survival." He was right—there *was* such a thing as pressing one's luck.

He looked at her intently. "I hope you don't think it's only that, Annja," he said. This time his earnestness made him seem about seventeen. "I have come to be very fond of you, these last few days. I hope that's not too forward of me."

"Forward?"

"Are you all right?" he asked.

"Oh—fine, fine," she said, dabbing her lips with her napkin. The fact was she'd aspirated some of her coffee in astonishment. "Just—that is, I think I breathed in a gnat."

"Have some more water," Wira said, refilling the glass for her. He didn't seem to mind having servants bring them food and drink, out here on this shaded veranda where the salt-tinged sea breeze blew cool. But he seemed impatient with the formality of waiting for someone else to pour for him when he could have the pitcher on the table and pour for himself whenever he wanted.

"Thank you," she said, smiling weakly.

He looked at her anxiously. She drank some water to reassure him.

"I have to go soon," he said. "There's training with my commandos, then buckling down to work." He genuinely seemed to find sitting at his desk handling the affairs of state more arduous than running ten miles in the tropical heat followed by two hours of intense combat training.

"I thought of something," she said. "Last night."

He cocked his head. "Yes?"

"About our problem with the pirate fleet, I mean."

"Oh," the Sultan said. He sounded disappointed.

"I don't pretend to be any kind of military or intelligence expert. But couldn't you try making the Philippines too hot for the Red Hand?"

"I take it you're not talking about climate change?"

"Only figuratively." She sipped at her coffee. "We need to get the Red Hand junks into international waters. Right?"

"Quite."

"And they're not likely to fall for an offer to make a swap on the open sea. But it strikes me, everybody's pretty keyed-up about terrorism these days.

And the Philippines have a real, live, active insurgency going on."

"More than one," Wira said.

"You told me the Rimba Perak terrorists hate the Red Hand and have fought battles with them. I don't know if Eddie Cao Cao's gang gets on any better with the Philippine terror groups. But as Purnoma says, terror makes for some pretty strange bedfellows."

Why did I have to go and choose that figure of speech? she thought at once with an inward groan. But the glitter in the Sultan's dark eyes seemed to be purely professional keenness.

"So it does," he said.

"I won't ask if you have intelligence operators in the Philippines, because I know it's a friendly nation and everything," she said. "But maybe you have contacts who could pass word to the Philippine government that the Red Hand is running guns to their own Muslim separatist guerrillas. And then maybe you could use a different third party to tip the pirates that the Filipinos are about to hit them on suspicion of terrorism. That should flush them right out into the open sea. Uh, so to speak."

"Frame them, you mean," Wira said thoughtfully.

"That's one way to put it. Yes. Frame them it is."

He slapped his hand on the table, making the orange juice and water slosh precariously in their respective pitchers. "Capital idea! Worthy of Lestari herself."

"Hmmph," Annja said.

He stood. "If you'll forgive me, I'll rush off. I

want to get Purnoma started on this scheme before I head out to train." He grinned. "I think you've solved our dilemma, Annja. I could hug you!"

Instead he almost raced into the palace. She sat looking after him.

"Yes," she said a little wanly, "you could."

ANNJA SPENT THE DAY in fruitless research. She'd started receiving answers on the queries she had sent out to various associates by e-mail, concerning any mysterious discoveries made during the Sixth Crusade. They weren't much help.

She found hundreds of Web pages making reference to the alleged event she had read about. Almost all were worded precisely the same, down to gaffes in punctuation and spelling. Meaning all were copied from a single none-too-informative original.

Common as that was on the Web, analogue-world libraries yielded similar results. Various entries in the religious-conspiracy genre detailed the same story in about the same words. One referred as a source to an eccentric history of the Crusades published in French in the 1920s, a copy of which actually existed in the Meriahpuri University library. It was delivered to Annja by courier, since she was not permitted to leave the palace without an escort. The book added elaboration without illumination.

Two of her contacts e-mailed her a reference to an English book from 1841. When, late in the afternoon, she got hold of scans of that account, it turned out the French one was an almost word-for-word translation of it. Cut-and-paste historiography was not an invention of the Internet age. She already knew that too well.

A query on alt.archaeology.com evoked a tidal wave of responses. Wild speculations and flames for her being so stupid as to waste everybody's time asking about such a self-evident fairy tale came out about fifty-fifty. The speculation ranged from the coffin containing the bones of Jesus, to the corpse of an alien from a flying saucer that crashed in Syria in the eleventh century and was recovered by the legendary Saladin. The latter account was almost a thousand words long and filled with remarkably authentic-seeming detail, not a word of which Annja found remotely credible. She admired the feat of fiction-writing.

Most of the small percentage of actual discussion revolved around the likelihood of Frederick II actually founding a militant order of knights—or at least of *religious* knights. That produced some fascinating details concerning his passion for astronomy, and his extensive menagerie. The closest to a consensus—that was anywhere near relevant to Annja's inquiry, anyway—was that of course he wouldn't. *Unless* something had turned up on his watch that actually challenged his irreverent outlook....

The rest of the posts once again went to confirm Annja's hypothesis that no discussion-thread remained on-topic for more than four layers of nested replies.

Annja ate dinner in her room as she waded through the thousand-odd replies in the newsgroups. She emerged into late twilight to learn from a passing aide that the Sultan had not yet returned to the palace. She headed downstairs to stretch her legs.

As she reached the foot of the broad stairs the Grand Vizier came up to her with his robes flapping like the wings of an agitated bird.

"Ms. Creed?" Krisna's ageless face looked more worried than usual. "You have a visitor."

"A visitor?"

The shaved head bobbed. "Out in the garden. If you please."

Frowning slightly, Annja followed Krisna out into the night. When she left the air-conditioned interior the garden air hit her like a wet perfumed blanket. "Who is it?" she asked.

"Someone to see you," was all he replied.

She frowned. For a wild moment she wondered if Hevelin and Sharshak had actually sought her out there. They were certainly bold enough to enter the very lion's den. She had a harder time imagining it would occur to them to do so. It wasn't that they struck her as unintelligent; they just seemed remarkably set in their ways of thought.

"Who is it?" she asked again.

"Please come," Krisna said, and despite her longer legs she found herself having to hurry, down the steps of a broad terrace and into the vast labyrinthine gardens.

Swarms of tiny insects instantly surrounded her, brushing her face, buzzing, biting, trying to invade her nose, mouth and eyes. *They* took her mind off wondering who her mystery visitor might be. Big moths with pale wings fluttered about the edges of perception; bats swooped past like animated shadows, slashing through the insect clouds.

Some places Annja had been were so polluted the residents joked about air you could see. Here, as so often in the tropics, you got air you could chew. With high-protein density, no less.

Something that chittered shrilly brushed her head. She flapped a hand at it, after the fact. She wasn't squeamish, especially about bats—which was a good thing, since she gathered these islands boasted some the size of winged poodles. But she drew the line at getting them tangled in her hair.

The hedges and vine-twined trellises suddenly opened out into a clear circle perhaps twenty feet across. A carved stone table and some metal chairs stood in the middle of it. Torches had been set up around it, trailing orange flames into the clear starry sky. The aroma of kerosene in their wells tainted the lush sweet scent of night-blooming flowers.

A man stood as if waiting for her. He wore a tropical-weight suit in what looked like shades of off-white. A white straw hat rested on the table by him. He had white or pale blond hair clipped close to the sides of a narrow balding head.

Krisna had vanished.

"Ms. Creed?" the man said. "Annja Creed."

Warily she stopped at the circle's edge. "Yes," she said.

"The name's St. Clair," the man said. "Cyrus St. Clair. I'm pleased to meet you."

"To what do I owe the honor, Mr. St. Clair?"

"Here. Sit. Sit," he said as he did. After a hesitation she followed his example, taking a place across the round table from him.

He studied her for a moment. His eyes were very pale. Their actual color was indeterminate in the dancing torchlight. He drummed fingers on the stone tabletop. It reminded Annja uncomfortably of a pallid giant spider dancing.

"Do you consider yourself a good American, Ms. Creed?" he asked.

She felt her expression harden. "I'm not sure it's any business of yours, but, yes, Mr. St. Clair. I do. Do you?"

He uttered a laugh that was more like a sort of abbreviated hiccup. "Testy, aren't we?"

"I don't know of any productive conversations that ever began that way," she said.

He laced long pale fingers together before him and leaned his elbows on the tabletop. "Your country needs you, Ms. Creed."

"The United States is, we're always told, the world's only superpower," Annja said. "I'm an archaeologist. And a reasonably obscure cable-television personality. I find it hard to believe I could make much difference to it, one way or another."

He shook his head. "I see you've fallen victim to the modern distrust of government," he said. "It's too bad. It's government that does the real good in this world. I wish you could see that."

"That doesn't make it any easier for me to see what good I could do for an entity as large as the United States government," she replied.

"With all due respect," St. Clair said with a tight smile that never threatened to involve his eyes, "it's not the person so much as the circumstances. You are close to Sultan Wira, Ms. Creed. No other American has gotten near as far."

Her eyes went narrow. "What exactly do you mean by that, Mr. St. Clair?"

"Nothing. Nothing at all. It's just that—well, here you are." He gestured at the fragrant night around them and by extension, she took in the palace grounds.

"And here you are, too, I notice."

He shrugged. "I have contacts in the palace," he admitted artlessly. "I actually get to talk to the Sultan whenever I want to."

"Then I hardly see why you're bothering with me."

"Ah, I said I *talk* to Sultan Wira. I didn't say he listens to me, did I?"

"And you think he listens to me?"

"What does he have you here for, then?"

"I'm not sure I like where this conversation is going, Mr. St. Clair."

"Hey. No need to be so touchy. I didn't mean anything by it." He leaned back and crossed his thin legs. "It seemed like a fair question to me."

She doubted that. She did not, on the whole, care much for Mr. St. Clair, or his insinuations. Especially that she should be overawed by his wholly implied connection to the might and majesty of the United States.

Still, the fact that he was able to make his way to this garden in the midst of the well-guarded palace grounds was better credentials than any piece of paper he might show her. And she saw no point, beyond recalcitrance, in being evasive about something that was hardly secret, and which he probably knew all about in any event.

"Sultan Wira has engaged my services as a consultant on archaeological matters," she said, "regarding certain artifacts he believes might hold particular significance to the Sultanate."

"That's it, huh? Really?"

She drew a deep breath and counted silently to five. "That's it. So I'm afraid whatever errand brought you here was a fool's errand, Mr. St. Clair. Unless it concerns ancient artifacts."

For a moment he looked at her intently. The hairs rose at the nape of her neck. Is *this* about the coffin? she wondered. What possible interest could the United States government have in a Medieval relic?

"On the contrary, Ms. Creed," he said. "You have yourself some unique leverage, here."

"To do what, exactly?"

"Make Wira see the simple truth that's staring him in the face," St. Clair said. "This is a little bitty country in a big bad world. This kid Sultan has done a good job cleaning up after the tsunami. Everybody acknowledges that. And he's lucked into a minor ocean of oil. But that just gets the big, bad rest of the world even more interested in tearing off a piece of what he's got."

"I don't think Sultan Wira is going to listen to me on the subject of oil rights, Mr. St. Clair."

He shook his head, rapidly, like a dog shedding water. "No. No. I'm just talking friendship. A man in Wira's position needs friends. He's got himself a terrorist situation here in this fly-speck country that could snowball way the hell out of control. Things could really boil over in a hell of a hurry."

Annja blinked slowly, trying to sort the jumbled metaphors out in her mind.

"That's all we're talking here," St. Clair said. "He needs a hand. The biggest hand in the world is stretching itself right out to him. Right out. And all I ask is that you see your way clear to helping him take that hand. Grab hold of it."

She stood. "I still think you overestimate my influence over the Sultan, Mr. St. Clair. Our relationship is strictly business."

He sat looking up at her coolly. "Is it?"

She frowned.

He shrugged. "It doesn't have to be."

"What do you mean by that?"

"The Sultan's a young man. You're a long-legged pretty all-American girl. People eat that sort of thing up around here."

"Now I know I don't like the course this conversation is taking, Mr. St. Clair. And I believe it's over."

"That other hoochie isn't holding back, you can bet your sweet little tail on that."

The crudity of his statement was so arresting she actually stopped. "Which hoochie would that be?"

"That one always slinking around, with the jeweled belly button. She's a Sufi, you know."

"Is she? Lestari? Is that who you're talking about?"

"That's her. You know what the Russians call the Sufis? The *fanatics*. They blame 'em for kicking their asses out of Afghanistan. And you know what? They've got a point, much as I'd like to claim all the credit for my colleagues."

"Providing all this is true," Annja said, "what has it got to do with me?"

"I just wonder if you're willing to do as much for your country as that little minx is for her false religion."

"If the United States government wants me to sleep with Sultan Wira for its sake, Mr. St. Clair," she said, "it's going to have to send me someone higher on the food chain to tell me so."

He sighed an exaggerated sigh. "Ah, Americans," he said. "We're so spoiled with all these precious *rights* of ours we don't want to do anything to stand up for them. Don't you think that kind of thing led to 9/11?"

"No," she said, "I don't."

He stood. "Do yourself a favor, Ms. Creed," he said, "and think about it."

"It doesn't warrant any thought, Mr. St. Clair."

He shrugged. "Well, then," he said, "for the sake of your friend the Sultan—and for your own—I'd suggest you just think again."

25

"Ms. Creed."

It was the respectful voice of a female aide. Wira had a cloud of them, of both sexes, all even younger than he and all quietly worshipful of him. Annja mildly marveled that he managed to keep such a level head, between the kind of power he had, and the kind of adulation he attracted.

She had just taken a nocturnal run around the interior perimeter of the palace walls, but was still all but snorting flames over her interview with St. Clair. She took a deep breath before she answered. She didn't want to take her anger out on an innocent aide.

"Yes, Miri," she said.

"The Sultan wishes to see you in his study at once, please."

She looked down at herself. Her lemon-yellow

top was soaked with sweat. But, it wasn't like Wira to say something like that without reason.

"I'm on my way," she said.

Wira and Purnoma stood peering down at the map display tabletop. It cast a soft multicolored glow on their dark faces. For once Wira had forsaken his stiff tunic for a loose flowing shirt of white silk, with billowy sleeves. Over his cavalry-style jodhpurs, royal-blue with red stripes down the sides, it gave him the look of a swashbuckler from another age.

Wira glanced up as she appeared in the doorway. "Annja! It's the most splendid news."

He came to her and caught her in a quick hug that made up in passionate intensity what it lacked in duration. "Whoa," Annja breathed, as he let her go. She brushed at a lock of her hair that had fallen loose to tickle her forehead. "What happened?" she asked.

"The Philippine government's reacting like a hollow tree full of hornets that's gotten knocked over by an elephant," Purnoma said. "They take anything to do with terrorism very seriously. Good call there, Ms. Creed."

"Our American guest has many unlooked-for qualities," a husky feminine voice said. Annja looked around. In the gloom of the study, where the walls of books sucked in the soft glow of track lighting, she hadn't seen Lestari standing to her left.

The woman glided forward. She wore a dark purple ensemble. An amethyst glittered in her navel.

Annja, who was less clothes-conscious than any woman she knew, nevertheless felt slovenly.

"It was a very good scheme," Lestari said. "I feel shamed I didn't think of it myself." She didn't look particularly ashamed, Annja noted. Nor as if much would ever shame her.

"The Red Hand junks are scuttling out into the Sulu Sea as fast as their engines will carry them," Purnoma said. He gestured at the tabletop. "Come take a look at the results of your handiwork."

Annja did. To her surprise she saw a dark surface, vaguely restless, with a number of red dots moving gradually across it. They didn't form anything she'd go so far as to call a formation. But they all clearly headed in the same direction.

"That is—" she began.

"Real-time satellite imaging of Eddie Cao Cao's pirate fleet," Wira said, grinning with boyish delight at spying on his enemy. He seemed almost indecently pleased with the whole thing. Beneath Wira's happy-lad exterior Annja thought she sensed more than a touch of the predator with his chase-reflex engaged in him.

She recognized it well. She had more than a touch of it herself. She felt her own pulse rising, the heat climbing in her cheeks. She owed her own debts to the Red Hand. She meant to exact some of the repayment herself.

"What you see are the heat-signatures of the

vessels' engines," Wira said. "They're not terribly efficient. Nor well-insulated, for that matter."

"How is this possible?" Annja asked.

Wira and Purnoma exchanged a glance. "The imaging comes from an Indonesian surveillance bird, currently operating over the Sulu Sea," Purnoma said.

"Indonesian?" Annja said in surprise. "I didn't know they had any surveillance satellites. I never heard about any such thing."

Purnoma showed her a grin. "There's a lot of things they don't show you on CNN," he said. "Especially in the black world."

"The Australians helped them build it," Wira said, speaking with fervor. "The Russians launched it for them."

She cocked a skeptical eyebrow at them. "And the Indonesians know you're borrowing this top-secret surveillance satellite? Last I heard you weren't on any too friendly terms with them."

Again a shared look, half guilty, half gleeful. "I think the phrase is, what they don't know, won't hurt them," the Sultan said.

"They have no systems built in to track unauthorized access, so far as we can find," Lestari said. She seemed indulgently amused by the enthusiasm of the youthful Sultan and the middle-aged intelligence chief. "The Australians are not as careful about such things as some people. Or as paranoid, perhaps."

"It's not paranoia," Purnoma said, "when people really are out to get you."

"Actually," murmured Lestari, "it can be. The world is full of people who imagine nonexistent plots against them, and fail to see the real threats."

Annja wondered what kind of response that would get. Muslim men weren't noted for encouraging backchat from women, no matter how liberal they liked to present themselves. Powerful men in the U.S. and Western Europe didn't always seem thrilled by it, come to think of that. She had found plenty of opportunities to talk back to authority figures, and by and large had made the most of them.

Purnoma only grinned. "Okay," he said. "So paranoids can have enemies, too."

"Why are you so sure the Indonesians can't detect the intrusion?" Annja asked. The long-term diplomatic and strategic interests of Rimba Perak didn't concern her except in the abstract. But Indonesia was a big, cranky, heavily militarized local power. If they spotted what was going on and decided to horn in, recovering the coffin could suddenly become exceedingly complicated. Impossibly so, perhaps. She doubted the Indonesians would give her the time of day, nor listen sympathetically to her archaeological concerns for the artifact's proper preservation.

Wira smiled at her. "Our software comes from Malaysia. And they are very careful about such things."

"Great," Annja said. "So now what happens?" Her heart was racing. Her hunter's blood was up. She *knew*.

"We go," Wira said. "The moment you made your excellent suggestion, Annja, I set the excellent Purnoma about the task of dripping the proper poisons in the proper ears. My next step was to put the navy and air force on full alert."

"They've been on standby since we lost contact with the *Ozymandias*," Purnoma said. "It won't take much to get them ready to roll. Singh's over at the ministry burning the midnight oil by the barrel right now. We're looking to intercept by tomorrow night."

"Air force?" Annja asked.

"We have a squadron of Harrier jets," Wira said. "The British sold them to my father. They were courting his favor rather heavily at the time. We recently upgraded them with kits from Singapore. They have full night and all-weather capability, and carry both laser and low-light television guided anti-shipping missiles from Germany. They will provide a nasty surprise for Eddie Cao Cao."

Annja felt a thrill of alarm. "You're not going to sink his fleet?"

"We're going to pound them hard," Purnoma said.

Wira did something with his little remote. A white light began to blink on and off, right next to one of the red heat-signatures.

"There's your GPS tracker, Annja," he said. "Our software has overlaid its return on the Indonesian feed. That's the ship that's carrying the coffin, although we haven't identified the vessel itself yet."

"Smart money says it's Cao Cao's personal ship, the *Sea Scorpion,* though," Purnoma said.

"But we can't be sure the transmitter is still with the coffin!" Annja said.

"What do you mean?" Wira asked.

"She means the pirates may have searched their treasure," Lestari said, "and found the transmitter."

"Wouldn't they just throw it overboard, then?" the Sultan asked.

"Not necessarily," Annja said. She wasn't sure whether she felt more resentful at the Sufi woman interrupting, or grateful for her support. "It might have occurred to them to place it on another vessel as a decoy, just in case of something like this."

"Eddie Cao Cao is paranoid," Purnoma said thoughtfully, "exactly because he has so many enemies. He hasn't survived this long in the business without a lot of old-fashioned cunning."

"In any event," the Sultan said, "while we have the surface fleet and the planes to give us cover, it's the commandos and I who'll be going in to secure the coffin."

"You?" Annja said with alarm.

Lestari showed her a cool smile. "Our Sultan desires to prove himself in the thick of combat. It's possible he watches too many action movies on DVD."

Wira frowned. "Really, now. I have my duty to consider."

"You have to be kidding," Annja said.

He blinked at her. "I do beg your pardon?"

"I shall leave you all to what I'm sure will be a most fascinating discussion," Lestari announced languidly. "Gentlemen, some words of caution—this Annja Creed is a woman of unlooked-for depths. Underestimate her at your peril."

She glided out, as always as if a thin force field cushioned her slippered soles from actually contacting the Persian carpet.

Annja frowned after her for a moment. I can't decide whether I've been complimented or threatened, she thought. Considering the source, it could well be both.

"Your Majesty," Purnoma said, "I've got plenty to do for this operation. I'd better go do it." He vanished, too, leaving his Sultan blinking after him in befuddlement.

Coward, Annja thought after the fleeing intelligence chief.

"Annja, I—" the Sultan said, turning to her.

"I can't believe you," she said. Her vehemence caught her by surprise. Wira, too, by the way he leaned back. "First you actually plan to destroy a priceless ancient artifact that might have untold historical significance—"

"It's a contingency plan only," he protested. "You know I'll do everything in my power to recover the relic intact."

"And now you're actually planning to lead the attack yourself, as if you were a commando."

He drew himself up. "I have completed the entire

commando training program," he said. "I regularly train with them, as I think you know. And if you believe the instructors went easy on me because of my status, I very much fear you don't know them. They're Sikhs, mostly."

Annja vaguely understood that perfected their hard-core accreditation. "Fine," she said. "So you're a commando. But these pirates are tough and vicious. I've seen them in action. Your men slaughtered them and they kept on coming. If you jump on them aboard their own ships they'll fight like cornered rats. You could get *killed,* Wira."

He stiffened. "I rather understood that was a customary risk of combat."

"But you're the Sultan. Rimba Perak depends on you. You've got mean, militant neighbors looking to swallow you up, big powers circling you like sharks smelling blood in the water, and a gang of internationally connected terrorists who want to set your whole country ablaze as a sort of beacon for world *jihad.* You can't put yourself at risk like—like some kind of subordinate. You can't."

He looked at her for a moment. His young face was set, although she would not say hard.

Then he smiled. "Why, Ms. Creed," he said. "How sweet of you. I didn't know you cared."

She drew in an enormous breath, uncomfortably aware of just how red her face was turning.

She glared at him. Then opened her mouth to say something.

Annja abruptly realized with a bucket-of-ice-water shock that she was arguing heatedly with a man who, no matter how enlightened he was, was still a despot—the absolute ruler of an exotic foreign land. In his own palace. And even though Amnesty International gave Rimba Perak pretty good marks for human rights under Wira—unlike his father—this was still his palace. And just as the ad campaign claimed for Las Vegas, what happened here would most definitely stay here.

Of course, she carried an American passport. And that conferred certain advantages. She could no longer count the times she'd been waved through foreign customs or interior checkpoints by authorities who proceeded to abuse their own countrymen and women, trying to pass the same point. But when it came to actually standing up for its citizens' rights abroad, she knew the U.S. government generally stood down.

The U.S. wanted Wira to play ball with them. If an American national happened to go missing after becoming a guest in the Sultan's palace, she could all too easily imagine the creepy Mr. St. Clair's flip response—*it happens*.

All this flashed through her mind as Wira stood with his mouth open and an expression on his face that reminded her of a scolded puppy. She understood from that that he hadn't decided to weld an anchor around her ankles and drop her off for the sharks in the South China Sea. But if she said any more—especially the kinds of things that were crowding into her forebrain, shoving and jostling each other and clamoring to be let out her mouth— that could change in a hurry.

She simply pirouetted, with angry ballerina grace, and stalked out.

To HER SURPRISE she was able to go to sleep fairly quickly. She'd had a long and grueling day, and the emotional outburst at the end had drained away what energy she had left. She took a shower, composed her mind and was asleep within moments of her head hitting the pillow.

A dark unknown interval later Annja snapped awake to the awareness that she was not alone.

She opened her eyes to slits. Moonlight through the open window gleamed along the unmistakable curved blades of swords.

26

Trying to keep her breathing as regular as if she was still asleep, Annja waited. She lay on her right side. The wall with the round-arched window in it was close to the bed behind her. She figured it was unlikely anybody was sneaking up that way.

She had at least three armed intruders in the room with her. Their eyeballs showed as fingernail slices of reflected moonlight above dark masks. Their swords had gently curved blades that widened toward the tips.

Two intruders advanced to her bedside. The third went to the foot. Their soft-slippered feet made only the faintest of sounds. She wasn't sure what sense had alerted her. Although now she could smell their sweat, acrid with adrenaline.

Wait for it, she commanded herself.

The man who had come up by her shoulders

raised his blade above his turban, grasping the hilt in both hands for a beheading stroke.

Strike.

Flinging the sheet off with her left hand she summoned the sword into her right. It sliced through the skin and muscle of the assassin's belly like a knife through warm butter.

So fast was the cut the swordsman probably felt no pain. Initially. She heard him gasp in surprise.

His sword clanged tip-first off the blue-tiled floor behind him. He began to scream as terminal agony landed on him in an avalanche of pain.

Annja continued the forehand stroke, bending forward with the strong muscles of her back and flat belly. Momentum and the blade's sharpness buried her sword a hand's-breadth into the second swordsman's side, just above his left hipbone.

She caught the hilt with her left hand, then thrust. The man howled as she drove the tip deeper. She felt its point tear through the skin of his lower right back.

It took no more than the strength of her arms and a twist of her shoulder to slice the blade free into the air. The man fell, thrashing and shrieking.

The man at the foot of the bed had fallen back. His mouth was an oval of horrified blackness against the dark face beneath his turban. Annja sprang to her feet. She ran down the bed at him, sword upraised.

The man flung his heavy blade to defend himself against Annja's downstroke. Steel rang on steel. The man's sword sounded a second, reverberating musical note as it flew from his hands.

He reeled back. Annja leapt off the end of the bed. She swung her sword around, out, up. Then she slashed downward and right to slash his arm.

He looked down at his bleeding arm. Then he looked at her and wailed in horror.

Annja went to the door and yanked it open. A man dressed in dark silk swung around to face her, sword in hand. His eyes went wide as he beheld a woman a head taller than he, confronting him from the open door with a sword in her hand.

It was the last thing he saw. She ran him through.

From above came shouts, the clash of weapons. *Wira,* Annja thought. A fresh adrenaline spike flashed like lightning through her blood and across her brain. Pulling the sword free she ran toward the sounds of battle.

Her charge took her up a flight of stairs carpeted in green and gold. A pair of palace guardsmen in tailored khaki battle dress lay facedown by the door to Wira's chambers in spreading pools of blood. From inside came shouts, the clang of steel on steel.

Hair flying, Annja vaulted the corpses and charged through the door. A pair of men in black silk clothing with green turbans and black cloth wound about their faces stood just inside with their backs to her. With a one-handed slash, diagonally left to right, and a two-hand return cut at the level of Annja's own shoulders both men went down.

She had already taken in the scene beyond them in a flash—a large bed at the chamber's far end, its clothes in disarray. The Sultan, bare-chested in brown silk pajama pants, stood his ground with a long scimitarlike blade in his right hand and a cutlasslike sword in his left. Both blades gleamed darkly in the yellow glow from bedside-table lamps, one of which had been upset and lay on the lush-carpeted floor. The young Sultan's hair, unbound, hung about his shoulders in a dark cascade.

Three figures sprawled about him, their blood seeping into the priceless rugs. A number of others circled in the shadows of the room's perimeter like a pack of wolves closing on their kill. Annja suddenly widened her eyes and sprinted recklessly forward right through the circling attackers—and straight at the Sultan.

From the corner of his eye Wira had seen the sword flash, saw the two unsuspecting terrorists fall. He turned toward Annja and her own eyes flew wide in amazement.

She ran past him. The assassin who had crept in through the window by the head of the great bed launched himself at the Sultan's unprotected back, his sword upraised in both hands.

Annja simply pushed her sword out in front of her as she reached the foot of the bed. Descending from his heroic leap, the terrorist fell right onto its tip. It slid through silk and skin and flesh with a deceptively soft crunching sound.

She saw the eyes go huge and round above the black facial wrapping as his momentum carried him down, impaling him on the blade. She grabbed the hilt with both hands, steering it to the right of her rib cage as his weight smashed into her and knocked her back and down. She heard floor tiles crack as the pommel hit

The black-clad man fell full atop her. The air rushed out of her. The light went out of his astonished, pain-filled eyes as he died.

Annja's blood was so supercharged with adrenaline that even having the air forced from her lungs could not slow her down. She drew her knees up beneath the man on her chest. He was dead weight, but he was small and wiry. She had six inches and a good twenty pounds on him.

She got her bare soles against his chest. The silk squished unpleasantly. She drove upward with all the strength of her long, lean-muscled legs. The corpse was driven right up the straight length of her blade and off to fall to one side. She felt a flash like a burn along her right shin and realized she'd cut herself on the sword.

She paid no mind. Arching her back she jackknifed herself to her feet. As her hair flew up in a cloud about her head, shot through with red highlights from the faint light, she saw a man charging in from her left.

She spun to face him, flinging up her sword. His blade clanged against the flat of hers. His eyes blazed with fury.

She whipped her shin up between his legs. The kick lifted him up onto his toes. The angry eyes bugged out. She whipped her blade free and cut him down as he bent over himself.

Glancing back over her left shoulder Annja saw two men rushing at Wira. He swung the terrorist's sword he held in his left hand up counterclockwise, knocking aside the weapon hacking at his head. His own sword slashed downward right to left across the masked face.

The second would-be assassin rushed forward, a step behind his comrade. Wira pulled the sword held in his right hand to his right across his body as his left-hand blade rang against the sword the black-clad man was swinging in an overhand stroke. He guided the cutlass down and to his right, pivoting his hips clockwise.

His right-hand sword swung up and chopped down. It split the black turban and the skull beneath. The man dropped to his knees and toppled to the side.

The nocturnal killers fell back to regroup. Wira glanced back over his bare shoulder at Annja. He showed her a somewhat manic grin.

"You do have unlooked-for talents, Ms. Creed," he said.

They were still outnumbered seven to two by the black-swathed swordsmen. "I've got this side," she said tersely.

Back-to-back they fought as the assassins darted in, tried to strike. Annja chopped down to cut through a blade slashing at her side. The swordsman fell over backward to avoid her counterattack. It worked—she didn't dare break away from the young Sultan for fear of being surrounded. The fallen assassin kicked himself backward. Then he caught up a sword dropped by one of his fellows who no longer had a need for it and rejoined the fray. But cautiously, this time, Annja noted. He was hanging around the edges as if awaiting an opening.

She heard steel ring behind her. Wira grunted. A man screamed. She dared not look behind as two men lunged for her, one from her left, the other coming around to the side of the bed to attack from as far to her right as he could.

She parried a slash from the man to her left, shaving a slice from the belly of his blade but failing to sever it. The man to her right thrust at her vulnerable side Anticipating his attack she was already wheeling toward him. She parried with the flat of her sword, blade down. The cutlass slid just past her hip.

Cat-quick, the man drew back his sword. Annja sensed more than saw the attacker to her left moving on her again. She pivoted, whipping up the point of her sword, stepping into her assailant and thrusting.

She caught him with arm upraised, the sword slid into his belly. The man screamed but brought his arm forward and down in a desperate hack at Annja's skull. She caught him right beneath the elbow of his sword arm with her left hand. Then stepping back with her right foot she torqued her hips sharply clockwise again, using her assailant's own momentum to hurl him past her by his arm and the three feet of steel thrust through his stomach. He slammed into his partner as that man attacked. Annja ripped her sword free as the two men fell in a tangle.

Another assassin charged. She turned and engaged him in a crashing, ringing exchange of cuts.

The door, which apparently one of the intruders had shut, flew open. Annja looked toward it even as she fenced with her foe. Men in battle dress burst in. They carried MP-5 machine pistols.

The uniformed men shouted in Malay. Annja parried high. Then she released her sword and front-kicked her opponent in the chest. He staggered back. The sword vanished into thin air.

The palace guardsmen opened fire. Their guns were shatteringly loud in the bedchamber. The man Annja had kicked backward was chopped down. The assassins still on their feet died.

The man who had fallen under his skewered comrade threw the body off him, leapt up and tried to bolt to the open window. As he reached it bursts of gunfire plucked at the back of his black silk blouse. He threw up his hands at the impacts. Then he toppled forward, out the window, to fall screaming to the lawn three stories below.

A guardsman ran to the window to look out after him. Others came crowding in through the door. Some moved swiftly to examine the fallen assassins. Others stopped to stare openmouthed at Annja.

"What?" she said.

"Look at yourself," Wira said, sounding amused.

Annja stood in a T-shirt and underwear, her long legs fully exposed. She was covered in blood.

She looked up at him, wide-eyed. "Well," she said, "it's the latest fashion."

27

Like the bedroom, Annja found the Sultan's adjoining bathroom large and luxuriously appointed. But not hopelessly gaudy or decadent, as she expected a South China Sea potentate's bathroom to be.

She showered for a long time. It took time for the multiple jets of water, which she had turned to stinging heat and strength, to flush away the sensation of having her skin covered in blood.

When she emerged from the shower stall she found a fluffy white robe and fresh towels had been placed on the green marble counter by soft-footed servants. Wrapped in a sense of floating unreality, she toweled herself mostly dry, put on the robe and wrapped her hair in another towel.

Then she emerged. The room had been completely cleaned. Sprays of fresh flowers, including lilacs, had been placed in niches on the wall, in planters on the floor and on most horizontal surfaces. They did a startlingly effective job of masking the harsh scents of disinfectants—which in turn did a pretty fair job of masking other, even less congenial smells.

The stained rugs were gone. The tile beneath cleaned up readily. The bedclothes were so fresh she could smell them. She suspected the very mattress beneath, huge as it was, had been replaced. With a little bit of express-elevator sensation in her stomach it occurred to her to suspect that somewhere in the great gleaming onion-domed pile of the palace, or the vaults beneath, was a storeroom stacked with replacement mattresses wrapped neatly in plastic, for just such eventualities as this. Cleanup after failed assassination attempts.

And, she supposed, those that succeeded as well. That was one thing that decisively linked the mightiest monarch to the most miserable beggar—when they fell, life went on. The major difference was the amount of energy other people put into pretending otherwise before getting on with it.

At the big bed's foot sat Wira. He wore new pajama bottoms, these of pale orange silk. His hair, still unbound, hung to either side of his face like heavy dark curtains.

As she came into the bedroom he raised his head and smiled at her. His smile had a haunted quality to it, as did his eyes.

"Thank you," he said.

"For what?" she asked, approaching. She got within six feet of him and stopped. She was unsure how to proceed. She felt cleansed but extremely drained.

He laughed softly. "Saving my life. It was a very professional attack. The intruders were inside the grounds in force before anyone discovered them. They left teams to delay my bodyguards getting to me. Almost long enough."

She came and sat next to him on the bed. That seemed harmless enough. He certainly didn't draw away.

"Why did they use swords?" she asked. She didn't bother asking how the assassins had gotten in undetected—it was an inside job. That was so apparent there seemed little point in bringing it up. Rooting out the traitor or traitors, and dealing with them—that was his problem, his and Purnoma's. She was pretty sure she didn't want to know the details, anyway.

"The *langgai tinggang*," he said. "That translates as, 'the longest tail feather of the hornbill.' Very poetic, really. It's a type of Dayak *parang*. You're familiar with the Dayak?"

She nodded. "Borneo tribesfolk," she said. "Some of them tend to be pretty resistant to the modern world."

She could feel his warmth. She smelled soap on clean masculine skin, realized he'd showered as well. She felt honored he had let her use his personal facility while he went elsewhere, even if it was one door down the hall, as was likely. The odd, courtly courtesy seemed so typical of him.

"You're very knowledgeable. Although I suppose it is your line of work. And 'resistant to the modern world' is a nice way of putting it."

"Being quick with a euphemism about native peoples is one of the skills we learn in anthropology if we don't want to be ostracized. Most times it's justified. Sometimes it goes too far. Were these men Dayaks, then?"

He shook his head. His hair brushed his shoulders. They were wide shoulders, she noticed, with well-defined musculature beneath bronze skin.

"Oh, no," he said. "Sword of the Faith. For some reason that's the weapon they've adopted as their literal sword of the faith. They fight with swords as a point of honor. As do my own forces, as you've seen."

He smiled a lopsided smile. "In a strange way, I believe the assassins were honoring me. Despite my embrace of Western ways, measured though it is, I am apparently worthy of a most traditional death."

"I'm a little surprised your guards didn't try to take any prisoners," Annja said.

"They did," he said. "The guards in your room. Neither in particularly good shape. The Sons of the Sword, as they call themselves, do not surrender. Nor do they talk. As I'm sure you realize, torture's no use for getting actual information. The mere threat works fine on the weak-willed—but Sword of the Faith weeds those out in ways you probably could imagine, but shouldn't care to, I think. For the others—" He shrugged. "Torture can serve for punishment, to terrorize others, or to generate false testimony."

"I know," she said. She didn't meet his eyes. For some reason she thought of Cyrus St. Clair, his narrow balding head, his pale indeterminate eyes, his white Panama hat.

"Also," the Sultan said, "I suspect my guards felt chagrined that they were so late to the scene—especially since they found their work being done for them by a foreign woman. A very beautiful one. With a Crusader-style broadsword."

He looked at her curiously. "Where did you get that, Annja?"

"What do you mean? I managed to wrestle one of the swords off the assassins who came to my room. I've practiced sword-fighting a lot. It's one of the reasons I decided to become an archaeologist. Even if my specialty did wind up being documents. And really—"

He smiled gently. "I know what I saw," he said softly.

Annja shook her head and tried to make her eyes go ingénue-wide. "Maybe I grabbed it off a wall. Events are a bit of a blur."

"Annja, dear," he said, "there are no straight-bladed, cross-hilted swords in this palace. I may be a modernist and a moderate, but I am a Muslim. To us, the cross-hilted broadsword is the dominant symbol of Crusader aggression. And all this begs the question, where did the mysterious thing go?"

She looked him in the eye. She noticed they had long lashes. Beautiful eyes. She felt her cheeks grow warm and her breath grow short. Her skin took on a tingling sensation.

"Does it really matter?" she asked, more breathlessly than she intended.

"No," he said. His own voice had dropped half an octave. "No, I suppose it doesn't."

He reached for her. Drew her to him with a hand on her shoulder. She turned to meet him.

Their mouths joined in a kiss. It went on and on. When they broke away she stood before him.

He took her hand, kissed her palm. "I have to go," he said. "A helicopter waits to take me to my flotilla, which is already under way. I won't see you until I get back. You may stay here as long as you wish. You've the run of the palace, my dear."

"Be careful," she said, before rushing out of the room feeling a flood of emotions.

Because she had learned the value of rest the hard way, Annja actually went back to sleep as Wira went off to dress and then head out as the first rosy light stretched its fingers over the city and the harbor overlooked by the bedroom window. She slept no more than an hour. When she opened her eyes, not exactly refreshed but at least more rested, Wira was gone.

She had her own arrangements to make.

Twelve hours later, she was slipping over the

gunwales of the power junk she had chartered, into a black Zodiac boat bobbing in the chop as a swollen red sun plopped into the dark Celebes Sea.

28

The weather scans showed a new storm system spinning its deceptively slow way south of the Philippines out of the wide Pacific. Annja didn't think it would reach them before morning. It would leave time. She hoped.

Waving goodbye to the worried-looking Philippine captain and crew whose dark faces lined the rail, she throttled up the outboard engine and putted away. Kind of sweet of them to worry about me, she thought, since there's nothing to connect me to their vessel. Some activity in accounts under names other than the one on her birth certificate had led to a pure cash transaction to hire a fast-powered craft out of the fishing town of Tawi-Tawi, off toward the end of the Philippines' long, narrow Sulu Archipelago near Rimba Perak's neighbor Sabah.

She had looked for a vessel with captain and crew

of the poor but honest class. Captain Delgado and his crew were a tough-looking bunch, to be sure. But nowhere on earth did the sea coddle weaklings. The ocean was big and powerful and heedless, and would swallow you without a trace for the slightest lapse in caution or judgment, or just on general principles.

The conclusion they'd come to was obvious from their whispered conversations. Who else but some kind of secret agent would hire them to transport her and an inflatable powerboat loaded with electronic gear to the middle of nowhere?

And that's where she was. Squarely in nowhere's midsection. In the dark, the little junk, whose captain was reluctant to display running lights, quickly vanished. Annja was left all alone with the warm thick air pressing against her face, the smell of the salt sea and the petroleum engine, the growl of the outboard and the gurgle of the wake, and an entire sky full of stars.

Before setting out she learned that the moon, in its half phase, wasn't supposed to rise in this part of the world until around 2:00 a.m. She guessed that would be the outside limit of the envelope in which Wira, bless his reckless heart, would make his move. Heaven knew what kind of radar or night-vision equipment the obviously well-capitalized Eddie Cao Cao had to equip his pirate fleet, or at least his flagship, the *Sea Scorpion*. But there was no point in the Rimba Perak navy making things easy on the pirates by allowing the waning moon to illuminate them.

So Annja steered the boat, frequently checked her headings against her GPS navigator, and tried not to dwell on how completely foolhardy this whole thing was. She had brought an emergency kit, a shortwave radio and some flares, in case she just got utterly lost. She knew if the storm caught her out here in the open sea they'd do her no good.

She didn't fear totally missing her objective. Much. Even though one thing she didn't have out here on her ridiculously tiny and remarkably fragile seeming boat was a means to track the transmitter she'd snuck into the crate with the coffin. After all, unless events veered wildly off course, her target was going to make itself, or be made about as obvious as it was possible to be.

Still, it caught Annja by surprise when the night flamed up before her. Out of nowhere the sky a few points off her port bow lit with a gigantic yellow flash. It was followed by two more, in rapid succession. Then an orange fireball rolled into the sky, and all kinds of lights began flashing. Tracer rounds arced gracefully. The sound of the first blast rolled over her like a wave, overpressure so powerful she felt it on her face.

It was an impressive sound-and-light show. *"Yes!"* she exclaimed, pumping her fist. It had all come together as she planned.

Then it struck her hard she was heading into the midst of that floating inferno.

"That's why I get paid the big bucks," she muttered, and cranked up the engine.

She made no attempt at stealth—speed was the plan. With all the flashing going on, to accompany the banging, and the orange and yellow flames billowing up already from a pair of junks, a small boat on the water was going to be obvious for anyone who cared to look. The kicker was, why would anyone *bother* to look for a random small boat? There were plenty of big, well-armed boats to look at instead.

Much more likely was that accidental gunfire would wipe her out.

What she was witnessing was like the biggest, best fireworks show ever. It was so utterly unlike anything she had experienced that she actually felt little fear heading into it.

She had seen sea battles before, on television and in movie theaters. But there had always been that wall of separation. Even in old footage from World War II, when those were real guns shooting and the flashes when the shells hit were tearing apart and incinerating real human beings, it had always been something happening a long time ago and far, far away and in all events on the far side of that uncrossable glass wall. It may have been real once; it wasn't real *now*. But the lights and noise and even smells that surrounded her, swallowed her, were so overwhelming they seemed a different kind of unreality.

A pair of banshee shadows screamed overhead, low enough to rock her boat with their air-wake. They had to be Rimba Perak jets. She passed within a few hundred yards of a seventy-foot junk afire to the waterline, with orange flames bursting up higher than it was long, underlighting an enormous coil of black smoke squeezing into the sky. She smelled burning fuel oil and barbecue. She knew way too well what that meant, and suddenly it was very real.

Panic rose inside her. She could barely breathe. The sudden massive adrenaline dump, combined with the smell of burning human flesh, overwhelmed her. She vomited over the side of the Zodiac.

Mostly.

When she finished Annja unscrewed the top of a water bottle, rinsed her mouth, spat. "Okay," she said, "I'm officially in deep now."

The only thing for it, clearly, was to plunge on even deeper. Because she was Annja Creed. And also because she'd feel like a *total fool* if she turned the Zodiac around and scuttled back into the middle of the ocean.

29

The battle itself exploded.

In an instant, it seemed, Annja found herself surrounded by ships churning the seas with ghostly wakes; raking up lines of spouts with heavy automatic weapons and geysers from misses by rockets, bombs or cannon shells. She had no idea exactly what sort of ordnance was going off. But there was surely a lot of it.

Ships blazed up with light. She saw huge muzzle flashes light the sky like sheet lightning. Explosions flashed, dazzling white. Flames rushed skyward like demons escaping hell.

There had been about twenty vessels in the Red Hand pirate fleet when last Annja saw the overhead imaging in Wira's study. The Rimba Perak navy had brought ten to twelve surface craft to the party. There was a mix of coastal-patrol vessels ranging in size

from mere armed speedboats to Singapore-made
bruisers, over fifty meters long and packing 76 mm
guns, 30 mm machine cannons, and ship-killing
missiles, along with the land-based Harrier attack
jets. Though the Red Hand probably outnumbered
the Rimba Perak forces in terms of manpower as
well as hulls, the superior firepower and discipline
of Wira's men would tip the balance in their favor.

The explosions made the air seem solid. Sometimes it quivered all around her, as if she were trapped
in clear gelatin. Other times it just banged on her like
big sheets of boiler plate. She felt fear that the sheer
high-energy, high-intensity *sound* produced by the
vast quantities of explosives going off all around could
permanently damage her brain, destroy her physical
coordination or even her ability to focus her thoughts.

Yet she had no thought of going back. Once
focused on her goal, she moved toward it inexorably.
She would only alter course if a better one suggested itself. Anyway, she was well and truly in the
middle of things here. The way back was as at least
as hazardous as the way ahead.

She steered around a piece of flaming wreckage
that appeared to be the remains of a lifeboat. A small
boat with Rimba Perak's green, gold and red
pennants fluttering from its stern sped within a
hundred yards to starboard, its twin guns raking a
junk on the other side of it. An RPG flashed in its
stern, setting off its fuel in a yellow fireball that
flew straight up in the sky as the boat lost way. A

burst of heavy automatic-cannon fire ripped the air above Annja, making her duck her head reflexively between her shoulders.

From the moment she had started to form the whole deranged scheme in her mind, listening to Wira and Purnoma and the sinister, lovely Lestari in the Sultan's study the night before, Annja had wondered how she was going to be sure which ship was her target. She had operated on the assumption that it would be pointed out to her in one or more of a number of ways.

So it proved. Just as she started to fear she could never escape the hell boiling over on all sides of her—that if a stray bomb or bullet didn't wipe her off the planet, a ship churning along at top speed would blindly run her down—she saw a big junk ahead, just starboard of her bow, steaming full speed away from the dogfight. It showed no lights. Nor, more significantly, did it show any sign of gunfire.

It didn't stay dark for long. Enormous spotlights pinned the junk like horizontal pillars of blue-white light. One of the big corvettes and a patrol craft half its size pursued to port and starboard, converging like sharks.

The junk dwarfed both. It was huge for a wooden ship. It must have been two hundred feet long, its sharply raked stern and bow rising improbably high against the black sky. Annja thought it must have immense engines to thrust it over the waves so rapidly, raising a big green self-luminous wake. Fast as it was, though, it was no match for the two sleek, modern Sultanate craft.

The junk's deck sparkled with muzzle flashes like a Chinese New Year parade. RPGs buzzed from it to flash against its pursuers' sloped armor, or hiss harmlessly into the swell. The Rimba Perak ships only returned fire with machine guns and Mauser machine cannon, instead of their missile racks or 76-mm deck guns. That in itself told Annja the fleeing ship must be the *Sea Scorpion*. And it must be carrying the coffin.

Unless all it's carrying is the transmitter, she remembered with a jolt of dismay. She turned her inflatable boat's prow toward it and pushed on at top speed.

In the general battle the grief was not all going one way. The pirates fought back with everything they had, big thudding .50-calibers and buzzing, sparking swarms of RPGs, as well as a constant hailstorm rattle of small arms. Off her starboard quarter Annja saw the long low shape of a Rimba Perak cutter ablaze from knife prow to stern. Even as she watched its magazine erupted in a colossal blast shot through with pulsating flame and flickering flashes as minor munitions cooked off. It broke in two and began sinking, with a hissing audible even above the cosmic racket of the battle, below the waves.

Ahead, the two Sultanate ships closed with the big junk. Annja saw what she thought were grapnel lines arcing toward the fleeing vessel. The pursuing ships came in right under the junk's looming counters. Men began to swarm up the lines and scale the sheer wooden sides of the hull. Grenades flash-cracked on deck. Assault rifles flared. Annja bit her lip as commandos dropped to the waves like dark fruit.

Wira! she thought. He would certainly be among the first to board.

She broke clear of the battle. It actually seemed strange not to be surrounded by volcanic upheavals of fire and noise. The big junk had lost way; she was gaining on it. Her heart sped up.

Sirens hooted from the Rimba Perak ships. They cast off or cut the lines holding them fast to the junk, which now lay dead in the water and was beginning to drift counterclockwise. The big corvette, which Annja felt certain was Wira's flagship, swung the huge blinding white eye of its search-light around.

Directly toward Annja.

But no, the beam did not strike her. It shone almost directly back over her head. At the same time the corvette's machine-cannon opened fire. Red tracers lanced above her with sky-ripping noise.

She turned her head. A hundred-foot-long junk was bearing down on her. The Rimba Perak search-light lit its crimson forecastle and the staring eyes painted on either side of the bow like a stage.

Annja's Zodiac moved faster. She was in no danger of being run down. But she saw faces, bleached pallid in the multimillion-candlepower beam, staring at her. Arms pointed right at her.

Kalashnikovs began to wink orange fire at her from the rail. Bullets kicked up little spurts of water all around her small craft. A heavy machine gun raked the water toward her, its thumb-sized bullets sending up water spouts as high as a house.

Annja watched in helpless fascination. Absently she tried to keep steering straight for the *Sea Scorpion.* The risk of being run down by the Rimba Perak warships, or plowing into the junk's squared-off stern, seemed the least of Annja's worries.

Above and to the right of the onrushing junk, a star caught Annja's eye. With everything else going on—all of it with a whole lot more immediate significance for her personal survival than astronomical phenomena—she wasn't sure why.

Then she realized it was getting larger and brighter. Rapidly.

The junk's whole stern blew up in a flash that lit the sky white from horizon to horizon. Annja saw debris, shattered planks and what she thought were twisting human bodies flying skyward in a pillar of yellow flame. With a whistling roar the Harrier jet that had launched the guided missile flashed over Annja's boat. The doomed junk, engine shattered, its tall stern enveloped in a fireball, began to fall away to its own portside.

Annja looked forward. The Rimba Perak naval craft had sheered off on diverging courses. She guessed they were intent on preventing pirate craft from coming to their leader's aid. Not that any seemed eager to do so, especially after the abrupt fate of the one ship that tried. A quick glance back showed the battle spreading out, as if the pirate fleet's survivors were scattering like a covey of frightened quail.

The *Sea Scorpion*'s stern loomed above her like a dark wooden cliff. She throttled back. The Zodiac's hard nose nuzzled the big ship to the starboard of its huge wooden rudder like an amorous dolphin.

She reached into her seabag for her grapnel gun. I'm getting to be an old pro at this, she thought, and brought it to her shoulder.

ANNJA WASN'T SURPRISED to find no one guarding the stern. Several still bodies lay about the deck, which was slick with blood and hazardous from bushels of empty shell casings, tinkling like tiny brass chimes as they rolled in shoals to and fro as the ship moved with the waves. Since both sides favored dark clothing for nocturnal operations, she had no idea who the dead were. Shouts and shots came from up ahead, seemingly up out of the hold.

She picked her way carefully forward to avoid slipping on the spent casings. Then she froze and ducked down in the shelter of a yard-tall coil of cable as thick as her arm.

Men were clambering over the starboard rail. Dark-clad men with dark masks hiding their faces.

They carried suppressed machine pistols. Sword hilts with cross-shaped guards jutted above each man's shoulder.

"Oh, dear," Annja said softly. Somehow, the Knights of the Risen Savior had joined the party.

The sloping deck offered plenty of cover for Annja to sneak forward. The Knights seemed focused single-mindedly on the noisy battle raging belowdecks. They showed no interest in securing the top deck.

Moving from hiding point to hiding point Annja found a hatch. It opened into darkness. She reached down, felt until she found a ladder. Then she climbed down, closing the hatch after her.

Black enfolded her. Her eyes adjusted slowly after the flash and flare of the naval battle. She reached tentative hands out to explore as her surroundings came dimly into view. She found herself in a world of closely fitted planking, a narrow gangway with a low overhead.

It smelled better than Annja had expected the inside of a notorious pirate vessel to smell. Apparently Eddie Cao Cao insisted on certain standards aboard his flagship. Assuming that was really where she was, of course.

That didn't mean it smelled good. She could detect stale sweat, bilge water, diesel oil, burned lubricants, various forms of mildew and mold. She also smelled disinfectant and layer upon ancient layer of varnish.

Yellow light spilling beneath a doorway ahead faintly lit the gangway. The noise of combat came from beyond it. Sword in hand Annja crept cautiously forward.

It was like being inside a living thing. Ships move. Not just in terms of rolling and pitching and yawing in response to the vast irresistible motions of the sea. But internally, flexing, shifting.

A big wooden ship did so much more than a metal one. It was Annja's first time on board such a ship, of such a size, on the open sea. All around her the junk shifted and creaked and groaned.

There was one thing she did not feel or hear—the throb of big nautical engines. Apparently either the pirates had shut them down, or the invaders had shut them off for them.

Listening at the door did little more than confirm that fighting was going on close by. Possibly right on the door's other side. She reached for the rope latch, pulled the door open enough to peek through.

A number of stacked crates and objects swathed in gray or blue plastic tarps stood stacked left and right. The space beyond them opened up into a large hold with a kind of gallery or walkway running around it. Lamps hanging from the overhead lit it badly.

There was no mistaking the crate containing the coffin in the hold's center. All around it men fought.

Dark-clad fighters pressed in from both sides, the Rimba Perak commandos from Annja's left, the Knights from the right. A knot of pirates was being forced back upon the crate. Only a handful remained. But they were fighting hard. Annja saw Knights and commandos die as well as pirates.

For whatever reason the shooting and grenades had been dropped in favor of hand-to-hand combat. Most likely everyone, pirates included, feared damaging the precious artifact they battled over.

Annja smiled slightly. Maybe Wira wasn't so eager to send it to the bottom, after all, she thought.

She could make out little more. A pair of pirates crouched before her, backs to her, in the passageway between the crates.

She saw him then—Wira. At first she didn't recognize him. Like his men he wore indigo battle dress, although his long hair was confined by a midnight head-rag like one of the pirates. Her heart jumped in her chest. He waded into the enemy ahead of his men, laying about with his sword. A huge pirate with an even bigger bare belly swung an outsize battle-ax at him. He ducked the blow, slashed the man across the shins. The pirate screamed, bent to clutch at himself. Wira split his shaven skull.

A tall figure dressed in a scarlet tunic stepped forward. He carried a pair of butterfly swords, single-edged weapons with metal knuckle-bows and short, heavy blades almost like cleavers. He had a square, handsome face and neatly trimmed black hair and beard. He called something in a commanding voice.

The pirates disengaged and drew back against

the crate. The fighting stopped. Apparently both Knights and commandos were willing to wait and see how events proceeded.

The two pirates crouched in front of Annja weren't, though. Unseen by the combatants, back there in deep shadow, they raised Kalashnikovs to aim at the young Sultan.

Annja glided forward. She struck twice. Her blade bit deep. Both pirates fell without a sound.

No one looked their way. Wira and the man with the two swords and the commanding presence came together in a clash of steel.

Eddie Cao Cao caught Wira's downstroke with his swords in an upward X. Before he could riposte the Sultan side-kicked him in the flat belly. The pirate leader slammed back against the crate. His powerful upper body swayed alarmingly over it.

Wira darted forward, slashing backhand for his opponent's chest. Cao Cao had feigned some of his loss of balance. He blocked across his body with his left-hand sword held upward. His edge skirled off Wira's. The pirate spun around, crouching, slashing for Wira's right knee with the blade in his right hand.

Wira jumped astonishingly high in the air. The broad blade swiped harmlessly beneath his boot.

As he came down he slashed a whirring blow at Cao Cao's head. The pirate lord blocked with his left sword. Then he slashed the young Sultan across the stomach with his other weapon.

Wira jumped back. A line of skin appeared, pale

against the midnight blue of his blouse. The middle of it was a shocking scarlet line.

Annja's shout was lost in the general roar of dismay from the commandos and—she thought—the Knights, and approval from the surviving pirates.

Wira seemed to freeze, staring down at himself as if paralyzed with horror, at the pain, at the sight of his own blood, at the shock of having his sacred person so violated. Annja felt sick. He should never have come there. She glanced frantically around for the rifles dropped by the men she had silently dispatched. Both corpses lay atop their weapons.

Grinning like a shark, Cao Cao advanced for the kill.

Cocking his right butterfly sword back over his shoulder the pirate thrust his left one for the Sultan's wide-open chest.

The young Sultan moved with shocking speed. His sword flashed across his body, right to left. It struck the stabbing blade and knocked it across his opponent's broad chest. Turning his wrist sidearm Wira slashed backhand right over the top of the pirate's sword arm.

His curved blade sliced Cao Cao's throat. Blood spurting, the pirate leader took several steps back. His head lolled to one side. He fell.

The hold was silent.

For a moment Wira stood gazing down at his fallen foe, chest heaving. Blood streamed from the gash across his belly, wetly glistening black against the dark fabric of his uniform. With a flick of his wrist he cleared blood from his curved blade.

Then he raised his head to look at the surviving pirates. Only five remained standing. The ragged men instantly threw down their weapons. Turning inward toward the crate they went to their knees and laced hands behind their heads.

Evidently they knew the drill. As well they ought. They'd inflicted it on others often enough.

For a moment Annja feared one or the other group would simply massacre the surrendered men where they knelt. She had no objection to cutting them down in the heat of battle. But killing in cold blood went against her grain.

Perhaps they merited death these men—they served with the most bloody-handed and merciless pirate gang in the South China Sea, which probably meant the world. But what if all wasn't as it appeared? What if they were recent recruits, maybe even conscripts whose obedience was secured by threats against their families? They had fought fiercely at Eddie Cao Cao's side. But had they any choice? When not one but two packs of highly trained, highly motivated and thoroughly ruthless killers swarmed aboard the great junk, the only available options were fight or die.

It was pure speculation, of course. Annja had no way of knowing.

As if noticing them for the first time, Wira stared past the crate, its yellow-pine sides defiled with shocking bright spatters of blood, at the Knights. The two groups, who had relaxed subconsciously at the fall of the pirate king, went tense. They glared at each other from blacked-out faces—dog packs contesting an alley.

Annja thought one of the Rimba Perak commandos swung up his submachine gun first. The Knights did likewise. Suddenly the rival forces were aiming at each other with automatic weapons, separated by no more than a dozen feet of deck slick with blood.

My turn, Annja thought. She straightened and strode forward from between the piled crates, right between the barrels of the too-ready guns.

30

"Gentlemen," Annja Creed said, projecting for all she was worth, "I, Annja Creed, hereby claim this relic in the name of science and the global archaeological community."

Wow, she thought. Is that totally the lamest, most pompous sentence ever, or what?

Many faces turned to gape at her. Even the pirates swiveled their turbaned heads on scrawny necks to stare at this unexpected apparition.

"Ms. Creed?" a young Knight burst out. No mistaking Sharshak, Annja thought.

"Annja?" the Sultan said.

On Sharshak's far side, farther from Annja but no farther from the fray, a Knight with broad shoulders and chest and a bit of a belly stood shaking his big square head. Behind his war paint and the black glop in his beard he seemed to be smiling.

"Well," Wira said slowly, still staring at her as if she'd sprouted antlers, "I have agreed to such an arrangement."

He looked at the Knights again, seemingly unconcerned by the black barrels of submachine guns pointing at him, and frowned. "But I am not sure circumstances permit it to be carried out."

"Well," Annja said in her brightest, brassiest voice, "if you boys are dead set on slaughtering each other to show who's got the biggest sword, then I suggest you take it up on deck, where you can die in the nice fresh air and not threaten any more damage to this priceless treasure."

They all stared at her.

Hevelin expelled his breath in a gust. "May God forgive me saying so," he said, "although I suspect our unsainted patron would heartily concur. Clearly there's no point in contesting who has the biggest sword. There can be no doubt."

"By Allah, you are right," Wira said. "It is most assuredly Annja Creed."

She felt herself blushing. "That's the nicest thing anyone's ever said to me, Wira. Sir Hevelin. Now, why don't we all remember our basic firearms safety and stop pointing those things at each other before someone gets hurt?"

Almost shamefacedly, both sides lowered their weapons. They didn't look at each other. They seemed embarrassed to.

I always wondered about the actual distinction

between ballsy and stupid, she thought. Now I know—if it works, it's ballsy.

"But wait," Sharshak cried. Annja's heart sank. His earnest young voice throbbed with genuine distress. That could only mean bad news.

"Where will you take our holy relic to determine its just ownership?" he asked.

Darn, Annja thought. "The only sensible place is back to Meriahpuri, in Rimba Perak."

His boy's face turned mulish behind the black paint. "I don't see how we can possibly agree to that," he said. "How can you trust this man?"

"The Sultan has signed a contract to abide by my decision," Annja said.

"But we haven't," Sharshak said. He shook his head. His eyes seemed to glitter suspiciously, as if tearing up. "Ann—Ms. Creed, we cannot permit you to hand our relic over to these unbelievers!"

Cosmopolitan though he was, Wira looked pretty grim at being called an "unbeliever." Annja could see tension winding the body language of both groups back up. The captive pirates, meanwhile, were turning into quivering masses. They knew if things headed south, they'd be caught in the cross fire.

"Hold it," Annja said. She tried to make her voice snap without raising it—to sound commanding without making any trigger fingers reflexively twitch. It seemed to work. People looked at her again.

It was a start.

"I set up this arrangement," she said. "I know for

a fact you're all honorable men, pirate scum excepted, of course. But I don't ask you to take my word for it. I'd stake my life on Sultan Wira holding to the letter and the spirit of his promises to me. In fact, that's exactly what I'll do. I guarantee this deal with my life!"

Everybody's eyes were wide again.

"That's a real touching offer," an all-too-familiar voice said. "Too bad you're gonna get taken up on it so quick, little lady."

"St. Clair?" Annja looked wildly around. The U.S. agent, looking cool and positively dapper in his ice-cream suit and Panama hat, had emerged from the shadows behind the Rimba Perak commandos. Crowding out on the narrow gallery to either side of him were men in green turbans with cutlasslike swords thrust through their sashes. Similarly clad men were popping up behind the Knights. All of them aimed Kalashnikovs at the two groups facing each other past the crate.

The Sword of the Faith had arrived at the party. Apparently, as counterterrorism specialist St. Clair's honored guests.

"All right," Annja said, "this officially sucks."

St. Clair looked her way and gestured. Hard hands grabbed her arms from behind.

The faces of Knights and the Sultan's commandos were stiff as they stared at the weapons held on them. Perhaps thirty men of both sides remained functional inside the hold. At least twenty terrorists surrounded them—more than enough, given that they had the drop on their victims and a height advantage so they could massacre them without cross-firing each other.

Through pregnant silence St. Clair strolled around behind his men to approach Annja.

"Ms. Creed," he said politely, "I can't tell you how good it is to see you here. It's kind of like hitting a grand slam. We scoop up the relic, the Sultan and you, all at one stroke. Very cool."

"I thought you worked for the United States!" she flared at him.

His smile was thin and icy.

"I do," he said. "It's policy. Maybe I'm goosing it along a little bit. But it's for the good old U.S. of A. I told you, amateurs couldn't understand."

He reached out to stroke a finger under her chin. She turned her face aside—mostly to prevent herself from snapping at his hand. I've got to pick my chance, she told herself. I'll only have one. If I even get that.

"What do you think you're doing?" she said. "These are Muslim terrorists you're palling with!"

"You noticed." He smirked.

"The war on terror is losing steam back home," he told her quietly. "We need to get the terrorists a win, here. One that won't hurt U.S. interests. Just a strong nudge, to remind the softheads back home why we fight. No hard feelings, okay? Like I said—policy."

"Policy," she echoed stonily.

"We got some *special* techniques in store for

you," he said with a leer. "You'll star in your very own torture video showing the world what barbarians these rag-heads are we're dealing with. You'll be queen of YouTube for at least a week. People will tear out their hair and scream for blood."

He turned to his ring of terrorists. "Kill them all," he said. Then he shrugged.

Orange fire and head-splitting noise filled the hold as the terrorists opened up.

The two terrorists held Annja's arms down to her sides. As St. Clair turned away and the other terrorists' guns thundered she summoned her sword. She flicked it down against the man to her right's leg.

Shocked, he shrieked and let go of her arm to grab at his blood-spurting calf.

She snapped the blade horizontal, and pivoted into the man on her left. She yanked backward hard with her trapped left hand to keep that arm clear. The sword cut into the man's belly and side. He fell, releasing her wrist.

St. Clair spun toward her. His hand was inside his jacket. He was clearly going for a handgun in a shoulder holster.

Annja used both hands to wrench her blade free of the falling terrorist. She flung herself toward St. Clair, cocking the sword to her right and then lashing out at waist level with all her strength in a desperation swing. She felt a moment of hesitation.

St. Clair's knobby hand came out holding a big

angular Colt 1911. His face twisted in a sneer. "Missed," he said.

Something made him look down. His eyes flew wide in horror as he began to register the pain. His stomach had been slashed open. The .45 dropped from nerveless fingers as his body toppled.

Annja's sudden explosion of motion had drawn everyone's attention, even the terrorists who had just begun to massacre the Knights and commandos. The gunfire faltered as the terrorists gaped at their leader's fate.

At least seven Knights and commandos were down. The rest suddenly turned and went for the terrorists with attack-dog fury.

Guns flared and crashed. But the Sultan's men and the Christian holy warriors had rushed in among the terrorists. They couldn't use their Kalashnikovs without cutting each other down. That wasn't stopping all of them. Some at the rear sprayed the scrum impartially.

Annja ran right toward the nearest terrorist. He looked her way. The expression on his face was total astonishment as he felt a whistling slash.

Several others saw her charging. She slashed one's rifle across the top of its receiver as he swung it toward her at waist level. He fired. Muzzle blast and the bullets' passage yanked at her shirt.

The gunman screamed and fell back, black shirt alive with blue flames, as hot gas jetted from the ruptured top of his weapon into his body and face.

The others threw down their rifles to draw swords. Annja cut down two before steel cleared their sashes. Then she was stuck in a wild melee against four terrorists at once.

All of the black-clad Sword of the Faith killers in their green turbans had stopped shooting. Annja had the impression of all-out vicious face-to-face fighting to her left. As she defended herself against wild swings and slashes she could only hope the superior training and discipline of the Knights and Wira's commandos could overcome the terrorists' numbers—and that they wouldn't wind up fighting each other, by accident or on purpose.

A foe tried a horizontal backhand slash at her neck from too far away. Too far, because when Annja parried with the flat of her blade, point-upward with her hand at the level of her own sternum, the spacing was ideal for her to flow into a rapid high-line lunge that sent her blade horizontally right between his eyes.

As he went down with his eyes rolled up toward his turban and weeping tears of blood, she engaged two more of his comrades. A third danced from foot to foot behind them, glaring at her with eyes more horribly fascinated than angry or defiant.

She glanced quickly left. Wira stood embattled with his back to the crate. He fought like a whirl-wind against three foes. He had picked up a second sword, as he had last night in his bedroom, this time one of his own men's. Around him lay a semicircle of fallen terrorists.

But for all the young Sultan's superb skill with twin weapons he lacked eyes in the back of his head. A new attacker leapt up on the crate, raced forward with sword upraised to split the unwitting monarch's skull. Annja shouted a warning.

It went unheard in the din of clashing steel, shouts, screams and agonized groans of the wounded.

Pain flashed through her face like fire as one of her assailants took advantage of her momentary lapse of attention to slash her across the cheek. She lashed out backhand in reflex. Her sword caught him in almost the same place. It cut through both cheeks and his nose. He fell screaming and clutching his ruined face.

A figure leapt up behind the man on the crate. The terrorist swung his blade at the Sultan's unsuspecting head. Flinging himself heedlessly forward, the young Knight Sharshak rammed his short sword through the terrorist's back.

The man slumped forward, dragging down Sharshak's blade. Annja mechanically parried as the man who had been jittering behind his comrades launched a wild cut at her head. He was reckless. He closed too far, allowing her to thrust-kick him in the sternum, driving him back several paces.

Furiously she rounded on the other man. From the edge of her vision she saw Sharshak kick the impaled man from his blade, falling off the crate to slam one of Wira's three attackers to the blood-slickened deck. Then the Knight leapt down at the Sultan's side.

Wira looked at him. His eyes widened in amazement. Then Sharshak thrust again—right toward the young Sultan.

Annja hacked her opponent's sword off in the middle. He stared at it in dumbfounded amazement until her return stroke spun him to the deck trailing a spiral of dark blood.

Sharshak's short sword went to the hilt in the belly of a terrorist who, seeing Wira distracted, had pressed the attack from the Sultan's right. The remaining killer slashed Sharshak across the left shoulder.

Wira cut the terrorist down. Sharshak wrenched his blade free. The man who had fallen under his slain comrade's weight grabbed him by an ankle.

Twenty feet away Annja saw a terrorist shoulder a Kalashnikov. Its muzzle-brake pointed at Sharshak and the Sultan. He was too far for Annja to reach with a sword attack. Screaming a warning as shrilly as she could she released the sword and stooped to grab a fallen rifle.

Wira and Sharshak looked around. Sharshak saw the terrorist aiming the assault rifle. Ignoring the man clutching both his ankles, pinning him in place, he knocked the Sultan sprawling with a broad sweeping blow of the back of his sword hand.

Three bullets of a wild burst slammed into his chest. He fell.

A moment later Annja caught the terrorist rifleman's head on top of the front sight post of her recovered rifle. She triggered a burst of her own. The man's face crumpled beneath his turban, vanished in a spray of blood.

She swung the weapon around, looking for targets. The last of the terrorists was being chopped down as she watched—oddly enough, by one of Eddie Cao Cao's surrendered pirates, who had snatched up a fallen commando's blade and lustily engaged the hated Sword of the Faith swordsmen. Two more pirates likewise stood shoulder-to-shoulder by their erstwhile captors. The other two had apparently died in the fighting.

Annja covered with her rifle until several commandos took up stations on the walkway covering the hold. Others ran to Wira to help him up. He shrugged them off, moved quickly to the fallen Sharshak's side.

Hevelin already knelt beside the young Knight. His right arm hung to the deck, its midnight-blue sleeve glistening with the blood that had soaked it and run down to turn his hand into a gory claw. Sharshak lay on his back with arms outstretched. His gray eyes stared sightlessly at the dark overhead. Through the paint on his face his expression seemed to Annja to be one of peace.

Hevelin raised his blacked-out face to meet the young Sultan's eyes. His own blue eyes ran with tears. Slowly he shook his head.

Wira laid his hand upon the older Knight's shoulder. Then, rising, he helped the older man to his feet.

Realizing the commandos were in a twitchy frame of mind, and might react poorly to a foreigner approaching their Sultan with firearm in hand, Annja carefully laid down the Kalashnikov. Then she came down to join the tableau where the two men, Christian Knight and Muslim Sultan, stood facing each other across the body of a young man who had died to save a recent enemy.

Both Knights and commandos held themselves warily, alert for a fresh attack. But their eyes were turned outward—it was terrorist reinforcements they warded against. Knights went among the fallen terrorists making sure they stayed down with quick sword thrusts.

The victors' body language no longer showed distrust of one another. They had fought, and won as comrades. It was a bond, Annja knew—since she shared it—as strong as family or nation or religion.

"Annja," Wira said. "I'm glad you survived."

"I am, too. I mean, glad you survived—both of you. And me." She looked down at Sharshak. "I only wish he had. He was a sweet boy."

"Many good men have died tonight," Hevelin said in a voice thick with emotion. "Some of the best I called my enemies, until mere moments ago."

"Enemies no longer," the Sultan said. "I am pleased to meet you, Sir Knight. I am Wira, Sultan of Rimba Perak."

He thrust out his right hand. Without hesitation Hevelin clasped it with his right.

"I am called Hevelin," he said. "I am honored to take your hand in friendship."

Somehow Annja lacked all heart to comment on the testosterone densely permeating the air.

"Annja," Wira said, turning gravely to her. "I withdraw all objection to the Knights of the Risen Savior taking possession of this relic. Pending your professional judgment, of course—as I agreed."

He swept his gaze back over Hevelin and his weary, bloodied comrades. "We may believe we serve different causes. But tonight we fought together for good. That transcends all in my eyes. Perhaps I am naive."

"I pray more of us might become naive in such a way," Hevelin said.

Annja stood, looking from man to man. Her eyes filled with tears. She blinked them sternly away.

"I honor both of you—all of you," she said, unable to keep huskiness from her own voice. "Since we have fought so hard, and so many have died, to secure it—what do you say we see what it is that's caused all this destruction?"

Wira looked to Hevelin. The old Knight shrugged. "It would be churlish to resist the request, under the circumstances," he said. "All here have earned the right to see what they sacrificed for."

Knights and commandos joined together to pry the lid off the yellow-pine crate. Several climbed inside, shifted out enough of the strawlike packing material to reveal the plain gray metal lid of the coffin itself.

It took four men, two from both sides, to lift the lid enough to slide aside so that all could see.

A collective gasp filled the hull. Annja's breath caught in her throat.

After a moment she shook her head as if to break a spell. "You can cover it when you're ready," she said. "I've seen enough."

Hevelin and Wira looked to her. "Cedric Millstone told me the Knights of the Risen Savior had prepared a special climate-conditioned vault to keep the artifact secure," she said. "Shortly before he himself was murdered, by St. Clair's little helpers, I suppose. Is it true your Order has such a facility in America?"

"It is, Ms. Creed," Hevelin said. "There it shall stay safe—safer than it has been for the better part of a millennium. And hidden well away from public view."

She nodded. "Then I think that's best," she said, as with a scrape of metal on metal the coffin was resealed, reverently, by the men in the crate.

"I never thought I'd say this," she said, shaking her head, "but I don't believe the world is ready for something like this."

31

No sooner had the coffin been transferred to Wira's flagship, the *Berani,* along with the wounded and the surviving Knights of the Risen Savior, than Wira received a shocking encrypted transmission from his capital. Lestari had brought proof to the Sultan's security chief, Purnoma, of the identity of the traitor who had allowed the assassins into the palace grounds the night before. It was the Grand Vizier, Krisna, Wira's friend and supporter since childhood. From diaries found in his apartments it seemed he was a far more devoutly fundamentalist Muslim than anyone had imagined.

Why he had helped his young charge for so long was anybody's guess. It would remain so. Although several of his confederates in the palace had been rounded up, the aged Grand Vizier had produced a hidden Kahr handgun and gone down fighting, taking two of Purnoma's men into death with him.

Annja saw the news hit Wira like a blow to the gut, as they stood in the red-lit electronic wonderland of the *Berani*'s high-tech bridge.

Annja gratefully accepted the captain's offer of his cabin to sleep, after she had cleaned up. There would be no rest for Wira or his crew.

SULTAN WIRA professed himself unable to pardon the three surviving pirates who had helped fight the terrorists. After all, they were wanted by a number of nations, for innumerable crimes. He ordered them confined to a cabin in the *Sea Scorpion* overnight.

But Wira did not order the door to the compartment in which the pirates were confined locked. Nor did he order it guarded. Nor did he order the several small boats bobbing alongside the pirate flagship, including the ones that had brought the Knights after their mother ship dropped them off and steamed away, to be watched.

In the morning the pirates were gone. So was one of the small powered craft.

No one seemed the least bit concerned. Annja knew she wasn't.

I don't know if what they did down in the hold redeemed them from whatever crimes they committed, she thought. But then again, I don't know it didn't. In this case, judgment was not hers.

She felt content with that, as she stood on the afterdeck of the sleek fifty-five-meter *Berani,* sipping a cup of steaming coffee with plenty of cream and sugar from the warship's galley. The sky was the color of the coffin. Ragged pale clouds skimmed gray waves beneath the overcast. It was surprisingly cold. Annja wore a long gray sweater that came down to the thighs of her slacks, and the ends of whose sleeves provided fine insulation for her hands as they gripped the metal cup.

A half-dozen wrecks, still drooling thin gray smoke, dotted the sea. One was a hundred-foot Rimba Perak motor launch. The others were Red Hand junks. Their high sides, once painted gaudy scarlet and gold, with huge eyes staring from the bows, were blackened and streaked almost beyond recognition.

The *Sea Scorpion* floated a quarter mile astern of the warship. Annja regarded it in the murky dawn.

She heard a step, looked around. Wira approached. He wore a black pullover similar to hers, loose black sweatpants and black athletic shoes. His lush blue-black hair was tied back in a neat queue from his tapering, handsome face.

He lit up as she turned and saw him. "Annja," he said, coming forward and raising his hands.

As if in a dream she raised her own. He took them. She barely managed to keep from spilling her coffee, but no thought of pulling away entered her mind. His kissed her once, lightly, on the lips.

She shivered.

"I'm proud of you, you know," he said. He let go of her left hand, to her relief, since it held her cup. As if leading in a dance he turned her to face aft, side by side with him.

"I'm proud of *us,*" he said. "All of us. We have shown that courage and goodwill can triumph. Maybe I'm childish, but that encourages me. No matter how small or temporary it may be."

She smiled and sipped her coffee. "I've found, Wira, that there's not much point in worrying about the continuance of evil and suffering in the world. They'll always happen. All we can do by reminding ourselves of that, when we do get a win, is discourage ourselves from trying the next time."

He nodded. "Imagine how terrible a place the world would be if we didn't try."

She sighed. "That's true," she said. "Yet I can't get too comfortable with it."

"How so?"

"Well, nobody wakes up in the morning and says, 'How can I be evil today?' Except for maybe a few especially messed-up adolescents. Even serial killers, even sociopaths without any real sense of right or wrong, tend to come up with rationales for doing what they do.

"It often seems to me that the most horrible things

are done by the people who are most passionately convinced that they're right. The good of humankind, or of the planet, can excuse a lot of bad behavior, it seems."

"Like my commandos? Or our former foes, the Knights of the Risen Savior? Or you and I, for that matter?" Wira asked.

"No. Or anyway, I like to think not. I mean, we fought for the right—for *good.* But you and the Knights fought passionately against one another. For good. And here's the real kicker—so do the Sword of the Faith terrorists. Don't they? Even Cyrus St. Clair. He did what he did thinking it was for a higher cause. I'm sure he died believing himself the greatest of patriots."

Wira frowned. "I find what you say uncomfortable," he said slowly. "But I cannot refute it. So what can we do, then? To ensure that we do not commit great crimes, in the name of the greater good?"

I wrestle with that all the time, she thought. She ached to tell him, to confide. The truth—the *whole* truth. To be able to share her deepest secrets with this man, this cheerful, quick-minded friend, this strong and vulnerable leader.

But she couldn't. And that was the problem. It had begun to gnaw at her belly last night when she should have been deep in the sleep of the exhausted.

"I wish I knew for certain," she said, shaking her head. "It seems pretty horribly unfair that one of the surest ways to turn into a monster is to try too hard to do the right thing."

"I wonder," the Sultan said. "Might the road to perdition be the easy route, the morally expedient route—accepting that the end justifies the means?"

"That could be," she said. She looked at his profile, well-chiseled and strong, as if to drink it in with her eyes. "I've never accepted that. Maybe that's what saves my soul."

He looked into her eyes and smiled. "But don't let's be gloomy," he said, suddenly seeming as boyish as he had wise beyond his age a few moments before. "You yourself said we needed to let ourselves have our wins. Let's celebrate this one."

She smiled, a bit wanly, and nodded, brushing back a wisp of hair the heavy sea breeze had plucked loose to tickle her nose and cheek. "You're right."

"I know your business here is virtually concluded, Annja," he said.

Here it comes, she thought.

"But I find I'm not eager to see you go. Why don't you stay? Not—professionally, as it were. As my guest."

"That's very sweet," Annja said. "And I'd really, really like to."

His face clouded. "I sense the unspoken *but.*"

She nodded. "But I can't. I have a life. A career. And a destiny. And it isn't here in Rimba Perak."

He drew in a deep breath. "Well, perhaps it might help if I—"

She held two fingers up to his lips. "Please," she said. "Don't even say it."

He quieted. He might have taken umbrage. She knew he wouldn't, and he didn't. Instead he looked hurt.

It tore at her heart.

"Wira." She reached to touch his brown cheek. He took her hand and kissed it. "I'm not what you need. You have your position to consider. Politics—national and regional. Even global. I'm a nobody."

He grinned ruefully. "It's no longer the fourteenth century, Annja. Marriages are no longer arranged for dynastic purposes."

The words hit her like a hammer in the heart. Blast him for finding a way to say it, she thought.

"All the same," she made herself say, "political considerations inform everything you do. They have to. I know how seriously you take your job. And anyway—you need someone who can be an adjunct for you."

He shook his head. "I'd never ask a woman to be no more than an ornament," he said. He grinned. "Even though you are highly ornamental."

"You're sweet. But even so, you need a woman who can assist you. Serve as diplomat—administrator—problem solver."

"Doesn't the ability to be my best bodyguard count?"

"How long could you keep from feeling resentment, if you felt—however politically incorrect or regressive it might be—that you were hiding behind a woman's skirts?"

He shook his head. "Naturally one likes to think better of oneself." But he didn't contradict her.

"Wira, I care about you. Very much. I have great respect for you. I *like* you." She sighed. "And that's why I'm leaving as soon as we get the details wrapped up for dealing with the coffin."

He pressed his lips together. She could feel the emotional pain and turmoil beat from him like sunlight off waves. There was nothing she could say to make it any easier on him.

To say nothing of her.

All this time the *Berani* had been bearing off to its starboard. Now it moved beam-on to the drifting pirate flagship. A naval officer in short-sleeved whites appeared and saluted crisply to the black bill of his cap

"Awaiting your command, Your Majesty," he said.

Wira had turned to snap to attention and return the salute in a way the toughest drill instructor could find no fault with. "Carry on, Lieutenant," he said crisply. "Execute the fire mission."

"Sir." The officer turned away and spoke quickly into his headset in Malay.

Wira turned back to Annja. He held wide his arms.

"Annja," he said, "since we have to part—"

She was already in his arms. She could hear no

more of what he said. The world had erupted in an Armageddon of noise.

Rockets streaked overhead, trailing tails of yellow flame garish against cloud. The *Sea Scorpion,* still holding the bodies of Eddie Cao Cao and his crew, and liberally splashed with the contents of its own fuel tanks, erupted in a colossal yellow fireball.

As the shockwave of the distant blast rolled over Wira and Annja, their mouths met in a final farewell kiss.

TAKE 'EM FREE
2 action-packed novels plus a mystery bonus
NO RISK
NO OBLIGATION TO BUY